We Never Swim in the Same River Twice

Middle East Literature in Translation
Michael Beard and Adnan Haydar, *Series Editors*

For a full list of titles in this series,
visit https://press.syr.edu/supressbook-series
/middle-east-literature-in-translation/.

We Never Swim in the Same River Twice

Hassouna Mosbahi

Translated from the Arabic by William Maynard Hutchins

Syracuse University Press

First published in Arabic by Dar al-Adab, Beirut, 2020, as *La Nasbah fi al-Nahr Marratayn*

Copyright © 2024 by William Maynard Hutchins
Syracuse University Press
Syracuse, New York 13244-5290
All Rights Reserved

First Edition 2024
24 25 26 27 28 29   6 5 4 3 2 1

∞ The paper used in this publication meets the minimum requirements
of the American National Standard for Information Sciences—Permanence
of Paper for Printed Library Materials, ANSI Z39.48-1992.

For a listing of books published and distributed by Syracuse University Press,
visit https://press.syr.edu.

ISBN: 9780815611691 (paperback)
        9780815657187 (e-book)

Library of Congress Cataloging-in-Publication Data

Names: Miṣbāḥī, Ḥassūnah, author. | Hutchins, William M., translator.
Title: We never swim in the same river twice / Hassouna Mosbahi;
        translated from the Arabic by William M. Hutchins.
Other titles: Lā nasbaḥ fī al-nahr marratayn. English
Description: First edition. | Syracuse : Syracuse University Press, 2024. |
        Series: Middle East literature in translation | Includes bibliographical references.
Identifiers: LCCN 2024009334 (print) | LCCN 2024009335 (ebook) |
        ISBN 9780815611691 (paperback) | ISBN 9780815657187 (ebook)
Subjects: LCSH: Tunisia—History—Demonstrations, 2010—Fiction. |
        Arab Spring, 2010—Fiction. | LCGFT: Historical fiction. | Novels.
Classification: LCC PJ7846.I6974 L313 2024 (print) | LCC PJ7846.I6974 (ebook) |
        DDC 892.7/36—dc23/eng/20240627
LC record available at https://lccn.loc.gov/2024009334
LC ebook record available at https://lccn.loc.gov/2024009335

Manufactured in the United States of America

Poetical idea: pink, then golden, then grey, then black.
Still true to life also.

Day, then the night.

—James Joyce, episode 4, Calypso, *Ulysses*

Man, my sons, is like the river. It has a current and
banks. It gives birth and pours into other rivers. It must
serve a purpose. Diminish the current, and the river
becomes a swamp.

—Augusto Roa Bastos, *Hijo de Hombre*
(Son of Man)

Contents

Translator's Introduction

We Never Swim in the Same River Twice by contemporary Tunisian author Hassouna Mosbahi explores the psychological impact of Islamist rhetoric and violence on a cross-section of individuals, primarily men, in Tunisia after the fall of the Ben Ali regime during the Arab Spring of 2011. The three main characters are Saleem, who will soon turn fifty and whose happy marriage to a teacher is threatened by his deteriorating mental health; Aziz, a homely looking retired postal clerk with a deep appreciation for literature and international cinema; and Omran, a writer and public intellectual who has lived large portions of his life outside of Tunisia and is corresponding with Sophie, a young Franco-Tunisian woman, back in Paris. These three men become friends over beer at a bar called The Corsairs in Bizerte, a coastal city of Tunisia, and during walks on the beach there.

The interplay between a character's personal life and a nation's politics has been a popular theme for Arabic-language novels for decades. In *We Never Swim in the Same River Twice*, as in Mosbahi's earlier novel *Solitaire* (*Yatim al-Dahr*), the comparison is not between the microcosm of a family and the macrocosm of a state—as it was in *The Cairo Trilogy* by Naguib Mahfouz or *Return of the Spirit* by Tawfiq al-Hakim. Instead, the interaction is between the political culture of Tunisia and the psyches of the novel's characters. The authors they read (for Saleem American ones like Carson McCullers and Henry Miller, who is also a favorite for Aziz, and Egyptians like Taha Hussein and Europeans like Montaigne for Omran) are an important element of their personal development as are the films they watch: American and European ones, for example, for Aziz.

We Never Swim in the Same River Twice is a sequel to *Solitaire*, not because they share characters but because they explore Tunisian society and the Tunisian identity before (in the case of *Solitaire*) and after (in the case of *We Never Swim in the Same River Twice*) the fall of the autocratic Ben Ali regime. Investigations into what it means to be male and the constraints that political events place on a society in general and men in particular are common to both novels.

Mosbahi in *Solitaire* follows a Tunisian scholar's musings through the entire day and evening of his sixtieth birthday. As he remembers scenes from his past, he also explores episodes from Tunisia's history. *We Never Swim in the Same River Twice* takes place during the Arab Spring, which brought an uptick in militant Islamism and common-garden hooliganism. American readers may find disheartening parallels in this novel to the surge of militant White Christian Nationalism in post-Trump America. Suffering in Palestine is, unfortunately, still a reality.

Saleem's agitated mental state deteriorates as he reacts to jihadist violence and realizes that even his natal village is off-limits for him. Aziz was orphaned as a child and had to hustle to stay alive. He never married, but as a youngster was embraced by a colonial French sugar mama. Omran adopts the dangerous role of a public intellectual and, like all the other main characters, is shocked by the jihadists' cultural terrorism. The characters' masculinity and rationality are so threatened by shaggy-bearded Islamists with black calluses on their foreheads that Saleem, Aziz, and Omran at times resemble Peter Pan's lost boys trying bravely to ward off attacks by pirates. An anonymous reader for Syracuse University Press noted perceptively: "The violence of the Islamists in the Post Revolution triggers in . . . Aziz the long buried chapter of The Battle of Bizerte of 1961 where thousands of Tunisians were killed by the French army still stationed in Bizerte, five years after independence."

Karim Hamdy, another perceptive peer reviewer for Syracuse University Press, suggested that the character Omran was inspired by the Tunisian intellectual Lafif Lakhdar, who died in 2013 in Paris: "Mosbahi knew Lakhdar well and considers him a mentor. . . .

Although fictionalized, many features of the character match Lakh-dar's life record." Noting the range of linguistic registers Mosbahi uses in his novel, which is primarily in Modern Standard Arabic but includes some Tunisian dialect and French, Hamdy added, "The entire work is conceived . . . by its author as a Sisyphus-like struggle by each character, and . . . the country/society itself, against an unre-lenting . . . downhill tumble from the high hopes and optimism of the early post-independence era. The narrative is . . . an ironic counter-point to the inevitability of constant change announced in the title."

A feminist trope is a woman's need to tell her story. *We Never Swim in the Same River Twice* is a Tunisian male version of this im-pulse, and the plot is driven not so much by interactions between the characters as by each man's reminiscences and reflections on the so-ciopolitical realities that have shaped his life. Except for Omran, the public intellectual, narration is usually in the first person. Saleem's first-person narrative, though, changes to the third person as his mental health deteriorates. There are momentous events in the novel, but since they are remembered or recounted, instead of narrated by an omniscient author, the tone is more elegiac than sensationalizing.

The river in the title is not one of Tunisia's actual rivers; it is Tunisia as a lived experience, a mob demonstrating, or a person's life as he recalls and recounts it. The body of water rippling around the edges of this novel (and *Solitaire*) is the Mediterranean Sea. In summary, *We Never Swim in the Same River Twice* is a daring novel that challenges happy talk about the Arab Spring and Islamism. The character Omran reflects sadly: "Like the boulder of Sisyphus, Arab history will always continue to roll back down the mountain. Every time the Arabs attempt to rise, they collide with a boulder that blocks them from awakening. . . . Any hope for change or release is extinguished, and history in the Arab World resembles a black hole that devours even distant glimmers of light."

Omran's biggest, most life-threatening decisions, in different decades, have been when to leave or return to Tunisia. Tunisian author Hassan Nasr's novel *Return to Dar al-Basha*, which was also published by Syracuse University Press (in 2006), relates the fraught return of Murtada al-Shamikh to Tunis and scenes of his childhood after he lived abroad for many years. In some ways this earlier novel prefigured tensions felt by the main characters in *We Never Swim in the Same River Twice*.

My first translation from Arabic literature was published in *Playboy* in 1975, and since then I have developed some strategies. I typically use italics for foreign words, to set off interior monologue, or to mark a narrator's switch from first to third person. I occasionally use bold type for emphasis. If an Arabic word is used as a technical term, I translate it by the same English word; otherwise, I use different English words to explore various aspects of its meaning. When it seems best to include an Arabic word in transliteration, I try to use its English equivalent in the same paragraph. I offset passages that represent diary entries and the like. I also capitalize nouns when they are used as names.

I am happy to thank the perceptive expert readers of my manuscript for Syracuse University Press and the editors there, as well as my colleague Dr. Saloua Ben Zahra for her encouragement of my interest in Tunisian literature, for identifying the Canigou Café, and for picking a favorite Tunisian river.

We Never Swim in the Same River Twice

Saleem

I must rise. . . . Yes, I need to get up, but my warm bed tempts me to remain stretched out and pretend I'm asleep. I hear taps on the window! It might be drops of rain. The cold may be bitter this winter morning. Here I am, visualizing in my mind's eye people racing down filthy streets to work, amid the screech of vehicles. The chaos must have reached its peak. Curses and insults are raining down from every direction; fists are flailing, and people are quick to quarrel at the slightest provocation. One person treads on another because conditions are bad, and folks no longer have any patience or an atom of affection or compassion. They are cruel even to children, invalids, and impoverished or handicapped people. All the same, I need to get up. Yes, I must rise. My wife left a half hour ago with my young daughter. She went off without asking how I feel or even saying good morning. My daughter did not give me a hug, as she used to. But it doesn't matter. Better days will come, and harmony will reign again. This is what I hope and desire with every bone in my body. For now, though, I must quit this warm bed and go to work. Otherwise, the agency's director will lose his temper and won't excuse my repeated tardy arrivals this time. I fear, though, if I do go outside, I'll be confronted by the frightening scenes that ruin my life and plunge me into dark nightmares day and night. Yes, that's how I feel. The moment I take my first step outside the building—or even beyond the apartment—I will panic, since I may encounter a neighbor whom I don't like and who doesn't like me. Then he will frown, and I will too. Each of us will silently curse his bad luck, which made him run into such an ill-omened, unlucky face first thing in the morning.

Occasionally, I commit a horrible mistake for which I pay a high price. One day I boarded a train heading to the capital at 8 a.m. and realized my mistake only in the final minutes before the train reached the last station. Yes, this happened. Even now, I don't know why I did that! I thought I would take the next train back, but an old friend, who had studied at the university with me, fell into my arms and embraced me warmly, as if he had been waiting for me. Then he invited me to have coffee, and I accepted without any hesitation. We sat in the Paris Café at Bab el Bhar, and he began to recount chapters of his life, which he termed "miserable." He focused especially on his divorce after his wife had poisoned his life and ruined it, almost driving him crazy. For two entire years, she had kept dragging him to various courts, as if he were a flimflam artist of some vile type. By the time the divorce was finalized, his spirit had almost ascended to his Maker. Now he was "restoring" himself and trying to regain his equilibrium, but the grave events that have flared up in this country, toppling the regime, have scared him. He has lost his poise again, worrying about what will happen tomorrow, the day after that, next month, or during the coming year. He assumes that an overwhelming majority of the people resemble him.

"And me? Mmmmee? I don't know either. By God, I don't know, my friend! I hope God sorts things out."

"How can you say you don't know?"

"Yes, I don't know . . . and you don't either."

"Yyyou! You haven't changed. For as long as I've known you, you've been a negative slacker. Even if the ceiling fell on the person dearest to you, you would shrug it off. You were like this when I knew you during our years at the university. The rest of us would go out on the streets to demonstrate and protest. But you—you would be in a rush to return to the university hostel and fall fast asleep, as if nothing concerned you: not the corrupt programs, not the fascist police who attacked the students and fought them with cudgels and tear-gas canisters, and not the daily injustices unleashed on our Palestinian brothers. Yes, you were a slacker, a coward, and an egotist.

You acted as if you were the only person on the face of the earth and the sole thing that concerned you was your own welfare."

Was I really that bad?

Yes, I was—and even more revolting and ugly than that. He had not meant to hurt my feelings; he simply spoke the truth. The fact is that I have never been good at anything except sleeping. And observing events dispassionately. Even the day they invaded Iraq, I refused to go out with the other students to denounce American terrorism. Worse still, I said something that made me seem to support that imperialist invasion! He heard me say something like that but didn't report me. He had not wanted to expose me. Had he, I would have been dragged down the street.

Perhaps he was talking about someone else.

No . . . no . . . never. . . . He was talking about me. He had been forced to wait for this moment to reveal the truth—to croon it loudly. Yes, I am a bastard: base, petty, and mean. I'll soon be fired from my job because I oppose the "Blessed Revolution."

"What blessed revolution?"

Ooohhh! Here I am playing dumb, always trying to make other people—now and in the past—think I'm an innocent, naive person incapable of harming an ant. That's enough! I must stop playing the filthy game of beating around the bush. I need to admit my flaws and faults; the time has come for self-assessment. No one will escape from it. Yes, no one will escape, and each person will get what he deserves.

I summoned the waiter and paid for both our coffees. Then I rose. He grasped my arm firmly, but I was able to free myself.

He screamed after me: "Scoundrel! I knew you wouldn't be able to stand the bitter truth."

Uuuuf! Since then, I haven't stopped biting my fingers; I should have shown him that the accusations he was directing at me applied to him—not to me, not by any stretch of the imagination. I should have reminded him of his black past and the secret reports he wrote to the university's administrators, denouncing students who instigated strikes and organized demonstrations . . . of how his roommate in the university district was found out and attacked one night and beaten so severely that he lost consciousness. Nonetheless, he never stopped spying and writing reports.

Uuuuf! I should have confronted him with those glaring realities and with numerous other ones—until he shut his mouth and fled like someone who has just farted in an assembly of distinguished shaykhs. Moreover, he was filthy and rarely bathed. That's why we called him "Dung Beetle." Everyone avoided him and wouldn't sit next to him in the lecture halls, cafeteria, or anywhere else. The foul odors of his obese brown body stank enough to make you sick, until you wanted to vomit. I feel sure that's why his wife divorced him. And perhaps there were other reasons. During our years at the university, he never stopped bragging about his virility, claiming he could rob five girls of their virginity in minutes. But a male friend caught him buck naked in a room at the university hostel one evening and immediately reported to everyone that his dick was the size of a fava bean. When this news reached her, beautiful Sarah, whom he had long annoyed with his advances, shouted at him: "Show me your prick, if you're really the stud you claim to be!" After that scandal, he quit bragging about his virility and, when he walked along with the rest of us, kept his head sunk between his shoulders, as if he were afraid of receiving a blow from Sarah—one that would smash his bones.

I left Dung Beetle haranguing himself in the Paris Café and began walking around Bab el Bhar, brooding about what I should do to relieve my heart and erase from my memory his trash talk and vicious lies.

It was calm and tranquil: so calm I imagined that the overwhelming anarchy that the "Blessed Revolution" had unleashed on us had finally cleared away and that its agents had returned to their lairs. But—suddenly—Bab el Bhar was flooded by huge crowds like great rivers. These groups weren't dressed the same, and their slogans differed. In front of El Masrah El Baladi, the municipal theater, Salafis were gathered; they wore Afghan jellabiyas and sported long shaggy beards; there were black calluses on their foreheads. They shouted "Allahu Akbar! God is Almighty! Allahu Akbar! Death to infidels, libertines, Jews, and Christians!" repeatedly and prostrated themselves as if preparing to pray. Other people, not far from them, were singing the national anthem, "Humat al-Hima" (Defenders of the Homeland), and waving Tunisia's flag. In a different area, young men demanded jobs with the frightening hysteria of a desert tribe's dog challenging a lost stranger. Directly behind them came middle-aged women raising a large banner on which was written: "The Equality of Women and Men Is the Foundation of a Civilized State." There were also silent, curious onlookers like hunting dogs waiting for the right moment to pounce on their prey. Eventually, all those large groups became agitated and stormed through the center of the capital like waves in the sea. From every side came screams of defiant alarm and incredulous anger. Then I noticed that all those disparate groups had united and begun lobbing stones, curses, stinging insults, and obscene taunts at police cars.

I tried to find an escape route from this spider's web in which I had landed, but my every attempt failed miserably. All these groups pelted me from right and left, and I felt I would die either from suffocation or from being kicked to death. Then a powerful wave propelled me into a bunch of ordinary people on a narrow street. I took a deep breath and raced for safety. I did not stop running until I reached the taxi stand, where I threw myself into a taxi. Because of the crowding and anarchy, this shared taxi was not able to leave the north of the capital for a long time. I took a deep breath and closed my eyes, hoping to take a nap, but my head, which was teeming with everything I had heard, witnessed, and smelled, wouldn't let me. I kept my eyes closed until the taxi had gone a long way. By then, I thought it would have reached the city where I have lived for more than ten years, so I opened my eyes and glanced out the window. The scenery was totally unfamiliar—as if the taxi were taking a route that I had never traveled before. I asked the young man beside me, who was busy with checking incoming messages on his cell phone, where the taxi was heading. He scrutinized me incredulously and then asked, "Did you climb into a taxi without knowing where it's heading?"

"No . . . I knew."

"Then why are you asking me?"

"Because I believe the vehicle is taking a route that doesn't lead to the city where I live."

"What is the name of that city?"

When I told him, the young man laughed out loud. He shouted to the other passengers: "Listen! This man climbed into our taxi without knowing where it was heading."

Everyone in the front seat turned to look at me as if I were sunk in shit up to my neck.

The driver stopped the vehicle and asked, "Where are you going?"

I named the city where I live.

"Who told you this taxi goes to that city?"

"I thought it did."

"Wouldn't it have been better to ask?"

"But where is this car going?"

"To Annaba, and we're almost to the border now."

His words were like a wall I had bumped into in the dark. I kept silent for a time as I gazed at faces that regarded me with scornful pity. Finally, I asked, "What should I do now?"

"This is your problem. You need to pay the full fare to Annaba and get out at the border station."

I did as I was instructed.

In the border station, I found a taxi that landed me in Tabarka shortly before nightfall. My first and last visit to this city had been many years earlier—more precisely in the first months of my marriage. My wife had insisted that we visit it to attend the summer jazz festival. She had fallen in love with this style of music during a two-week visit to New Orleans in the United States with other students from her English-language faculty at the university. Since that time, she has been a devotee of jazz and knows about all the jazz greats—male and female. She says that jazz music soothes and "melts" her until she becomes as light as a butterfly. During that brief trip, she danced night and day with African Americans on the sidewalks of New Orleans. She also returned a fan of American literature: Hemingway, F. Scott Fitzgerald, Richard Wright, Henry Miller, and Carson McCullers. I too fell in love with jazz music after those days in Tabarka—days that may have been the happiest of our marriage . . . Oh! How magnificent Louis Armstrong's voice was as his black silhouette twisted in the summer moonlight while the sea murmured, breezes wafted the fragrance of Star and Arabian jasmine blossoms, and I held the hand of my wife, who was swaying, with her eyes closed, in ecstatic musical delight!

After each night's concert, we would hurry back to our room in the Mimosa Hotel and make love until we became dizzy with pleasure. Oh, how beautiful those days were!

Thanks also to my wife's influence, I fell in love with American writers—especially Carson McCullers, who seems as fictional a character to me as those portrayed in her marvelous novels. I was troubled by her rare illness, which claimed her life halfway through it! I never tire of reading her novels. I even had a dream about her once—something that hasn't happened to me with any other writer.

She came to me on the beach of the city where I live, shortly before sunset. She was barefoot and wore a dress like the one described in her play *The Square Root of Wonderful*. It was a "white ball dress with a million teensy little tucks."[1] Her wine-red hair was carefully combed, with bangs spread over her forehead, like her pictures on the covers of her books in the French Livre de Poche editions.

At first, she stood looking at the sea as its hue started to change from light to dark blue. Then she turned toward me, smiling, and began to speak in the way Earl Shorris described when he visited her after she had contracted the illness that ended her life on September 29, 1967. He wrote: "She spoke with great difficulty, searching for the syllables of words, finally pronouncing them through the rifts of her dewy voice, forcing her mouth to give her a gracious, melodious harmony."[2]

She began by asking me, "Tunisian, now that you've finished reading all my books, what do you have to say about them?"

"I like them a lot . . . especially *The Heart Is a Lonely Hunter*."

"Oh . . . many people don't believe I wrote this book when I was in my twenties. Which characters did you like in it?"

"The mute and the young girl, who might be you. She roams the city to collect information about events happening there, to discover its secrets and mysteries. When she is tired, she sits down to play the piano, while her father, a watch and jewelry salesman, listens to her and drinks a cold beer to tame the fiery heat of summer in the South."

She smiled and replied, "I wanted to become a renowned pianist . . . but words stole me away from melodies and tunes."

I remembered she wrote in *Illumination and Night Glare*, the autobiography she dictated from her sickbed, that she longed "to get away from Columbus and to make my mark in the world." Initially, she wanted to be a pianist, but when she realized that her father could not afford to send her to a major conservatory, she abandoned a musical career and "told him I had switched 'Professions,' and was going to be a writer."[3]

I told her, "But music has always remained part of you. Every sentence you write contains a sweet music!"

"I'm happy to hear you say that."

I reminded her of this paragraph in *The Heart Is a Lonely Hunter*:

Biff stood transfixed, lost in his meditations. Then suddenly he felt a quickening in him. . . . [I]n a swift radiance of illumination he saw a glimpse of human struggle and of valor. . . . His soul expanded. . . . He saw that he was looking at his own face in the counter glass before him. . . . And he was suspended between radiance and darkness. Between bitter irony and faith.[4]

She gasped with admiration, and astonishment shone in her gray eyes, which fascinated her grandmother enough that she referred to her as "my gray-eyed grandchild." Her grandmother sold a valuable diamond and emerald ring so Carson McCullers could travel to New York City and enroll in an institute to learn to write. When she returned to her birthplace, Columbus, Georgia, she met Reeves McCullers in a friend's apartment. He at once struck her as enormously handsome, and she wrote:

> He was the best looking man I had ever seen. He also talked of Marx and Engels, and I knew he was a liberal, which was important to my mind, in a backward Southern community.[5]

"What do you think of my other novel, *The Ballad of the Sad Café*?"

"It's brilliant too. All its characters are weird, in an astonishing way."

She wrote it under the inspiration of a scene in a bar on New York's Sand Street, where Walt Whitman had lived. One day, when accompanied by two male friends, she witnessed a massive woman embrace a diminutive, hunchbacked man.[6] A few weeks later, while she was writing a story about Frankie Addams, the idea for *The Ballad of the Sad Café* leaped into her mind. Then she abandoned Frankie Addams and began to write *The Ballad of the Sad Café*, inspired by that scene—oblivious to the summer heat wave scorching the earth and people in Columbus. When she finished writing it, she placed the manuscript before her parents and went out to roam through the city. On her return, she could see their pleasure in their faces.

I asked her about Annemarie.

She sighed deeply, gazed at the sea, which had begun to turn black, and replied, "Remembering her hurts me more than any other memory!"

She remained silent for a moment. Then she added, "I loved her madly, as much as I loved Reeves."

They met in New York. When Annemarie Clarac-Schwarzenbach entered the room, McCullers thought her face would haunt her to the end of her life: "beautiful, blonde, with straight short hair. There was a look of suffering on her face that I could not define." McCullers was reminded of the meeting between Prince Myshkin and Nastasya

Filippovna in Dostoyevsky's *The Idiot*. Like the prince, she was over-whelmed by feelings of "terror, pity, and love."[7]

After she began a relationship with Annemarie, she learned that her friend was addicted to drugs and had journeyed to the East, visiting Egypt, Syria, Lebanon, and Afghanistan, in search of relief from her pain, anxiety, and chronic psychological problems. Annemarie revealed many of her secrets to Carson. She explained that she was German and that her mother had become disgusted with her on discovering she used drugs, sympathized with Communism, and loved women as beautiful as she was. Because her mother beat her severely, Annemarie ran away from her family's home more than once. Eventually, through a friendship with an aristocratic German family, she was able to flee to the United States of America. As a token of her love for Annemarie, Carson dedicated the book *Reflections in a Golden Eye* to her. During World War II, Annemarie's condition deteriorated. She attempted suicide and was hospitalized. After that, she returned to Europe and joined the Free French Forces led by General de Gaulle. They sent her as a correspondent to the Belgian Congo. From there she sent a letter to Carson McCullers in which she said:

> When I came up the Congo from Leopoldville, seven days on
> a small river boat, I got very frightened looking day and night
> at the jungle, it is just like an ocean of green, walls of green on
> both sides of the stream, green all around, and no open space,
> no horizon.[8]

Annemarie spent twelve days in a military camp. Most of the forty men who lived there were elderly "and didn't react any more." After that, she traversed two hundred miles of thick, tangled rain forest and

> found a wide area cleared, planted, inhabited by only two
> whites. I got a big straw covered house all to myself.

The last letter that Annemarie sent to McCullers was from Switzerland. In it she asked Carson to grant her permission to translate

Reflections in a Golden Eye. She also encouraged Carson to keep writing: "Write, and darling, take care of yourself, as I will."[9] A few weeks after that, Annemarie fell off a bicycle into a ravine, lost consciousness, and died in a hospital in Zurich.

I looked at Carson and found that her beautiful gray eyes were filled with tears.

"Sorry!" I exclaimed.

"The problem is that I weep feverishly whenever I remember her."

Trying to distract her, I asked, "Have you written something new?"

Her face became even paler, and she replied, "I want to write, but they won't let me!"

"Who?"

"The Heavenly Guards."

"Are there Guards in the next life?"

"Yes . . . and they are even more brutal and vicious than any guards on earth . . . more alert and watchful. No gesture escapes them. They even know what you're thinking. They tell us: 'You band of writers, poets, and philosophers: accept your fate. Don't wear yourselves out. Don't think you can continue doing what you did on earth!'"

After pausing for a time, she added, "Oh . . . how I want to read splendid, thrilling books the way I did when I was alive. My mother would send me out to buy what we needed for lunch or supper, and I would return with a book. Of the books I remember, there was one by Katherine Mansfield. I was so curious that I started reading while I was still on the street! I also loved the books of Thomas Wolfe, who was a Southerner like me."[10]

For some moments she remained lost in deep reflection. Then she continued: "One author I love is Richard Wright. I met him when we were living in a shared house in New York. He, his wife, and their son lived with us. . . . During that period, it was hard for Blacks to find a decent apartment. But our relationship became firmer in Paris, where he moved to live, after he was troubled by increasing White racism. He loved my books a lot; he said I was the White Southern writer who best described the lives of Black people. I was so furious about the humiliation to which Blacks were subjected that I began to identify with them. When I became so ill that I couldn't move, Richard Wright visited me in the American Hospital of Paris and comforted me. He said that his mother had suffered a similar stroke, which had not prevented her from raising a number of children.[11] I was shocked and greatly saddened by his death. That caused me to be frightened at how fragile human life is."

I wanted to talk some more, but Carson McCullers suddenly vanished, and I found myself alone with the sea, which was overwhelmed by the night's darkness.

Oh! How beautiful those days were!

My wife and I lived blissfully, with no grumbling or vexations, none of the quarrels that can spoil conjugal life and transform it into an inferno. We were so compatible it made our friends uncomfortable. Jazz and American novels. Especially Carson McCullers's amazing novels, which lightened the burdens of my monotonous job at the insurance agency, where there were a lot of numbers, computations, spreadsheets, and tense, tiresome, upsetting meetings, from which we emerged as frustrated and shattered as if we had spent a night in a cramped cell with no ventilation.

But now . . . oh, now! How sad I am about our situation. Our married life is scarcely tolerable. Like Biff in Carson McCullers's novel *The Heart Is a Lonely Hunter*, all I see in the present and the future are "blackness, error, and ruin."[12]

Tabarka was lonely and virtually deserted. Most of the shops were closed or closing. A few residents were hastening to their homes as if afraid of some imminent danger. Is this what the city is like in the winter?

I withdrew a hundred dinars from an ATM and found a nondescript hotel. The sixty-year-old owner was smoking by himself, and a cup of coffee sat in front of him. His bald head and his crafty, cunning glances reminded me of the Egyptian actor Mahmoud el-Meliguy, whom I loved when I was young. I inspected the room and headed for the exit, planning to go out and search for a restaurant to quiet the croaking of my empty belly. The hotel's proprietor yelled at me: "Where are you going?"

"I'm really hungry and want to go to a restaurant . . ."

"Oh . . . you don't seem to know that a curfew will come into effect in a few minutes!"

"Aaaah . . . you're right!"

He was silent for a time and then said, "Listen, I'll check in the kitchen. I may be able to find something from lunch."

He was gone briefly. Then he returned to tell me he had found some spaghetti with ground beef. After reheating it, he placed a plate before me.

I quickly devoured the spaghetti while the owner of the establishment watched me with crafty eyes and smoked.

Once I finished eating, he asked, "Would you like something to drink?"

I hesitated a little and then ventured, "Beer!"

"Oh, I'd like a beer too."

He opened the fridge, which I noticed was full of beer bottles. He brought me one, opened it and another one for himself. Then he sat down opposite me, feeling reassured.

"The first one's on me," he said with a smile.

"Thanks!"

"You look tired."

"That's true. I had a terrible day!"

"Why?"

"I'd rather not say; I want to forget it!"

"You're right. In any case, we are all experiencing our worst days currently. As you see, my hotel is empty. An entire week may pass without a single visitor, and there is nothing to suggest that matters will improve. Instead, all signs indicate that the situation will continue to deteriorate. . . . Don't you agree?"

"I don't know."

The hotel's proprietor was convinced that conditions would grow worse. The entire country was roiled with anarchy, protests, struggles, and strikes, and people feared that even worse was ahead. What frightened people most was the breakdown of public security. That was exemplified by the increased number of crimes and fires that were deliberately set and by the looting of goods in broad daylight. Bearded zealots did not hesitate to strong-arm and terrorize people who disagreed with their fatwas and prohibitions, which were as numerous as lice on dirty heads. He knew a young man from a village near Tabarka—the sole support of his mother who had diabetes. "The poor guy! They grabbed him when he was returning home one evening. They took him to a forest where he spent an entire night as each assailant tortured him in some different way. These torments culminated in them amputating his right hand, after they accused him of secretly drinking wine. Now the poor lad is lying in the hospital—leaving his mother with no one to care for her." He knew the young man well, because the fellow had worked a whole year at the hotel. Thus, he could swear a triple oath that he was innocent of the charge. But the bearded gents continued to act as if they were the masters of the city. "They do as they want, and no one can stop them. In fact, some folks may encourage them and incite them to perpetrate even more atrocious crimes." Yes, he had heard they had established an emirate in the South of Tunisia to enforce their weird laws—as if Tunisia were Somalia or Afghanistan. Had he nourished doubts about me—he knew how to size people up by their faces—he would never have offered me a beer, because the bearded ones sent spies to hotels, both small and large, and then attacked them and set them on fire. "Our country has endured nerve-racking periods, but the current crisis is the worst and most dangerous for all levels of society. Lord, spare us!"

During our third beer, the hotel manager's phone rang.

"Good evening. . . . No, not at all. I'm with a guest who loves beer as much as you or I. Come along. There's nothing to fear."

In a matter of minutes, a woman in her thirties appeared before us. From my first glance, I guessed her profession.

The owner of the hotel rose and embraced her. Then he told me, "This is Lulu. She's been my dear friend for many years. Isn't that so, Lulu?"

Lulu smiled and nodded her henna-tinted head in agreement.

I shook her hand.

After she sat down, the hotel's proprietor opened a bottle of beer for her and lit her cigarette.

"There's nothing to be ashamed of. I'll tell you frankly that Lulu worked in a brothel in Kairouan. Four weeks ago, the bearded ones attacked that brothel and drove away everyone who worked there, after scolding them and taking all their money. Poor Lulu telephoned me, weeping bitterly, and I didn't think twice about inviting her to stay with me until conditions improve."

The hotel owner hugged Lulu, smiled, and said, "Lulu's a sweetheart and is very dear to me. I love her very much!"

He kissed her lips. "Your lips are sweeter than honey, darling Lulu."

He kissed her again and then told her, "Darling, tell our guest what happened to you in Kairouan, so he'll know what's become of our country!"

Lulu took a long drag on her cigarette, drank half the glass of beer, and then released a fiery sigh.

Before the terrible attack, the women of the brothel in Kairouan had endured days and nights of terror, because thieves and perverts had exploited the breakdown in public order to rape and steal from them more than once. The day of the final attack, at the conclusion of the Friday communal prayer in the Great Mosque, the imam shouted to the worshipers, "Hear me: any man who participates in the destruction of the house of sin in the heart of our holy city will please God and His Prophet in this life and gain paradise in the hereafter!" Then dozens of bearded men with black calluses on their foreheads armed themselves with daggers, swords, clubs, and axes and attacked the brothel. The elderly madame, who was always cheerful and who supervised the establishment's safety, became so frightened when confronted by those hate-filled mobs that she fainted. Then they forced their way into the building. Those bearded zealots used the playbook of the previous thieves and perverts and stole all the money and jewelry they could lay hands on as well as other valuables. Then they brought out the prostitutes, who found themselves virtually naked in the street on a cold night when not even the police could protect them. Lulu and five of her friends were able to flee from the city to the wasteland of the desert, where they spent the night. Some of them broke down at first, weeping and wailing. But Zuzu, who was well known for her gaiety and optimism even in the most trying times, shouted to them, "Come on now . . . that's enough tears, Girls. We love life, and they hate it. Isn't that so?"

Then she raised her voice in song, belting out marvelous popular songs. The other women stopped weeping and started to sing along. They danced until dawn broke over the desolate plains of Kairouan.

The three of us stayed up drinking until 3 a.m. I slept, but not too well, until 8. I thanked the hotel's proprietor for a beautiful evening. Then I bade him farewell and rushed to the station. This time, before I climbed in a car, I made sure that it was heading to the city where I live.

Aziz

Should I go out? No, no, no . . . I won't go out. Rain, rain, rain: once the city is drenched, it becomes a pigsty and walking down its streets is a painful torture a person imposes on himself. If I ventured out, I would return to my apartment shaking with fever; that's what happened a year ago—this same month. I had to rest in bed for an entire month. Yes . . . that's what happened. For this reason, I won't go out. I will not venture outside, even though it's true that I like going to that café with a view of the sea and drinking coffee while I flip through the gap-filled pages of my life or read the newspapers. I might take a walk on the beach to meet Omran and listen to his ideas, which delight me and open windows in my mind on things that previously were concealed, hidden, and unknown in this country and in the souls and hearts of worshippers. But I shan't go out for fear of contracting a chest inflammation. A man like me, of my age, can easily succumb to such a malady. That's why I won't go out. This afternoon, I'll watch a movie, stretched out on the sofa in the sitting room. This evening, I'll prepare a light supper and open a bottle. I'll start drinking while I listen to soothing music. Before going to bed, I'll try to read some pages of the novel by that American author my friend Saleem likes. Oh, Saleem! The poor fellow seems to be losing his equilibrium. I don't know why. He no longer cares about his appearance. He was always spruce and cheerful but now looks like a tramp on the verge of a nervous breakdown. He has avoided me for weeks, as if I were his implacable enemy. His wife, Nadia, met me on the street one day and didn't greet me. In fact, she quickly crossed to the other side once she noticed me. That suggests she may be quarreling with Saleem and that some evil has begun to destroy their exceptional harmony. I love Saleem and respect his wife a lot. I want nothing for them and their beautiful little daughter but happiness and bliss. I await the day Saleem regains his equilibrium and vitality so I can invite him to have a drink at The Corsairs Bar.[13] At such a time, he may open his heart to me and tell me frankly what has happened. As long as I have known him, he has always trusted me and never hidden any of his secrets from me.

I won't go out. No, no, no . . . I won't. I need to accustom myself to staying at home, because going out has become expensive. Everything has grown dearer, and dangers have started to threaten young and old alike. Every day I hear things that scare me and plunge me deep into fears and worries. Yesterday I heard that the bearded ones had attacked a cinema in the capital. No one is safe from being harmed by them. Dozens were seriously injured and taken to the hospital. Here, a week ago, they set fire to a liquor store and threatened to kill the owner if he dared to reopen his shop. Yes, this is what they did. I think they will never stop doing these things, because one of their leaders placed a cowboy hat on his head and announced that the time had come to proclaim the Sixth Caliphate. I've never understood what they mean by "Sixth Caliphate"! The only caliphate I know was a system of governance in ancient times. It spread its influence over many lands and different regions. Caliph Harun al-Rashid established himself in his magnificent chamber in Baghdad's grand palace. He boasted of his power and influence: "Wherever it rains, remember to pay your land taxes to me!" I don't know how you could enlarge a small country like Tunisia, which is seven hundred kilometers north to south and two hundred east to west, to create a Sixth Caliphate. I asked Omran, who understands these thorny subjects, but he just smiled sarcastically. That made me think the man with the cowboy hat is raving about matters beyond his ken and understanding. But it seems that people like the bearded men are proliferating nowadays as their fatwas become more numerous and their demands more diverse. To the best of my knowledge, their caliphate is summed up by those demands. We may wake up one day to find a caliph seated cross-legged on a throne, spreading terror, with gallows erected everywhere, committing horrible massacres, while claiming the populace are deviants and that justice will be established by the blade of the sword. Yes, this may happen one day, because, in this dusty age, wonders and miracles still excite astonishment and amazement!

My telephone rang. My friend Murad is feeling sad and wants to meet me, but I pretend to be sick and postpone our meeting to another day. The truth is that I don't want to meet Murad, because his complaints have multiplied lately, especially after the bearded ones attacked his brother's son. That happened exactly a week ago, shortly after the evening prayer. Veiled men broke into their house, which is beside mine, dragged his nephew Raouf out of bed, and began beating him violently while they shouted, "Allahu Akbar! Allahu Akbar! Allahu Akbar! Death to the accursed Communist, the enemy of God and His Prophet!"

I don't know whether Raouf really is a Communist, since I've never heard him say anything or seen him do anything suspicious—neither before nor after the fall of the old regime. He may have revealed that he harbors "red" ideas in his head, which is shaped like an egg. It's true that, from time to time, he's tempted to attend meetings of the new parties, but he doesn't comment on them or chatter about them endlessly the way his uncle Murad does. What I've observed since he was a child is that he's an amiable, shy, goodhearted, and well-mannered young man, and a diligent student. He may not have any male or female friends, since he stays home throughout the school holidays and remains planted for hours in front of his computer. He is a cinema buff like me and is especially fond of Westerns. For this reason, I often invite him to my apartment to watch shows we like on the foreign channels. Once I told him jocularly that he looked like the character Gregory Wilks, who likes to call himself "Joe" in the film *Last Day of Summer*. And he really does look a lot like him, because he is tall and so thin that his ribs show clearly on his chest. Like Joe, he has large ears and a large nose, which fills his boyish face. The veins on his hands show clearly, like an old man's, and his nervous glances suggest that he suffers from some inner turmoil. I soon noticed that Raouf was enraged by that comparison, because he thought I meant he resembled Gregory Wilks not only in appearance but in his homosexuality and psychological complexes, which grew worse after a security camera caught him masturbating in a class. After that Raouf never watched films with me again. When I met him in the street, he would greet me coldly and walk faster, for fear that I would stop him and start a conversation, as I used to. Now Raouf is lying in the hospital and, according to what I've heard, suffers from fractures and other serious injuries.

I acknowledge that I didn't rush to save him; I let those creatures humiliate and beat him, spit on him, and threaten to slaughter him like a sheep for the Eid. My cowardice in failing to help him can be explained. I had drunk half a bottle of Kudia wine, and the alcohol was starting to make me dizzy and wobbly. If I had gone out to save Raouf, those raging beasts would have realized that I was inebriated from the way I moved. They would have raided my apartment and found all the bottles I've drained and those I haven't. They might have found the porn magazines in my bedroom with pages portraying beautiful actresses and models, soiled by my imaginary trysts. Besides, what could a frail old man like me have done against creatures armed with clubs and swords, people certain they are sent by heaven to punish libertines and apostates? Don't these excuses suffice to justify the fact that I trembled like a frightened mouse until those creatures left the residence of my friend Murad's family shouting "Allahu Akbar! Allahu Akbar! Allahu Akbar!"? When Murad returned home at ten that night, he began screaming loudly, threatening to wreak painful vengeance on the perpetrators while his aged mother and spinster sister moaned. Then suddenly, Murad stopped screaming, his mother and spinster sister stopped weeping and wailing, and the house was blanketed by the heavy silence of a household at the end of a period of mourning. I thought Murad would come chastise me, but he didn't. Even though I had urgent errands to run, I stayed home the next day to avoid finding myself face-to-face with

Murad, or his sister, who hates me intensely, as if I were responsible for her spinsterhood!

My poor friend Murad! He is abstemious, like me, and satisfied with his small share of the world. He exhibits no ambition or greed. He doesn't flatter other people, especially not the rich and powerful. He's always laughing and cheerful, despite the many trials he has endured. Someone else might have lost his head or succumbed to some disorder that left him like a rag tossed by the wayside. He might have perpetrated foul acts that led him to an unsavory end. But Murad, who has retained his equilibrium, is jocular, playful, and self-deprecatory. He is a person who believes he's none too bright—a short-legged donkey anyone can easily ride. I know all the misfortunes he has suffered, even though he rarely refers to them or talks much about them. I suspect that the greatest of these misfortunes struck his youngest maternal uncle—Saalim. After his father died of heart failure, Murad, who was fourteen then, was forced to drop out of school to support his impoverished family and tend to its affairs. He had to work ill-paid, menial jobs that did not really supply his family's needs. When Murad's youngest maternal uncle, who was twenty-eight then, noticed that the family of his dearest sister was in worse straits every day, he came to live with her and started to conduct himself as if he were her family's primary support and did not reject the request of any member of that family, unless it was something he could not afford. This made Murad's mother very happy. She prayed day and night that her youngest brother would be successful at work and marry a good girl who would provide him happiness and contentment and bear him children to assist him during his lifetime in the best possible way and serve as his heirs after his death. Murad was naturally very happy to have his youngest maternal uncle in his family's home, especially since Murad liked his uncle Saalim more than Saalim's four older brothers. Saalim also treated Murad like a dear friend, sharing with him all his heart's emotions and secrets. He liked to sit with him, spending the evening, and discuss many different topics—especially politics, which fascinated Murad more than any other subject. For this reason, Murad never tired of reading newspapers and magazines from Cairo and Beirut and keeping up with the news on the radio and the television channels.

Saalim worked as the assistant for a wealthy merchant called Hajj Qasim. This man trusted Saalim a lot, more than any other person working for him. For this reason, he sent Saalim on business trips to different parts of Tunisia. From these, Saalim accrued material gains that helped him advance and improve his situation. His boss honored Saalim, entertaining him in his home, and seated him with members of his family, even his three beautiful daughters, without any reservations. What the passage of days would eventually reveal was that shy Saalim, who was fond of sad songs, films, and TV serials that contained tear-jerking scenes, bitter disappointments, and bloody injuries, had fallen in love at first blush with the middle sister. This love continued to sear his heart for many years without his confiding it to anyone, not even his sister or her son Murad. The object of this insane love, al-Hajj Qasim's daughter, who was named Thurayya, was herself unaware of it. When she eventually heard, she slapped her chest and shouted: "Ooooooh . . . the poor dear!" This was something she might have said had she found herself face-to-face with a mouse caught in a trap in a corner of their spacious residence.

Saalim really was a poor dear and, despite his infatuation with her, had never dared gaze into her eyes! In her father's house, he played the part of a faithful, dutiful servant—nothing more. He never said or did anything that contravened a guest's code of conduct in the home of his benefactor. When he heard about the marriage of Thurayya to the son of one of her father's friends, Saalim lost his bearings completely and could not tell East from West or South from North. If al-Hajj Qasim sent him with merchandise to Béja, Saalim would take it to Mateur or El Kef. If al-Hajj Qasim asked him to go to Sousse, he would head to Mahdia or Monastir. He made substantial bookkeeping errors that drove al-Hajj Qasim crazy and caused him to lose his temper. He would say hurtful things he had never said to Saalim before. In the end he let Saalim go, explaining, "My boy . . . commerce is no place for dummies and slackers!"

Once Saalim was fired by his former benefactor, his equilibrium suffered even more, and there was a scary gleam in his eyes. Now, when he walked in the streets with a shambling gait and gazed at the people around him, he imagined they were weird, large insects walking on their heads. He would race and flee because he believed buildings were swaying and about to collapse. He would cross a street filled with cars without looking right or left. Then curses would rain down on him like arrows in ancient wars—insulting his mother and calling him the worst possible names, without him reacting in any way. He would keep silent for hours on end—distracted, totally oblivious to what was happening around him—and then suddenly start yelling loudly, burst into monotonous sobs, rip his clothes apart, or beat his own head until it bled. At times he disappeared suddenly; then after an exhaustive search by the police, he would be discovered wandering aimlessly in a rugged desert or asleep in some wasteland. Even though he once spent weeks or months at a time in a psychiatric hospital, his condition did not improve. In fact, it deteriorated. Murad had to look after his uncle, who was no longer able to care for his own hygiene or bathe and dress without Murad's help. This became especially true as he aged and succumbed to multiple illnesses, which kept him bedridden most of the time.

In addition to all these calamities, Murad suffered one more: his older brother and his brother's wife died the same year, leaving in his custody their son, Raouf, who was ten at the time. Murad had to raise and nurture him until he entered the university. Now Raouf is a law student and hopes to become an attorney. Naturally, Murad, his mother, and his spinster sister, who is over fifty, are proud of this clever grandson, who makes them feel confident and reassured about the future of their family, which had seemed destined for extinction. In fact, he provides them prestige they had never dreamt of. For this reason, they are continually supplicating God to keep every evil and harm far from Raouf and to guide him to beneficent safety with no false steps or aggravations on the way. Aaaah! How my friend Murad has suffered! One calamity after another, and no glimmer of salvation on the horizon!

It's now after 1 p.m. I'll stretch out on the sofa. I'll watch the film *Australia* some other time. The heroine in it is played by the astoundingly beautiful Nicole Kidman. I love this film a lot because it transports me far away . . . very far away. I also love the brown child who is Nicole Kidman's companion from the movie's beginning to its end, a kid who experiences one adventure after the other with her while accompanied by his elderly, half-naked grandfather, who is able to solve life's puzzles and surmise what dangers and surprises the days will bring.

Omran

The rain did not prevent him from going on the walk he took every morning. That was a hallowed practice he would never abandon unless his body failed him. This morning he thoroughly enjoyed it, and his heart filled with euphoria and spiritual bliss as he sauntered along the beach in the rain beneath a cloudy sky. He always experienced these same feelings when he sensed he was uniting so totally with nature that he might actually be a tree, cloud, raindrop, blade of grass, wildflower, star, straw carried by the wind, fine transparent fog, seabird, or wave retreating and then rolling back while repeating its poignant song that was reminiscent of the sighs of a heartsick woman lover. His daily walks did not merely awaken these feelings but also roused his mind from its languor and lethargy. After each outing, he felt that his mind was refreshed—livelier, clearer, and deeper.

After his walk, he ate breakfast: black bread with olive oil, a glass of milk, and two spoons of honey. Now he sat calmly, listening to the patter of raindrops on the windows and the roof. He would like to yield to this sweet serenity, which he had enjoyed since he freed himself from the horrible insomnia that had tormented him for five months. During that period, he had never experienced more than an hour of sleep a night, or not even that much. Instead, he had passed the entire night exploring a white labyrinth where nightmares and dark thoughts leaped at each other like plague rats. Attempting to escape from that insomnia, he had gone for lengthy walks along the banks of the Seine in Paris and not returned until he felt fatigue seize hold of him. Then he would take the Metro back to his apartment in the Nineteenth Arrondissement. He would soak in the tub for a long time before he stretched out in bed, hoping to enjoy a sweet sleep that would last the entire night. He would close his eyes and wait. Even though his eyelids felt heavy, sleep would refuse to come, and once more he would find himself wandering in the white labyrinth. When he had almost lost his mind over this, his physician, after exhausting every other remedy, inquired: "How long have you lived in exile?"

"Twenty years."

"What form of exile is it?"

"Voluntary."

The physician reflected for a long time before asking, "Will you accept my advice?"

"What is it?"

"Return to your homeland."

"What's the connection between my returning there and my insomnia?"

"I sense that returning there will cure you of this torment!"

He left the doctor and walked along the Seine from the Eiffel Tower to the Arab World Institute. At its entrance he met an old friend, someone he had known since they both lived in Beirut dreaming of a revolution that would bring the Arabs back into the flow of history. The two men walked to the Jardin du Luxembourg. Spring was beginning beautifully, and the weather was excellent. They sat on a bench facing a fountain and discussed the most important books recently released in Paris. At a certain moment, his friend said, after scrutinizing his face, "You look preoccupied and tired. What's the matter? Are you working on a new book?"

"No, insomnia has tormented me for months. I've been on the brink of insanity more than once."

"Have you seen a doctor?"

"Yes."

"What did he tell you?"

"He advised me to return to my country."

"Perhaps he's right!"

"Do you think my insomnia could be related to exile?"

"It might be . . . I read once that exiles suffer from many maladies and that insomnia and insanity are two of them."

"So, should I return to Tunisia?"

"Why not?"

He spent the night brooding about the matter. Early the next morning, he telephoned his brother, who worked in Tunis as an attorney, and asked him to arrange for a return visit free of political and administrative vexations. A week later, his brother phoned him—delighted and happy—to tell him he could come home anytime he wished. Thus, he returned to his homeland, after an absence that had lasted a quarter of a century, with only a small valise containing some clothes and his favorite books.

The day he arrived his brother took him to their family home outside El Kef. His elderly mother embraced him. She moved with difficulty and wept bitterly. After dinner, he threw himself in bed and slept until noon the next day. He ate a light breakfast and ventured out to hike trails he had scampered over, barefoot or wearing well-worn shoes, as a child and a teenager. When he felt tired, he lay down under a shady tree, recalling what Ovid had said during his exile on the Black Sea: "It's not about a return merely to Rome, but to a certain street, a certain house, and to a space on a shelf besides those of your brethren."[14] Then he slept until the sun was ready to set.

Enjoying the calm of the countryside and a long sleep free of nightmares, he spent two months in his family home. Then he returned to Paris and found himself totally cured of his painful insomnia. Since that time, he had begun returning to his homeland at least twice a year. After his mother died, he found that he enjoyed coming to this coastal city in the fall or winter and living in the little seaside house his brother had bought as a family summer home. He did not know anyone who lived in the city, but one evening while he was walking along the shore, a man around forty had approached him and asked hesitantly, "Aren't you Mr. Omran—the intellectual who lives in Paris?"

"Yes . . ."

"This is an enormous surprise!" the man said, literally jumping with joy.

"And you are?"

"I'm Saleem . . . I work for an insurance company here, in this city. I've read many of your books and always pay attention to your excellent articles in the newspapers and magazines."

"I'm delighted to hear this!"

"Mr. Omran, you're an exceptional thinker!"

"Please, don't exaggerate!"

"Not at all, Mr. Omran. This is true. I've learned a lot from you!"

Saleem succeeded in gaining Omran's trust from this first meeting, even though Omran had a reputation for being chary with friendships. Thus he welcomed Saleem to his house during each of his stays in the coastal city or strolled along the beach with him while engaging in thrilling conversations about books, music, and the state of the nation. He was well informed about them and their secrets. At times Saleem came alone, but on other occasions he was accompanied by his friend Aziz, a short, ugly, elderly man distinguished by his wit and intelligence. Aziz had an amazing memory and an acerbic tongue that enraged anyone who did not enjoy black humor or withering sarcasm. Like Saleem, he was a bookworm and loved the cinema. He enjoyed recounting the plotlines of his favorite films— those of Fellini, Visconti, Coppola, John Ford, Martin Scorsese, Elia Kazan, and Sergio Leone. Once when Omran asked, "Which is your favorite film character?" Aziz had replied with a chuckle, "Charlie Chaplin, because he has provided me many laughs in hard times, and Clint Eastwood, because I've always wanted to be as handsome, powerful, and capable of killing my enemies as he is . . ." After a short silence he added, "I also love Simone Signoret, especially in the film *La vie devant soi*!"

During that visit, Omran had noticed that Saleem's life seemed unsettled enough to suggest a deep personal crisis, one perhaps caused by the serious events facing the country then. Two days ago, Aziz had visited and told him that Saleem had started to avoid visiting or speaking to him for some unknown reason. Saleem also seemed to be engaged in endless quarrels with his wife and neighbors. He had heard too that Saleem's boss at the insurance agency was grumbling about Saleem's many absences and poor performance.

Omran experienced a calm sensation as smooth as silk. From time to time, he would close his eyes and dream, traveling far away in his imagination and recalling memories of his past—significant and insignificant events. His inner life shielded him from the turmoil of the external world, protecting him from its evils and lies and warding off the desolate loneliness that so clearly was his inevitable destiny. After all the bitter experiences he had survived and the various trials he had suffered, he simply wished to live alone and be self-sufficient, enjoying every moment, every hour, and every day. He could not afford to waste the remainder of his life on fantasies, the way he had in his youth. For this reason, he chose to focus on what was most important: his own private world. Recently he had come to regard sensual pleasure as his bellwether and guide. He also enjoyed reading works by philosophers who reflected on the physical world and lit his way forward whenever he felt lost in a thorny labyrinth or dark tunnel. He read these philosophers early in the morning, when his mind was still clear, or before falling asleep. Actually, he was rereading them, having first read them when young. Reading them again, he felt he was able to comprehend them properly, now that he was older and had been schooled by his experiences and tribulations.

He was currently reading the essays of Montaigne. Before his morning hike, he read: "For us to do philosophy means learning how to die."[15] He believed that Cicero, whose saying this was, had been correct. When we learn how to die, we learn how to live and how to grasp what is essential and necessary for us to live, liberated from fantasies and lies or any feeling of false grandeur that might cause us to forget our weakness, fragility, and flaws. Montaigne was also right to say that man, when he learns how to die, also learns how to rid himself of all the shackles of pressure and force, from all vestiges of slavery.

Last summer he had visited a friend who lived in Bordeaux. One hot afternoon, his friend drove him to Montaigne's chateau in Bergerac, and they toured Montaigne's Tower, where the French philosopher wrote his *Essays*. Montaigne had lived and worked there, after designing his tower to allow him to devote his time to reading, writing, and contemplation nonstop. He afforded himself seclusion, to avoid the outside world's hustle and bustle, turmoil, and bloody conflicts. He also took care to strip the tower of any display of luxury or opulence; instead, it was a house where an ascetic shielded himself against the evils of the world. From time to time, Montaigne would look down on his garden and at other views from that tower before returning to his private world, which continued to occupy him more than anything else. Within it he did not fear loneliness, finding it more tolerable than its absence. In his solitude, Montaigne had no companions to discuss or debate with—except for ancient Greeks and Romans, who were his guides for living and thinking. He was steered by them as he recorded his own thoughts and ideas and inscribed their aphorisms and memorable sayings on the ceiling. The solitude of the tower did not keep Montaigne from acquiring an expansive and deep view of all the concerns of existence. Instead, it protected him from all the contemporary struggles, wars, and pandemics that devoured hundreds of people every day.

After visiting the tower and strolling around the chateau, which was closed to visitors that day, Omran leaned his back against the trunk of an old tree and stretched his legs out, hoping for a rest that would allow him to plunge deep into his thoughts. The silence around him was unparalleled. It was a silence that gave birth to wisdom and allowed a person to plunge into his interior world and explore its topography and caches. At one moment, he heard Montaigne whisper to him: "We think only about what we want to think about and when we wish to. Thus we assume the color of our surroundings like chameleons. What we know at this stipulated hour, we change once and again, retracing our steps: this is nothing but a fluctuation and transformation."

Montaigne remained still for a time; then he whispered: "Thus if I speak of myself by differentiating and specifying, that is because I consider myself by differentiating and specifying. All contradictions proliferate in me according to roles, according to approaches. Thus I am a disgrace, shameless, chaste, licentious, taciturn, diligent, brittle, proficient, a dunce, cunning, good-hearted, a liar, a profound scholar, an ignoramus, liberal, stingy . . . I see all this plainly in myself, always as I change and vary."

Thunder grumbled, and the downpour intensified. The roar of the stormy sea grew louder, and the wind blew insolently. Then the trees whinnied like horses preparing to race.

He was certain that his deep readings of Montaigne, Spinoza, and Kierkegaard had made him examine reality objectively, unhurriedly, and neither too optimistically nor too pessimistically. For this reason, he nourished reservations about what was termed the "Arab Spring," which many people heralded. He wasn't enthusiastic about the popular uprisings it brought.

During his youth, comparable upheavals had shaken him, bringing him glad tidings of better times. In fact, he had even supported military coups, mistaking them for revolutions. His disenchantment had been bitter, though, once the coup leaders quickly became more tyrannical and corrupt than the rulers they had overthrown. Now, he remained convinced that, like the boulder of Sisyphus, Arab history will always continue to roll back down the mountain. Every time the Arabs attempt to rise, they collide with a boulder that blocks them from awakening. Then they sink once more into the dark recesses of a past that refuses to transition to the present and the future. Despair hovers over hearts and souls once more and a sense that history is a train, which has broken down in a desolate, monotonous desert. Now people are a herd, wandering aimlessly! Elites have lost their compass and go astray in their spider's web of impotence and vapidity! In this terrifying void, dark forces emerge from their flask to attack societies with jaundiced fatwas that criminalize all those who reject them. Any hope for change or release is extinguished, and history in the Arab World resembles a black hole that devours even distant glimmers of light.

Saleem

Three p.m., and the rain hasn't stopped pouring down. I'm still in bed. I don't know what the director of my agency will do to me tomorrow! I should have phoned his secretary to tell her I'm sick, that my daughter is sick, or . . . But I must use a different excuse, not ones I've cited before. It must be a convincing excuse; otherwise, the director's anger will be staggering this time, because my absences are mounting; they are obvious to him and my colleagues at work. But what will I do? What can I do? My condition is still troubled. In fact, it may be growing worse and more disturbed every day. My mind is muddled, and the fear . . . oh, the fear! Fear is like a dark specter that pursues me all the time, peering down at me at any moment and on every occasion, ruining my life, spoiling my relationship with my wife and my ties with other people, condemning me to live in constant anxiety.

This fear has tyrannized me since that incident! My wife invited her friend Amira to attend a small party we gave for our daughter's eighth birthday. Amira, a divorcée, lives with her son, Yusuf, who is fourteen. She is a beautiful, charming woman who teaches French, and my wife and I are always happy when she visits us. Conversing with her is enjoyable, especially when we discuss the cinema, music, and theater. I don't know the reason for her divorce. My wife may not either, because she mentioned that Amira does not like to reveal the secret recesses of her personal life and conceals a lot. This made me honor and respect her even more. It sets her apart from those women who are always grumbling, complaining, and croaking like frogs in stagnant ponds, exposing the faults of their husbands,

attributing to them 100 percent of the blame for poisoning their conjugal life—while pretending that they themselves are angels whom
evil fears to approach!

I said: we invited Amira to our daughter's eighth birthday party,
and my wife prepared a fancy dinner. I placed a bottle of champagne
in the refrigerator so we could toast our health. But Amira didn't
arrive at six as she had promised. We waited for her until seven; then
my wife phoned her, and she didn't pick up. My wife tried to contact
her more than once. By eight-thirty, we felt certain she would not
come. Then we celebrated our daughter's birthday, even though we
were worried about Amira, who always honors her commitments. By
the time we went to bed, we assumed that something had happened
to her.

When I returned home the next evening, my wife was trembling
with fear and her face had turned the color of an old lemon. She told
me that Amira had prepared to come and was waiting on the sidewalk for a taxi. Then, suddenly, a bearded man, possibly a criminal
who had just escaped from prison, accosted her and began to pepper
her with stinging insults like: "You're a stinking whore, an infidel,
a fallen woman! You need to be taught a lesson so you'll return to
the strait path." Then he struck her so hard she fell to the ground,
where she remained, unconscious, for some minutes. The amazing
thing, though, is that no passerby came to her aid. They just walked
on by, as if oblivious to her. When she regained consciousness, she
went back to her apartment, stumbling from pain and the terror of
the blow. When her son saw the condition that she was in, he started
to shout for help. Then the woman next door called an ambulance.
Amira spent a night in the clinic, and the physician advised her to
rest for a week. My wife found that she was in a terrible state and
said the shock might cause her friend to suffer a terrible nervous
breakdown. The increasing number of attacks on women has only
heightened her trepidation, and all the victims were women who
were not wearing hijab. In the mosques, imams in their Friday sermons and other exhortations incite men to trail any women who
aren't "legally" dressed, claiming that the Shariah requires women to

turn themselves into black blobs! My wife fears that what happened to her friend Amira will happen to her as well. Yes, that might occur, because the bearded ones believe in disciplining women who do not submit to the Shariah dress code, which they say pleases God and His Messenger and guarantees for its enforcers a paradise filled with houris and eternally youthful lads.

That evening we didn't eat, and even our young daughter went to bed satisfied with just a glass of milk. My wife and I tossed and turned in bed until late that night. We awoke early the next morning with swollen eyes, looking like we had spent the night on a bed of thorns. When I heard my colleagues at work discuss attacks on female students, female artists, and female instructors at the university and secondary institutions, and chat about bearded men kidnapping adolescent girls in some African country, my fear became so intense that I was unable to produce the report my boss had ordered me to draft. That was the first time this had happened. Afraid some harm would befall my wife, I phoned her more than once, telling her to be cautious and to avoid walking by mosques where bearded men congregate and offer people books about punishment in the tomb, jihad, and the characteristics of the Muslim woman.

After I finished my day's work at the insurance agency, I decided to visit Omran, who had arrived in the city a week earlier from Paris, where he has lived since his youth. Now he is seventy-five but still enjoys good health and vigor, astonishing mental clarity, and an astounding memory, which allows him to cite maxims of philosophy, lines of poetry, whole paragraphs from precious books, and the histories of ancient events. I respect him a lot and value him and his ideas, which he has garnered both from extensive and diverse reading and from his own experiences. Omran has survived many ordeals and enraged many regimes and prominent personalities, not only in our country but in many other Arab lands. His bitterest enemies are the bearded men, who brand him not only "an infidel" in their statements and manifestos but also "a freethinker" and "an enemy of God and His Messenger."

They have threatened to kill him more than once. Despite all this, he has remained true to his beliefs and loyal to his principles; he is determined to defend them, even if that means sacrificing his life. I always tell Aziz—and my other friends—that Omran is the greatest thinker our land has produced since Ibn Khaldun. What pains me and makes me sick to my heart is that his books are not as widely circulated or famous as those about punishment in the tomb and other such silly booklets. In fact, he's almost entirely unknown. I suspect that my friend Aziz is the only other person in this city to have read him, and he did that on my advice. I asked Omran once why people don't know about him in our country. Then he borrowed a line from the poetry of al-Mutanabbi and told me, smiling sarcastically, "I am here a stranger in face, hand, and tongue."[16]

I found Omran standing in his small garden, wearing a gray hat, a black scarf around his neck. He was sunk in contemplation of the colors of the sunset spreading over the sea. He welcomed me warmly and asked how my wife and daughter were. We entered the parlor and sat down at a table holding a bottle of mineral water and a blue notebook, which he may use to record his observations, thoughts, and comments. I was expecting him to broach events in our country and the "Arab Spring," but he didn't. Since our first meeting, I have noticed that he avoids delving into this subject, which currently preoccupies people of all classes and points of view. I did not want to upset him by bringing it up.

He told me that he was rereading the *Essays* of the French thinker Montaigne and that he had found in them spiritual comfort for our stormy era of dangerous upheavals. For an hour, he did not stop talking about Montaigne. From time to time, he would bring out a copy of that thinker's *Essays* and read a paragraph or two. The fact is, though, that I did not focus much on what he was saying, because I was busy thinking of how to encourage him to talk about the fears that had begun to keep me awake after the attack on Amira. Finally, I left him, feeling concerned and depressed. I stopped at The Corsairs Bar for a beer and did not return home until ten.

I found my angry, outraged wife waiting for me.

"Where were you?"

"I was with Omran."

"Why didn't you telephone me?"

"I became caught up in the conversation and forgot. Sorry!"

"But I called you more than once. Why didn't you answer?"

"I took my phone, but it wasn't charged."

"Please don't do this again!"

"I promise!"

"I'm tired. I need to sleep. Your supper's on the table in the kitchen."

I just ate the salad and put the spaghetti with seafood in the refrigerator. I opened a bottle of Magon wine and began to drink, sinking into my worries and fears. I didn't go to bed until the dawn call to prayer resounded.

Aziz

The film *Australia* is excellent! It was just as if I had never seen it before. For two whole hours I totally forgot who and where I am. Once again, Nicole Kidman was astonishing and enchanting, whether furious or calm, sad or happy. Now I feel I've awakened from a beautiful dream to face my miserable reality! Elderly, bald, and ugly, I live in a sad solitude where my only consolation is provided by the patience, dreams, and fantasies that films and books afford me and by a fertile imagination that allows me to have sex with the most beautiful women while I masturbate. Not even Nicole Kidman has escaped. Ahhhhhh . . . Hhhhhha! What a degenerate, childish old man I am!

My lively imagination has allowed me to tour the world without being forced to step outside my apartment! Thanks to books and films, I have experienced many famous large cities: Rome, Paris, London, New York, Berlin, and Venice. When I discuss these cities, a person listening to me would think I've lived in them for years, like one of their citizens—while the fact is that I rarely travel. I hate the capital and avoid going there. When I'm obliged to do that, I come back more frustrated than a fisherman returning with an empty sack and feel more kicked around than a fig in a bag. I visited al-Mahdiya once, and its seaside cemetery enchanted me so much that I wished I could be buried there. I remember spending a day in El Kef. A friend took me there one morning and brought me back that evening, so drunk I could not tell East from West or North from South. For this reason, all I remember of it now is the filthy bar where I became inebriated and the faces of some of its patrons. One was a youth whose age I could not determine. He was poorly dressed, shaggy-haired, pale-faced, with a roving glance, and so thin you could see his bones. He drank avidly while belting out the songs of Edith Piaf and Jacques Brel. A huge man beside me devoured an enormous mound of roast lamb and informed me—as sweat oozed from his plump, flat face— that this young man had returned crazed from Paris, where he had been studying, and that no one knew why he had gone mad!

After I retired, I considered visiting various cities, especially those in the South of Tunisia, to become acquainted with the desert's climate and the way of life of its people, but I soon changed my mind. It's true that occasionally I feel constrained by my life in this city, where I was born. All the same, I have no desire to leave it or move away. In this respect I resemble a husband who no longer loves his wife but cannot abandon her. Besides—what's the point of travel? Why endure its headaches and pains when books and films allow me to become acquainted with the most famous cities of the world while stretched out on the sofa in my little home? I should add that I am a creature of my habits and faithful to a few places in this city. For three decades I had my hair cut by the same barber and stopped going to him only when he died. I like to buy meat, fish, vegetables, and grain from the same store. I've enjoyed having a drink in the same bar—The Corsairs—since I was fifteen. I was still legally too young to enter it then but was born with an old man's face. People thought I was almost twenty when I was twelve, and when I was thirty, they assumed I would soon turn fifty. Now they may think I've aged enough to die and leave my place to someone better and more useful than I am.

The rain is still streaming down, and I hope it doesn't stop. If the sky clears, I'll be obliged to go have a few drinks at The Corsairs. Perhaps I'll drink too much and stagger home, bumping into the wall on my right first and next the one to my left. That's what I did when I was young, and after I matured as well. Now I'm old and suffer from many infirmities; occasionally, the pains of gout become intense and confine me to my bed for weeks at a time. The doctor has advised me more than once to stop drinking. I have, for a week or two, but eventually hasten to The Corsairs and don't leave until the city seems to be shaking as if from an earthquake!

I satisfied myself with an omelet and a glass of orange juice and then went back to bed. The neighborhood is strangely silent—as if its inhabitants had migrated elsewhere. I wonder how my friend Saleem is? Where is he now? I sense he didn't go to work today. He has missed work repeatedly, and his condition has suddenly deteriorated. No one knows why! I don't understand why he's avoiding me and doesn't want to talk to me, even though he always used to tell me I was his dearest friend in this city. I still love him and consider him the finest person I've ever met. Since I befriended him on his arrival in this city some ten years ago, we've never quarreled or been upset with one another. Our congeniality was always exemplary, and I still remember our first encounter clearly.

That was toward the start of autumn when people were preoccupied by the terrorist attacks in New York and the war in Afghanistan. The Corsairs Bar was teeming with customers that Saturday evening. I was in a distant corner, drinking beer. Before me was a copy of Henry Miller's *Black Spring*, and I planned to continue reading it, but the ruckus raised by the drunks prevented me. At some moment, a handsome, dapper man, who seemed to be modest, self-confident, and in his forties, approached and asked whether I would mind if he sat down in the empty chair across from me. I had no objection. At first glance I grasped that he was a stranger to the city. He ordered a beer. From time to time, he would look at me and at *Black Spring*.

Finally, he told me, "I read that book and liked it a lot."

"I'm just at the beginning. It seems entertaining."

He drank his first glass, relaxed, and recited from *Black Spring*, by heart, a sentence I had jotted down in my notebook of favorite quotes:

For me the book is the man and my book is the man I am, the confused man, the negligent man, the reckless man, the lusty, obscene, boisterous, thoughtful, scrupulous, lying, diabolically truthful man that I am.[17]

That brilliant sentence was enough to build a sturdy bridge between us. We were soon cordially engaged in an enjoyable, spontaneous conversation about books and films, as if we had been friends for a long time. Our friendship strengthened when each of us discovered how similar we are in our tastes, since we love pretty much the same books and films. I felt happy and proud to have made the acquaintance, purely by chance, of someone I enjoy sitting and conversing with about literature and the cinema. I say "happy and proud," because the people in this city who consider themselves cultured treat me with contempt and mock me privately and in public. They say I'm just a postal clerk who tries to conceal his defects and deficiencies by referring to the titles of books and films, if only to distract people from his ugly looks and short stature. Yes, this is what they say about me in my city. Each of them looks down at me from atop the pile of his university degrees as if I were a detestable mouse that had snuck into their libraries to destroy them and ruin their treasures and valuable masterpieces!

At first I was enraged by their lies, sarcasm, and scorn; now, though, I ignore all that, especially after I exposed some of them and discovered that they know nothing about the most important books. If they have heard of them, all they know are their titles and what they're about. Moreover, they had read books only grudgingly, to get their diploma. I, though, read because books have always helped me maintain my equilibrium and bear the painful hardships I have faced in my life. The truth is that I don't like what experts and degree holders say about books, because for the most part their comments are cold, tedious, boring, artificial, and totally devoid of anything that would encourage or spur us to read books. On the contrary, their comments alienate us from books. The fact of the matter is that I hate these phony intellectuals. It's the "eloquent" person I despise most. My reference to him as "eloquent" is sarcastic, because I think he is a humorless chatterbox and that his affected eloquence deadens every one of the senses. He goes to such extremes that I want to slap him about in front of the idiots who open their mouths wide in admiration for his countless banalities. The expert loves to stand at the front of assemblies, his belly bulging with fat and inflated with gas, to discuss ancient poets and authors who employ multiple words and expressions that are obsolete and survive only in massive, yellowed dictionaries consulted solely by mummies like him. He does this with all the delight of an archaeologist excavating tombs to show people piles of decaying bones. He typically looks down on me and demonstrates his dislike and disgust for me—as if I were a fly disturbing his rest and relaxation during a siesta. Uuuuf! But why am I talking about him? He can go to hell, and the worst of luck to him!

I'll return to Saleem and say that I grew certain, as I spoke with him, that he is not one of those experts. Instead, he loves books just as much as I do and discusses them the way a lover talks about his sweetheart.

That first evening the stranger held out his hand, shook mine warmly, and said, "I'm Saleem! What's your name?"

"Aziz."

"I'm delighted to meet you!"

"Me too."

We've met repeatedly since then, mainly at The Corsairs. Over the course of time, I have disclosed to Saleem many different aspects of my life, as he has done for me too. I know he is from a small village in the countryside beyond Kairouan and that he worked in an insurance agency in the capital. Then he was transferred to work in a branch office in this coastal city. I also learned that he is married to a woman who teaches English. As our relationship grew firmer, Saleem did not hesitate to invite me to his apartment on various occasions. He would always tell me, "You're my only guide in this city, my docent for everything beautiful in it!"

Omran

He prepared tea with mint and reread the letter he had received the previous day from Sophie:

My dear Professor,
I know you don't like the expression "my professor," but allow me to use it, because you really are my spiritual professor. I have learned a lot from you and by following your guidance. I have started to regain my equilibrium and love for life, after almost tumbling into an abyss from which I would not have been able to escape.

To start with, I wish to tell you that I have repeatedly tried to telephone you, but you did not pick up. I went to your apartment, sensing that you might be ill or busy writing. But the concierge at the apartment building said you had traveled. Where? He didn't know. When I was passing in front of the Arab World Institute that same day, I met your Lebanese friend, and he told me you are in Tunisia. I know you like to go to that seaside city in the north of the country every fall but wondered how you could think of going to Tunisia when the country is experiencing life-threatening disturbances including ones fomented by your enemies—the bearded men who have threatened to kill you more than once and to create a new caliphate. For this reason, I beg you, my dear professor, if you really are there, to reply to my letter as quickly as possible so I won't worry about you. Since I always trust you, your good judgment, careful analysis, and clear-sightedness, I want to ask what you think of this "Arab Spring," which the media here and everywhere else in the world discuss endlessly and rather positively?

As far as my condition goes, I can say I am a lot better than last year. I am keen to benefit from your precious advice, especially about what to read. Recently I finished the novel *The Golden Ass*, which you advised me more than once to read. It really is a brilliant novel, as you told me. You were right when you said it resembles other great works of literature like *The Odyssey*, *The Metamorphoses*, *The Thousand and One Nights*, *The Decameron*, Diderot's *Jacques the Fatalist and His Master*, and *Don Quixote*. The stories in *The Golden Ass* overlap, intertwine, and embrace each other, transporting the reader to worlds that seem strange and amazing, even though they reflect human life in its different aspects and facets. You were also right when you asserted that this novel, which was written by a native of the region where you were born and raised, influenced great contemporary authors like Borges, Kafka, Marquez, and Günther Grass. While I was reading it, I did not forget to pause when I came to the chapters that you told me accurately describe the sorry condition of the Middle Eastern man through the ages. The most amazing chapter may be the one in which the donkey describes the trials and dreadful torments it endured when an evil knave forced it to climb a rugged mountain carrying a huge load of firewood—more than an elephant would carry. With each step the donkey's hooves struck rocky projections, and the servant boy never stopped beating him and mistreating him in the worst way until his hide was scored and lacerated in many places. At moments when the ass almost fell, the knave didn't try to assist him. Instead, he tortured him even more vexingly, striking him viciously with a heavy stick. He even fastened stinging nettles with poisonous burrs to his tail to force him to climb the mountain! The ass here does represent—as you said—the Middle Easterner, who is forced by tyrants to endure one ordeal after another, from a difficult birth to a difficult death.

I would like you to know as well that I have read lots of books about the ancient and modern history of Tunisia. I have also begun to listen to Tunisian music. Ma'luf music makes me feel spiritually peaceful, calm, and tranquil. I sense now that I have been reborn and that the real Sophie has started to free herself from the other Sophie, who got lost in labyrinths while she searched for herself, for her identity, and for the meaning of her life. . . .

Yes . . . this is how I am now. All because of your influence! In conclusion, I wish you a happy stay in the city by the sea. Till we meet again—hopefully soon!

Your spiritual daughter, Sophie

He had met her three years earlier. At the beginning of autumn, when wan Paris resembled an elegant forty-year-old princess, before *la rentrée*, the beginning of the school year, had unleashed its feverish tempo, he had strolled for a long time by the banks of the Seine. Then he had found a seat in the Luxembourg Gardens and enjoyed the warmth of the fall sunshine and the beauty of the trees, which had started to turn yellow in preparation for the leaves' descent.

During his excursion he had been struck by the beauty of a mixed-race girl crossing the Pont Neuf in the opposite direction. At that time, he had remembered something that had happened to him when he was an adolescent.

Each summer, at the beginning of the harvest season, a nomadic group, including men and women, would arrive from the lower plains to work in the fields, hoping to make enough money to feed them during the long winter. Throughout the day, under the blazing sun, they would labor in the fields while singing monotonous, mournful songs, which he loved hearing. At times they made him feel like crying, for reasons he did not understand. At noon one day, he prowled through the fields for a long time before suddenly finding himself face-to-face with a youthful man and a young woman no more than twenty. They were clearly newlyweds, but poverty had not allowed them to enjoy a full honeymoon. The woman's beauty had astonished him at first glance, and her savage femininity had scared him. He had sat in the shade of a carob tree and begun stealing glances at her as she leaned over and deftly and quickly gathered ears of grain. She wore a traditional gown, a *maliya*, without any lingerie, and it accentuated her breasts and disclosed hidden parts of her provocative body that caused him to tremble like an apple tree swaying in the wind. Lust raged through him, burning him for hours without his being able to extinguish it. The flame of his desire flared higher when she flashed a smile at him while her young husband, who seemed sunk in some perennial depression, wasn't looking.

He became obsessed by her and began going every day to the same place to watch her industriously harvesting. From time to time she would look up from the stalks of grain and smile at him in a way that stoked the fire of his desires. As days passed, he was no longer satisfied to watch her from a distance but followed her and her husband in the evening after they stopped harvesting. When her husband was distracted, she would turn and set him afire with a look, a smile, or a gesture so saucy and lascivious that he stayed awake all night. All he could think of was her wild femininity and her breasts dancing beneath her robe. Once, when the couple was returning from the field at twilight, he approached her and stole a quick kiss from her sweet lips. Her husband may have sensed that something reprehensible had occurred when he wasn't looking, because he turned around, raising his scythe in the air as if to harvest the head of the perpetrator. For some moments, the husband stood there frozen, aiming glares at him like arrows capable of quickly severing his joints. Then he walked away deliberately. The wife, though, took some steps and then turned back, expressing, with a smile and a wink, her desire for another kiss.

He returned home quickly, afraid his heart was pounding loudly enough for all the Bedouins returning from the fields where they had been harvesting to hear. That night, after supper, he headed to the shack of a shaykh who was over seventy but still enjoyed good health and musculature that showed he had been strong and powerful in his youth and middle age. He always wore a black *qashabiya*, a hooded robe, except when the summer heat became intense. He was eccentric and had never revealed where he came from, not even which region, or how he supported himself. He was leery of everyone and welcomed no one into his hut. If he did speak to this person or that, he limited his words to a bare minimum. Should anyone attempt to trick him into speaking longer or explaining something, he would immediately turn his back and depart. His stern features suggested he was one of those old men whom life had so tested and tried that they were content to stay in their own private world, one they needed to protect like a precious treasure. Omran's mother told him that this old man had arrived in the village during a bitter winter with heavy snowfall and had lived in a cave in the slope of a hill. Once spring arrived, he had built a shack in a ravine. He would occasionally disappear for a week or a month and then return. On fine evenings he would sit in front of his shack and begin to perform, on a reed flute, haunting melodies like those that herdsmen play in the desert. On some nights, he would sing songs full of heartbreak and an ancient love's wound that refused to heal.

Since he was fascinated by the strange and mysterious characters in the short stories and novels he read with gusto and enjoyment during that period, he started hovering around the shaykh's shack, especially during his summer vacation, in hopes of discovering something that might allow him to penetrate the old man's world, which seemed shrouded in secrecy. Once, at the end of the harvest season, when he was passing near the shack shortly after sunset, he heard the shaykh call to him. He obeyed this invitation, but his heart was pounding as if he were about to write a difficult exam. He found the old man seated cross-legged by the entrance to his house, smoking a cheap Haluzi cigarette. In front of him was a brazier on which a teapot was murmuring. The old man asked him graciously and fondly about his studies at Ez-Zitouna University, the shaykhs with whom he studied, and life in the capital. From his comments and brief references, Omran realized that this old man knew the capital, was familiar with its neighborhoods and streets, and must have lived there for a long time or perhaps was one of its native sons. The shaykh, though, quickly started talking about the southern desert as if he were one of its people. Then he launched into a lengthy discussion of numerous other cities, as if he had grown up in each of them. He described all these places in astonishing detail but was stingy with anything that might illuminate his own secret world. The shaykh would drop some hint only to obliterate it quickly, leaving himself invulnerable to anyone keen on deciphering the enigmas and puzzles of his life.

His soirée with the shaykh lasted a long time, and he did not return home until late—to find his agitated mother waiting up for him in the courtyard. After this, he spent many more evenings with the shaykh, who became his only friend in the village that entire vacation. During their encounters, the shaykh, who nonetheless remained a puzzle that excited both Omran's anxiety and doubt, recounted amazing adventures he had experienced at different times of his life. To bear witness to everything he had suffered and endured, the shaykh would show Omran scars from the many battles he had fought; these were clearly visible on all parts of his body. Omran could never tell whether the shaykh had participated in those horrendous battles as a soldier, a brigand, in self-defense against ferocious cruel-hearted enemies, or to defend his people and tribe. He noticed that the shaykh never talked about women. If he ever began, he would release a hurt, fiery sigh that suggested old wounds that had still not healed. Then he would quickly jump to another topic.

That evening when he was blazing with the fires awakened by the dangerous kiss he had stolen from the lips of the Bedouin wife, he headed to the hut, wanting to share his secret love with the shaykh. The old man welcomed him as cordially as ever and offered him a glass of mint tea. Then, after scrutinizing Omran's face for a long time, the shaykh remarked, "You seem to be head over heels in love, my boy!"

Trembling, he narrated to the shaykh what had happened to him with the young Bedouin wife. After he finished, the old man bowed his head thoughtfully. Then he asked Omran, "Do you want this woman?"

"Of course . . . but how could I get her?"

The old man smiled in a cunning and crafty way and replied, "Listen . . . tomorrow when they return from harvesting, I'll distract her husband by talking to him and draw him away far enough that you can approach her and set up a rendezvous with her for later that night, after he's sound asleep."

The plan succeeded, and, after he stole another kiss from her, the wife promised to meet him in a place he specified.

That night, after everyone else was fast asleep, Omran stole from his house and hid in the specified location, feeling agitated, his heart throbbing, his body shaking as if he had a fever.

Time passed as slowly as a heavy cart drawn by a stubborn ass. At times he thought he saw someone, but the specter quickly vanished in the soft summer gloom even as waiting tortured him with the teeth of its saw. Then, suddenly, dogs began barking, and there was a horrible hullabaloo like that caused by a sudden night attack of thieves on the village. He froze from terror and felt his body turn to stone. The shaykh immediately emerged from the darkness to tell him in a whisper that he needed to scamper home, because his mother and brother were worried about him and had come out to search for him.

By the next morning, the young bride and her husband had disappeared, and that summer was worse than any he had endured before.

Every time they met, the shaykh would offer him this advice: "One's first love must be bitter, my young friend, or it wasn't real!"

Seated on a wooden chair in the Luxembourg Garden, he relived the scenes of that distant event with his eyes shut. When he opened them, he saw, seated on the chair opposite him, the mixed-race girl who had crossed the Pont Neuf heading the other way. She was smiling at him.

Is she smiling at me?

Yes . . . she is smiling at me, because there is no one behind me or to my right or left!

Am I experiencing a daydream?

The girl rose, approached him, and asked whether she might sit beside him.

He felt agitated but said, "Please do!"

"I would like to speak with you. Would that upset you?"

"Not at all!"

She had seen him for the first time at the Arab World Institute in a symposium called "Islam Today." What he had said about "The Mournful Muslim" had impressed her and she had wanted to introduce herself then, but he had vanished when the session ended. Since that day she had been longing to meet him. Then, today, she had been thrilled to encounter him crossing the Pont Neuf and had followed him.

"I am yours to command!" he declared with a smile.

Her name was Sophie. She was studying philosophy at the Sorbonne but had stopped attending lectures because she was experiencing a severe personal crisis.

"Why?"

She warned him that it was a long, painful story.

"Never mind." He was ready to listen to her!

Her childhood had been happy. Her father was a physician, and her mother taught French literature in the Jussieu campus of the Sorbonne. Every summer she accompanied her parents to Spain, Portugal, or Italy for the summer holiday. The small family's life had always been filled with happiness, delight, and contentment. Her parents rarely quarreled. When they did, they resolved their differences easily, without any shouting or rupture. But when she was sixteen, a crisis struck her and ruined her life, plunging her into a series of nervous breakdowns. One hot summer day, she was crossing place du Châtelet with her mother when a man in his forties, who appeared to be North African, appeared before them. Her mother stopped, looking dumbfounded and frightened. She clearly did not know what to do or say. The stranger calmly began speaking to her mother in a language Sophie recognized; she had heard it spoken in districts and markets where there were a lot of Maghribis and Arabs. Her mother, who was trembling and scowling, did not reply and stared at the man as though he were an ill omen. Then she suddenly shouted at him in French to leave her alone. The man became very agitated, and his face turned pale. He seemed to stagger from the insult he had received. After some moments of silence, he opened his mouth to speak again, but her mother prevented that by screaming again and attracting the attention of passersby, some of whom stopped to watch this drama. Indeed, one of them, who also looked North African, seemed ready to intervene at any moment. The first man continued to look at Sophie's mother sadly and silently. Then he departed with unsteady steps and disappeared into the mouth of the Metro.

Upset by what had happened, her mother had lost any desire to go to La Samaritaine to buy summer clothes. Instead, they returned silently to boulevard de la République and their apartment, where her mother spent the rest of the day in her room with the door closed. She did not emerge until Sophie's father returned from work. Then her mother looked as though she had just quit a severe, exhausting torture session!

This bizarre incident upset Sophie, but she did not wish to bring it up with either her mother or her father. For many months, questions and doubts continued to sting and scorch her, night and day. Did her mother have some type of relationship with that North African man? If there was some tie, was it an old love affair or family kinship? But how could it be an amorous or family relationship when her mother had always presented herself as French? Sophie had never heard her mother speak any other language besides that of Molière or do anything that wasn't entirely compatible with French social customs and traditions. She appeared to be more committed to these even than her husband and exhibited an intense disdain for anything related to Arabs. She wouldn't go to Arab restaurants, attend Arab parties, or watch their plays or films. But if he weren't linked to her mother, how would that stranger have dared speak to her in his native language? What topic could he have addressed with her that would have caused her to scream so angrily and furiously at him? What made her wonder even more and deepened her doubts was the fact that her mother never alluded to or made any reference to that incident; she continued to act as if it had never occurred.

Weighed down by these questions, she went late one cold winter afternoon, when Christmas was around the corner, to the apartment of Madame Simone, who was one of her mother's closest friends and who taught history at the same university. She lived alone, preferring consensual relationships to marriage, "which slays the emotions," as she put it. When Sophie was a child, she had often accompanied her mother on visits to Madame Simone, who had given her a lot of toys and books and treated Sophie like her own child. When Sophie grew up, she typically visited Simone alone to enjoy listening to her bons mots and stories derived from her many voyages around the world and multiple experiences with men of various races.

Madame Simone welcomed Sophie with customary delight, asking, "What will my beautiful young girl have to drink?"

"Orange juice."

Madame Simone placed the orange juice before Sophie and made herself some coffee, into which she poured a little cognac. She asked Sophie about her parents, plans for Christmas and New Year's, courses at the Institute, books she was reading, and the films she was watching. Then she asked, "My dear Sophie, is something bothering you?"

Without any hesitation Sophie recounted the incident at place de Châtelet.

Madame Simone sighed deeply, studied Sophie's face carefully, and then said, "My dear Sophie, I have advised your mother many times to disclose this fact to you, but she has refused categorically!"

"What fact?"

Once again Madame Simone sighed deeply. Then she said, "My dear, your mother is Tunisian! That man is her brother. Although he lives and works in Paris, she refuses to meet or speak with him."

"Why?"

When Sophie's mother was a student at the Sorbonne, she fell madly in love with Sophie's father. Eventually, they agreed to wed, even though her mother's family was conservative and deeply committed to their stern traditions. They thought her mother's marriage to a Christian would be a disgrace and a curse, unless the young

Frenchman converted to Islam. Her father had naturally refused. Despite Sophie's mother's tireless struggle to convince her family, they remained opposed and threatened to disown her if "she committed this heinous crime," as her father put it. In the end, Sophie's mother had chosen to sever her ties with her family and marry her true love.

Madame Simone remained silent for a time and then said, "Your mother is a courageous woman, and I believe she was right to do what she did. Her one error has been her total suppression of her origins and her refusal to tell even her daughter."

She left Madame Simone's apartment in the worst possible shape and headed back to the apartment building on boulevard de la République, conscious that within her lived another girl with roots and a personal history different from her own. That other girl had been inside her—from Sophie's birth until the moment Madame Simone revealed this bitter secret—but had been forbidden to announce her existence. Now she wished to emerge from the darkness in which she had been imprisoned for many years. This other girl would help and assist Sophie to rebel against the deception to which she had been subjected. Yes, she had been deceived, but now everything was shattering, withering, and fading, and her mental equilibrium, which had shielded her against pitfalls and psychological crises was breaking down and disintegrating. Yes . . . inside Sophie, whose parents had raised her to be stereotypically French in language, conduct, aspirations, was a twin sister, who had been denied, ignored, forgotten, and scorned. This other girl would need to emerge from her gloomy imprisonment to enjoy the vibrant light of day. Sophie would rush to save her sister and lift the darkness from her. That was what Sophie would do and persevere in doing.

Her relationship with her parents changed. She rarely shared a conversation, meal, or excursion with them. Unbeknownst to them, she started spending time in neighborhoods frequented by many North Africans—areas like Belleville, Goutte d'Or, and Barbès. Driven by her enormous curiosity, she began to prowl through their markets, sit in their coffeehouses, and listen to their language and songs. She was not deterred from this by the sexual harassment or provocative actions she experienced. She paid no attention to the young men who deliberately called out dirty comments when she passed. In the Belleville market, she wasn't disgusted when she felt a hand touch her buttocks and then turned and collided with a middle-aged man with a shaggy beard, a face ravaged by alcohol abuse, and broken teeth. More than once she sat in Goutte d'Or in sleazy coffeehouses frequented by old men, whom despair clearly haunted and whom years of living abroad had devastated. They survived in "The City of Light" as pitiful, dark ghosts. They passed the time playing cards, chewing over memories of the distant past, and listening to sad songs that reminded them of a homeland that no longer remembered them and that they no longer knew. When riots of North Africans flared up in the banlieues of Paris, she had taken the Metro and traveled there to watch them firsthand, defying the fires, the tear gas, and the violence of the young, masked rioters, who reminded her of the rock-throwing children in Palestine. She wasn't deterred by the warnings of her dear friend Chantelle. Instead, she increased her penetration of that strange world, which continued even then to provoke fear and fright, in order to meet young women who possessed French nationality but wore hijab or niqab, believing that this would protect their identity, which was threatened in "the land of the Christians." There were others who—like her mother—denied their heritage, refused to speak their mother tongue, and resented anything associated with Arabs and Muslims, because they were so firmly committed to their French identity. They had turned themselves into artificial, deformed creatures who nauseated Sophie! Eventually, she became convinced that neither the girls wearing hijab or niqab nor the girls who hid their identity had succeeded in attaining a healthy balance that would prevent them from losing their equilibrium and falling. Instead, they had been satisfied with a fraudulent, artificial equilibrium that might break at any moment—like a frayed rope! In the end, they were victims of the forced migrations their fathers had taken from their homelands and now lived suspended between "here" and "there."

During her first year at the Sorbonne, her life soured even more, because her parents began to quarrel bitterly and eventually separated. Their separation did not have much impact on her father, who soon resumed his normal, tranquil life, free of any vexations. Accompanied by a beautiful Algerian woman about fifteen years his junior, he started making the rounds of restaurants, parties, soirées, and cinemas—just as he had done with her mother during their happy years of marriage. The separation had caused her mother, though, to lose her equilibrium, beauty, sweet smile, and crazy love for life. She had sunk into a chronic depression that, in a short time, prematurely transformed her into a pale, wizened old woman. To forget her cares and crises, which mounted day by day, she became addicted to smoking and drinking strong spirits. She had trouble sleeping, and the light remained on in her bedroom until dawn. She would awake care-ridden, in an ill humor, fed up with herself and with life. At any moment she might yield to a black fury, smash plates and glasses, and then weep bitterly. Last year, a few days before Christmas, she had tried to kill herself, and it was a miracle that she had survived! By the time she left the hospital, she was a skeleton without any spirit.

Two days later, Sophie had gone to the Arab World Institute and heard his eloquent lecture: "The Mournful Muslim." When he had finished speaking, she had sensed that he was the only person who could help her find a safe exit from the thorny labyrinths into which she had stumbled.

Saleem

Now it's five. Shucks, time passes swiftly when I rave nonstop. But I need to leave before my wife returns from work. I must go out. I'll return an hour or two later, pretending to be exhausted after a long day at work. I'll walk for a time and then drink a glass at The Corsairs, alone, because I can no longer stand the company of even my best friends. Not even Aziz. And this is true although that poor fellow has done nothing to anger or annoy me. All the same, I've avoided talking to him for weeks or meeting him—I don't know why. I may figure it out, someday. Then I'll apologize, and affection and harmony will be restored between us. We may even be better friends than before!

The rain has stopped pouring down, and the clouds have begun to disperse, leaving gaps between them here and there. On the western horizon, the sunset has sketched a dark tableau gleaming with phosphorescent purple lights. As night approaches, traffic in the streets has diminished, and the number of pedestrians out has dwindled. Winter's desolation is spreading over the city.

I continued walking until I found myself on the shore. I began to gaze at the turbulent sea. Then, suddenly, there was an unexpected movement behind me. I turned to see a huge black dog with its mouth wide open, preparing to pounce on me. I was so terrified that I closed my eyes while I waited for the dog to rip open my belly and wolf down my guts. I would die a miserable death like homeless people whose only refuge is the wasteland. Moments passed but nothing happened. When I opened my eyes, I saw a man with a long, shaggy beard, not that dog. He wore a gray Afghan-style jellabiya and stared

55

at me so spitefully you would think I had killed his father or his mother. I decided to put some distance between myself and the threat he posed, but he began to follow me, looking like he meant to harm me. I quickened my pace as my heart seemed ready to jump from my chest. When I reached the bridge between the sea and the old harbor, I turned to see the black dog charging toward me at an insane pace. I screamed for dear life, raced away, my feet rising almost as high as my head, but soon fell. I may have blacked out on account of that brutal fall, since I no longer remember what happened next. When I came to, there was no trace of the dog or the Afghan man!

I entered The Corsairs Bar. The few patrons present stared at me as if they had never seen me before. I leaned my elbow on the bar, and the bartender I call Charley (I don't know what his real name is, although I may have heard it more than once, but I always forget it) poured me a beer.

He scrutinized my face and asked, "Have you had a fight with someone?"

"No. Not at all!"

"But . . ."

"But what?"

"There are bruises and scratches on your face."

"Oooh . . . I fell down."

"How did you fall?"

"I fell . . . I fell down . . . there by the old harbor bridge."

He continued to gaze at me with concern.

"Yes, I fell down. I fell there on the bridge. I stumbled and fell. It was dark, and the rain . . . the bridge was wet! Wouldn't that explain a fall?"

"You're right," admitted Charley, who had powerful biceps and loved football stars, Westerns, Brigitte Bardot, Ornella Muti, Belmondo, the original James Bond, Muhammad Ali Clay, Adel Emam, and Nancy Ajram.

"Yes, I'm right. Can't a man fall down?"

"Why are you angry? I merely wanted to draw your attention to your wounds."

"Thanks."

I looked in the mirror behind Charley and saw that there really were bruises and scratches on my face. If my wife saw them, she would subject me to a searing interrogation that would sour our relationship even more. I asked Charley for a paper towel. I dampened it and then began to wipe my face. But this made the bruises and scratches even more visible and uglier than before. I was scared. I would need to delay my return home until I was sure my wife was sound asleep.

Someone patted me on the shoulder. Who could he be?

Oh . . . it's Hameed who works in the agency with me. I hate him, and he may hate me too. But neither of us shares his feelings with the other. I'm sure that any affection demonstrated by either of us is phony.

"How are you?"

"Not bad."

"You didn't come to work today . . . isn't that so?"

"Yes."

"Why not?"

"I was sick."

He studied my face the way Charley had. Then he asked, "Did you have a fight with someone?"

"Ask Charley. He'll explain it to you."

"Why should I ask Charley?"

"Because he knows the answer."

He exchanged scornful looks with Charley and then told me, "You're weird today . . . my friend!"

I shouted at him angrily, "You're not my friend!"

Once more the few patrons looked at me. In the mirror behind Charley, I saw Hameed's head, which looked like an old donkey's with large teeth. Uuuuf . . . my God! Are these more waking nightmares? I glanced at the mirror again. Hameed was reflected there, looking like himself, the way he usually did. He was gaping at me with his mouth open wide. His eyes were staring at me as if I were a savage beast!

"Leave me and my affairs alone!" I shouted at him. Charley winked at him, and Hameed moved away, humiliated, his head down, as if he had peed in his pants.

I ordered another beer.

"No way," said Charley.

"Why not?"

"You've drunk five in less than half an hour! I think that's your limit. Isn't that so?"

"Have I really drunk five beers?"

"Yes. The empty bottles in front of you prove what I'm saying."

"Fine. May I drink one last beer?"

"You may have one more, but I beg you not to act up again. We're not used to seeing you in this state!"

"What state?"

"I mean you're unusually touchy today."

"Sorry!"

Charley placed the sixth beer in front of me. I drank it quickly and then rushed off into the cold night without saying good-bye.

Aziz

I no longer hear the patter of rain on the window. It may have stopped falling. But I won't go out. I don't feel like it. Since I retired, old age has turned my body into a pile of decaying bones, fraying muscles, an exhausted heart, and a compromised temperament. Now I'm obliged to remain in my apartment, especially on cold or rainy winter days. When I do venture out, I pay a high price. That's why I choose to stay home tonight. I'll read instead, listen to music, or watch films. Watching a film or two may be as good as it gets! I always prefer the old films that entertained me when I was a homeless boy, living in the streets. I would want to shelter from the summer's scorching heat and seek protection against the winter cold in cinemas, and there were many in those days. Nowadays they have all vanished except for a single theater, which is also threatened with extinction. Everything is changing with insane speed. Each year deluges us with wonders and miracles that draw us away from our old world and cast us into a new one, which they claim will provide a more comfortable and easier life. Actually, it corrupts our life and turns it into a tedious, mechanical game, devoid of enjoyment or happiness! But what shall I watch tonight? Oh . . . the best thing would be to watch one of those many films in which revenge is taken against evildoers, traitors, and horrible people with black hearts and sick souls. There are many such folks these days, and they make our life even worse. Should I watch *Once Upon a Time in the West* by Sergio Leone? It's an excellent film, especially the beginning and the end. How much I would have liked, when I was a homeless kid, to take revenge on my enemies, one after the other, the way Charles Bronson does. Then, finally every person who had tormented me would be forced to bite the dust the way Henry Fonda did after he killed Charles Bronson's brother. But I've watched this film more than ten times. So, I need to think of another old film that will entertain me as much as *M* by Fritz Lang did yesterday. I remember watching this film when I was twelve after I received five hundred milliemes from Madame Marie-Rose the first time I accompanied her to the market and helped her clean her small house and garden in the Corniche neighborhood, the old French district. I saw that film in the Paris Cinema on a cold winter day like today. When I left the theater, I started searching the faces of passersby for a grown man with a churlish heart who was killing children in their prime. On rue d'Espagne I saw a huge adult with broad shoulders. He wore a gray overcoat and a gray hat. He was walking very slowly; so I followed him. When he stopped in front of a primary school to watch the pupils as they left, I thought I would run at once to the nearest police station and inform on him. But the man immediately ambled away at his slow pace. Beneath the sky, which was covered with black clouds, he resembled a huge sea turtle!

When he reached the small garden opposite the Casino Cinema, he turned suddenly and cast me a look that terrified me. Then I raced away. During the next days and nights, that huge man's image pursued me. In fact, I dreamt one night that he was trying to strangle me. Once when I was walking down the street to the grand souk I saw him clasping the hand of a beautiful girl who was about ten years old. I approached them with extreme caution. When they reached a stationery store, I heard the girl tell him, "Dear Papa, I would like you to buy me pencils and a new school bag."

The man leaned down to kiss her affectionately and said, "I'll buy my beautiful gazelle whatever she wants!"

Yes, I really enjoyed that Fritz Lang film yesterday. The child killer in it reminded me of a dangerous criminal called Nasir. He snuffed out the lives of fourteen children, and the media in our country referred to him as "The Serial Killer of Nabeul." For many years this short, rude, bald man committed heinous crimes with amazing sangfroid but without attracting the attention from any of Nabeul's citizens, who trusted him and made no secret of their admiration for the careful way he completed all the chores assigned to him, especially agricultural work. He lived among them as a loner who concealed all his secrets and carefully avoided assemblies where there was much discussion. Each crime he committed encouraged him to commit more. His serial killings terrified not only the inhabitants of Nabeul and the cities and villages nearby, but all the inhabitants of the country, far and wide. For this reason, every family kept an eye on its children, fearful that they might be kidnapped one day, like the children slain in Nabeul. He felt proud and happy when he heard people discuss his crimes in the markets and coffeehouses. He would whisper to himself, "Ahhhh, ohhhh . . . if only they knew. I'm the only one who does!"

One day someone noticed him riding his motorbike with a child of about ten behind him. That person became suspicious. The next day, news spread through the city of Nabeul that a ten-year-old boy had disappeared suddenly and that his poor family had not found any trace of him. The witness immediately headed to the police station to reveal what he had seen. When al-Nasir was arrested, he confessed to all his crimes. He did that calmly, deliberately, without displaying any reaction, emotion, or regret—as if he were recounting ordinary events that were totally unexceptional. Attempting to justify his crimes, he revealed many details of his life, going back to his youth. He had not known who his father was and had met him only when he was in his thirties. As a child, he had lived with his mother, who was an itinerant sex worker who offered her body to anyone who fed her and compensated her with funds to help meet life's challenges. He had entered the trade at a young age to earn his living. When he turned twenty, he traveled to France but returned penniless four years later. He spent a year in Libya only to leave it frustrated, with nothing in his pocket then either. When he was thirty, he raped a twelve-year-old girl after her family refused to let him marry her. He said that he had loved that girl madly and that the disappointment he suffered ignited in him a fiery desire for revenge against the people of Nabeul, his mother's birthplace, and especially against its

women, who fled from his ugliness and mocked his premature bald-
ness and short stature. They had treated him like "a stray dog," as
he put it. During the ten years he spent in prison, his father, whom
he had never met, visited him, wept bitterly, and promised to help
him when he got out of prison. But his father died of cardiac arrest
a month later. Then the feeling that he suffered from a never-ending
curse intensified his hatred for the inhabitants of Nabeul.

When released from prison at the age of forty, he decided to perpetrate all the crimes he had plotted while incarcerated. One day he
saw a girl of about eight standing in front of a school looking anxious, with tears in her eyes. He approached her and asked sweetly
why she was nervous and weeping. She replied that she was waiting
for her mother, who was late. He put a piece of chocolate in her hand
and offered to take her home. She did not object. On his motorbike,
he took her to a deserted place and raped her in a deep gorge. Then,
after strangling her, he buried her. And that was the beginning.

In his confessions, al-Nasir said, "My first crime made me feel
proud and self-confident, and the pleasure I felt murdering her was
comparable to that of the rape. I remember going out that night to
tour the city until a late hour. I felt like shouting at the top of my lungs
to the residents of Nabeul: 'The hour of vengeance has arrived for all
the whores, villains, eunuchs, and impotent bastards of Nabeul!'"

Back then I scrutinized the justification for his crimes provided
by the "Blood-Shedder of Nabeul," realizing that I might easily have
become a killer and first-class criminal like him. Oh! What a miserable childhood I experienced in that God-forsaken, dirty neighborhood in the heart of the Medina, where most inhabitants were
petty seamen, porters, peddlers, or unemployed. These people were
ignored and forgotten by both the lords of the earth and the gods of
the skies! When I first became conscious of the world around me, I
realized that I was the only kid I knew who lacked a father. I lived
with my mother, who returned each day, exhausted from working
in other people's houses, to a wretched room where the walls oozed
from the humidity. My mother's brother, a sailor who was away
on the high seas for most of the year, had given it to us. During

his lengthy absences, his gray-haired wife, whose neck resembled a plucked chicken's, meted out to us various forms of torture and insults. I did not learn I had a father until I was six.

At noon one beautiful spring day, the second day of Eid al-Adha, I was strolling through the city with my maternal uncle and his four sons. We were walking along the quay at the old harbor when a tall, thin man approached. He had a narrow nose, small eyes, a thin mustache, and gray hair. This stranger reminded me of a heron—a bird that is called in Tunisian dialect "Hajj Qasim" and in literary Arabic "Sad Malik." He held out his hand to my uncle, who hesitated momentarily and then extended his too. Their cold handshake showed that they were not on good terms. The stranger kissed my uncle's children. Then he embraced me warmly and affectionately and thrust a coin in my pocket. When I felt it, I found it was a dinar. Without saying a word, he headed off in the opposite direction to ours. I didn't want to ask my uncle about this strange man. That night I told my mother what had happened, and she burst into tears.

Once she calmed down, she told me, "Listen, youngster, that man is your father!"

I stood up straight, as if a fire had scorched my butt, and shouted at her, "My father!"

She sighed and repeated, "Yes . . . he is your father!"

"Why have you hidden this from me?"

She burst into tears again. Then she hugged me and said, "I don't know, my little man! But you should know that your father is a corrupt, depraved, and cruel-hearted person. He left me when you were still a babe in arms to marry another woman as debauched as he is. Since then, he has never asked about me or you . . . as if you weren't his flesh and bone! He's a scoundrel, and I'm going to return the counterfeit dinar he gave you!"

Early the next morning, my mother took my hand, and together we walked briskly to the western area of the city. We stopped in front of a house, which had a dirty door and windows and cracked walls that made it look like a deserted ruin. My mother pounded loudly and repeatedly on the door. Finally, a thin brown woman with frizzy hair and a wan expression opened it. My mother threw the dinar coin between the woman's legs and shouted angrily at her, "Tell your husband that my son isn't a beggar!"

On the way back to our wretched room, my mother asked me, "Did you see what a loser your father is? He left me, a girl who turned all the boys' heads in our neighborhood, for a prostitute as desiccated out as a burnt log!"

That night, after supper, I asked my mother, "Why did you turn all the boys' heads in the neighborhood?"

After casting her mind far away, my mother said, without looking at me, "I was the most beautiful girl in the neighborhood!"

I studied her face, which was so layered with cares and carved by wrinkles that it resembled a cracked piece of dry clay, and asked, "Was my father handsome?"

She reflected briefly, sighed, and replied calmly, "Yes, my little man. If he hadn't been, why would I have married him?"

I was silent for a time and then inquired, "If you were the most beautiful girl in the neighborhood and my father was handsome, why was I born ugly?"

She embraced me fondly and replied gently, "You're not ugly, my little man."

"But all the guys in the neighborhood insult me for being homely."

"They're jealous of you, my little man."

Before I went to sleep, I looked at my face in the mirror. Then I crawled into bed, convinced that the children in the neighborhood were right.

Starting the next day, unbeknownst to my mother, I started spying on my father, from a safe distance. It became clear to me that he had no steady job. One day he would work as a porter at the harbor. The next day he would sell sandwiches on the quay. In spring and summer, he became a house painter, doing interiors and exteriors. In his spare time, and he had a lot of that, he enjoyed lounging in squalid bars, from which he would emerge with a staggering gait, talking nonsense and singing naughty songs. On numerous occasions I passed close to him, but he never noticed me!

When I was eight, the catastrophe occurred that snatched me from my childhood and turned my life into a string of nightmares and disasters. One winter day, a terrible storm blew in, shattering trees, disrupting traffic, and cutting off electric service to some neighborhoods. Late that evening, my mother returned from work shivering with fever, her face a faded blue.

She said, "Listen, my little man, heat up your supper yourself. I can't. I need to go to bed early. Perhaps God will grant me release tomorrow!"

I did as she asked and then fell asleep too.

In the morning, my mother did not wake me the way she usually did. When I touched her, I found she was as stiff as stone!

Omran

Night fell. He heard only the clamor of the surging sea and the roaring winds.

He lit two candles and began pacing back and forth thoughtfully. Then he sat down and wrote this note to Sophie:

> Your letter bringing me happy news of your improved condition truly delighted me. I now feel certain you have begun to emerge from the terrifying whirlpool that almost inflicted bodily harm on you. My hope is that you will continue restoring the rest of your ego, which has suffered for a long time from loss and anxiety and which successive crises came close to shredding.
>
> With reference to my situation, there is nothing that should concern you. I am happy to be here. What is currently happening in this country does not frighten me. To the contrary, it may inspire me with new thoughts. I will share these with you once they mature and crystallize. For this reason, I may prolong my stay here longer than during prior years.
>
> Stay well.
>
> Sincerely,
> Omran

He stretched out on the sofa and soon was lost in thought.

During a time of puritanical zealotry, the only thing a person who lacks power or supporters can do is continue writing—in hopes of clarifying his thinking and crystallizing his positions with all the daring, integrity, and veracity he can muster, while keeping as far as possible from any type of falsification, fabrication, or exaggeration. He believed that this "Arab Spring" people championed would lead to new forms of subjugation. The dark forces, which hoisted their leader aloft when he returned from exile as they chanted, "The full moon rises for us,"[18] would strive to impose this tyranny by various means and stratagems to turn history's clock backward again. Saleem and Aziz had informed him that violence had intensified in all parts of the country, and this certainly did not surprise him. He had learned from history and his own experiences, at different stages in his life, that violence is the ideal means for dark forces to spread their influence and to terrorize people until they obey these blindly while imagining that they possess the absolute truth and that their duty is to defend "the sacred," even if these dark forces legislate destructive violence in appalling forms. Therefore, the first rays of this "Spring" would quickly vanish, and a winter of despotism and tyranny would spread its gloom once more.

He was certain that enemies who had been lying in wait for him for decades would not hesitate to harm and perhaps kill him, the way their predecessors had dealt with anyone who differed from them in opinion or belief. But death, which had confronted him more than once, no longer frightened him. The worst death he had ever experienced had been his father's, one distant autumn day.

He had been fourteen then and was enrolled in Ez-Zitouna University in the capital. With his brother, Béchir, who was two years younger, he had lived in a wretched hotel in the Hafsia neighborhood in the Medina. It sheltered vagrants, thieves, and drug dealers who had just been released from prison or were on the lam. Every night, some of these men binged, drank to excess with whores, and sang dirty songs until morning. Occasionally, fierce battles erupted between them, and they brandished knives and exchanged blows. Then the hotel's owner was able to restore order only with great difficulty. Once, they killed a prostitute with whom they had copulated every night, and she had mooed as loudly as a cow being slaughtered. The next night they carried her corpse away in the dark to bury her in El Ghorbah cemetery, where homeless people and unidentified corpses are interred.[19] That frightful incident had terrified him and his brother. Then he asked a relative who lived in the capital to take them somewhere safe, and the man had quickly rescued them from that stinking hellhole.

At the end of the academic year, he returned to their hamlet with his brother, and both were overjoyed by their brilliant success in the end-of-year exams. Their father slaughtered a goat in their honor and hosted a banquet to which he invited their relatives and loved ones.

As always, he passed the day roaming through the fields and woods, covering extensive distances. He had moved swiftly since childhood and hardly ever stopped moving, except in the still of the night. He was proud of his superior speed and liked to say he could run faster than a horse. On the day of his circumcision, he had fled fearfully from their house, and his family had been forced to chase after him for more than an hour before they finally apprehended him. Even when he was young, he had not been deterred by heat or the cold, which became increasingly severe and bitter during snowstorms in the winter. He once walked through the snow in shoes with holes, and his right foot started bleeding. He would later tell a friend in Paris that he had enjoyed seeing his red blood on the white snow, comparing his enjoyment then with that of reading a favorite poem.

Toward the end of the summer vacation, he endured a frightening nightmare when he wandered through the fields. He imagined he saw his father's corpse on a stallion that had once thrown its owner who had named it "Runaway," because it was so hard to break. His father had often said, "I have a feeling that this horse will be the death of me!"

Trembling as if feverish, he sped home to find his father in excellent health and a good mood. That night he experienced another frightening nightmare in which he saw his maternal uncle slaughter a lamb his father had bought the previous week. A few meters away, women were keening around his mother, who seemed a lifeless black lump.

Before the end of the summer holiday, he went to visit a maternal aunt who lived in a hamlet about ten kilometers from theirs and spent the night there. Early the next morning he left her feeling upset, with a troubled heart. As he approached his family's house, he heard laments and keening. While he stood there, frozen to that spot, the earth seemed to quake beneath his feet. Then he shot home, wailing with terror, to find his father's shrouded body on a mat surrounded by his family.

At noon that same day, his father was carried on the back of Runaway, the spirited steed, to the distant cemetery, and the sheep he had purchased was slaughtered to feed those attending his funeral. Omran later wrote in his diary:

> The demise of my father when I was fourteen was a terrifying blow. I have never been able to mourn him properly till now. My father died in our isolated hut. When I returned to the capital to begin my second year at Ez-Zitouna, I would go every evening to the "afternoon" market, which was patronized by peasants from poor neighborhoods inhabited by rural migrants. Whenever I saw a peasant wearing a burnoose, I would race to get a closer look at him, on the off chance he was my father, whom I had buried in our hamlet's cemetery. That shows I didn't think he had died! This condition almost drove me crazy!

Saleem

I got home shortly after or before ten. I don't know which! Without turning on a light, I proceeded, feeling my way. But, suddenly, the apartment was shaken by a violent convulsion. I stood frozen to the spot, dominated by an intense fear. After a few moments, the light flashed on, and the exquisite vase was on the floor, in smithereens. At the door of her bedroom, I saw my wife, terrified, her hair disheveled, her eyes red. She glanced at the shattered vase and then burst into tears. I felt my heart shattering. I remained, frozen, where I stood—like a thief caught red-handed. Ooooooh! What rotten luck! I no longer seem capable of doing anything except ruining my life and upsetting the person I love the most. Now that the vase has broken, I am certain that my relationship with my wife can never mend; it will only deteriorate.

My wife slammed the door of her bedroom, and I headed to the kitchen. I found nothing there for me to eat—not on the table or in the fridge. There wasn't even a trace of the bottle of wine I had purchased two days before, if my memory served me right. My wife may have thrown it in the trash. Yes, she definitely had, after she saw me living and acting like a homeless wino. If I hadn't been drunk, the vase she loves and has always guarded from any harm—because it was a present for her thirty-fifth birthday from her friend Amira—would not have broken. Uuuuf . . . what rotten luck!

I headed to the sitting room. I planned to lie down on the sofa and try to sleep. Then I remembered that Isam, my older sister's son who is studying law in the capital, had telephoned three days ago to tell me that my younger brother's seventeen-year-old daughter had killed herself. How? Her family woke up one morning to find a note in her room. It read: "I no longer want to live." Everyone was amazed; she had stayed up conversing with them until eleven the night before and during the previous months had expressed no concern or worry. What could have driven her to renounce life voluntarily? Some members of her family thought she was testing their feelings for her. Did she hate or love them? Her father didn't pay much attention to the matter, saying that his daughter liked to pretend to be a rebellious teenager. Only the girl's mother wailed with terror, certain that her daughter had killed herself for some unknown reason. People spread through the fields and woods, searching gullies and valleys for any trace of her. When the search had exhausted and wearied them, they telephoned their relatives in the neighboring villages and in Kairouan—even those who lived in Sousse and Tunis—to ask for news of her. A week of searching and telephoning continued while her mother wailed and keened night and day. Finally, someone noticed the stink of her body emanating from an abandoned well.

On the phone, my older sister's son also informed me that, during his most recent visit to the village for Eid al-Adha, he had witnessed a heinous crime. He had been standing at the taxi station of El Alaâ, waiting for a shared taxi, when a bald man wearing shabby clothing approached a young woman who was carrying her young daughter in her arms. Pretending to admire the beautiful child, the man brought out a knife and slashed the girl's neck as her mother and everyone else waiting at the station watched. The poor mother fainted from the shock and fell to the ground. My nephew was still haunted by that weird nightmare event, which would torment him for a long time.

My nephew also confided to me that incidents of suicide had multiplied in our village and neighboring ones over the last three years. Most of the victims were young women and men approximately twenty years old. Their methods of suicide differed and varied. One young man had thrown himself down an abandoned well, like my brother's youngest daughter. Another had set fire to his body. Someone else had taken rat poison, and one youth drank Javel.

Adults in the village had no explanation for what my nephew called this "strange phenomenon," and it was extremely odd. During my childhood and youth, our village never experienced a single suicide. Despite all their poverty, calamities, and trials, people considered life a precious gift that should never be squandered. When death snatched one of them, villagers raised their voices in prayers and supplications to affirm to God again that they would always remain compliant with His commandments, since He is Clement and Merciful to His righteous believers. I reflected for a long time on this matter, surmising that modern methods of communication had brought to the inhabitants of our miserable village a virtual world that inspired lethal schizophrenia. My sister's daughter and the others chose suicide because they were no longer able to reconcile the virtual world, which enchanted and fascinated them with the lifestyles of the big cities and rich countries, with their rural reality, which differed little from the hell imams discuss in Friday sermons. For them at this point, clinging to life would mean clinging to a painful torture each person imposes on himself. I am sure that this virtual world drives many to climb aboard vehicles of death in hopes of reaching the promised paradise they see on the screens of their mobile phones, on television channels, and other forms of telecommunication. If not that, they cast themselves into the snares of the terrorist organizations and become suicide bombers who dream of a paradise in another world, where they will enjoy rivers of clarified honey, extraordinarily beautiful houris, and boys who never grow beards!

After our conversation, it struck me that my nephew only telephones to inform me of a death or some other painful occurrence. Not once has he contacted me to give me glad tidings of something that will delight me or make me feel uplifted. In this respect he resembles Kairouan's necrologist, who ruins its inhabitants' mornings by touring its streets and alleys to announce the names of those whose spirits have been seized by the angel Azrael and the hour of their burial in al-Janah al-Akhdar Cemetery. My nephew's underlying goal may be to force me to visit the village, sit down with its inhabitants, meet those born during my long absence, and recite the Fatiha prayer over the graves of my mother and father and of other relatives whose funerals I had not attended. A fact, which I did not dare acknowledge to him or anyone else, was that, after my mother died twenty-five years ago, I promised myself not to visit my village again. By then I had completed my university education and was busy looking for employment. That was why I had needed to stay in the capital during our summer vacation. I received news of my mother's death at the beginning of autumn.

I rushed to the bus station early in the morning only to find it so packed with customers that I felt scared and considered waiting to travel until early the next morning. But, suddenly, a crush of passengers, exchanging curses and insults, propelled me into the bus. I was dripping with viscous autumn sweat and sat next to a hunchbacked farmer in filthy clothes. He was frowning, and his body odor made me dizzy. So I fled from him to search for a seat at the rear of the bus. My plight then resembled that of a person who flees from a drop of water only to find himself beneath a downspout, because I ended up seated beside a short soldier so rotund that he resembled an overstuffed sack. He had a huge head, a snub nose, and thick, pendulous lips. Throughout the three-hour trip from the capital to Kairouan, he was constantly smoking or devouring sandwiches and boiled eggs. I felt like punching him to force him to stop eating in such a disgusting manner! Whenever that thought occurred to me, he would turn my way, his mouth open like a hungry beast of burden, and cast me a baleful glare. Then he would start smoking and eating again.

From Kairouan to El Alaâ, the bus was packed with even more passengers, and I was obliged to give my seat to an old man who groaned painfully from exhaustion and the heat. Once we had passed Haffouz, the bus broke down, and we had to wait two whole hours for it to be repaired. We did not reach El Alaâ, which was covered with autumn dust, until late afternoon. I must acknowledge that I hate El Alaâ intensely, even though I spent part of my adolescence there. I hate its dust, cactus hedges, pickpockets, wayward youth, one-eyed senior citizens, chatterbox shaykhs, and the grown men who congregate all day long near the bus station to play Kharbaqa,[20] the card game Chkobba, or al-Ronda while smoking cheap cigarettes and keeping an eye on travelers, to satisfy their curiosity and to whet their desire for slander, gossip, and calumny. The moment I got off the bus, they began to torch me with mean-spirited glances that disconcerted me enough I stumbled. It was a miracle I kept myself from falling.

Beneath the ancient olive tree at the beginning of the road to our village, I stood and waited. During that era, the road wasn't paved. People traversed the seventeen kilometers between El Alaâ and our village on foot, on a donkey or mule, or in one of those Peugeot 404 lorries that some people brought back from Libya after working there. I waited for an hour. Shortly before sunset, as silence spread over the desolate, sandy gullies where cactus hedges rose like dark legions portending disasters and calamities, a middle-aged man wearing shorts and a shirt of the type called "denim dungaree" approached and asked me, "Where are you going?"

"To Al-Dhahibat."

"Five dinars."

"That's a lot!"

"Five dinars is a better deal than spending the night outdoors in the middle of nowhere."

He's right, I told myself and climbed into the lorry.

I arrived at our house in the dark of night. Sadly and silently, my brothers and the men of the village embraced me. My four sisters and the other women began to wail and keen again and kept that up for almost half an hour after my arrival. Then I learned they had waited for me all day. When I was delayed, they had been forced to bury her without me. Next, my oldest brother, Mansur, started narrating the details of my mother's final hours. He said that the morning of the day she died she had summoned all her sons, daughters, grandsons, and granddaughters. Then she had started examining their faces, one by one. When she noticed my absence, she burst into tears and asked, "Where's my dear Saleem? I want to see him before I die!"

Her spirit had ascended late that afternoon.

When everyone else went to bed at midnight, I left the house to roam through the fields. Once I grew tired, I stretched out beneath an olive tree and began to sift through memories of my mother. I saw her dark blue eyes sparkling with affection when she placed a piece of bread, a hardboiled egg, and a few olives in my book bag before I rushed off to school early on a chilly dawn. I heard her sing mournful songs while grinding wheat during the fiery heat of midday. She appeared before me in the guise of a judicious man after my father's death; she had planted and harvested the wheat and picked the olives and almonds. I surprised her when she was weeping silently, feeling anxious and fearful about her eight children's future—four males and four females—the oldest of whom wasn't twenty yet, while the youngest was three. These images succeeded each other, in color at times and black and white at others. At one point my eyes filled with tears, and I sobbed, staring at the void she had left, as if I were peering into a deep pit. When the horizon shone with dawn's colors, I fell asleep and did not wake until the sun was high overhead!

During the four days I spent in my village, I visited my paternal aunt Fatima, who had lost her eyesight now that she was over ninety. I found her stretched out in bed in a darkened room redolent of the herbal incense she burned to relieve her pains. When they informed her that I was there, she asked her daughter-in-law to prop her up with a pillow. Fondly and affectionately, she began to caress me, saying, "Oh, everyone I love has left the village, and I can no longer inhale their pleasant scent. I think of them all the time and dream about them. How dearly I would like them beside me when I say my final farewell, which I think will not be long delayed!"

When I visited him, my paternal cousin Sa'eed, who was one of the rich men of the village, informed me that the drought, which had lasted many months, had led to widespread hunger and wiped out the livestock. Not even chickens had escaped its bane. During the summer, when the heat was ferocious, the wells and springs had run dry. Then the villagers had gone to Haffouz to complain to the authorities. But those officials merely listened nonchalantly to them. When the villagers grew angry, the guards shot into the air to threaten them. Then they left and returned to the village, feeling scorned and disappointed.

My last day there, before sunset, I went alone to the narrow, deserted gully they call "Camel Gully." It leads to Makthar, through a forest called "the Empty Mountain Pass," skirting the Awlad al-Siba', a tough group of ruffians who have often engaged with the people of my village in fierce battles, which are mostly about insignificant affronts. All it takes is for one of their cows to intrude on our land (or one of our donkeys on theirs) for cudgels to be raised and blood to flow. Early one rainy autumn, men and women whispered to each other that al-Arabi, a son of my aunt Fatima, was threatened with death, because the men of Awlad al-Siba' discovered that he had fallen in love with one of their beautiful girls. Al-Arabi suddenly disappeared, and for many months we did not see his face. One cold winter night the dogs barked, making a row, and I poked my head out from under a heavy blanket long enough to hear my father tell my mother that al-Arabi had returned to the village.

My last morning, I departed in the truck belonging to One-Eyed Ammar, who had been incarcerated more than once for smuggling. On the way, Ammar kept complaining about the policemen who repeatedly arrested him. He cursed their mothers and fathers and insulted their grandfathers as "sons of a whore." He complained: "They destroy my home and leave my children hungry! I feel certain they would have continued torturing me if I hadn't bribed them, like everyone else. But they won't get anything from me except what's between my thighs! Huhhhhhh! Dogs! By the head of my Lord Who created and established me in the worst possible way, they won't get anything from me, not even a millième! Do you know anyone important—there in the capital?"

"Why?"

"I want to tell him about the injustice and corruption rampant in these famished, rural areas. Perhaps he'll do something."

"I don't know."

He glared at me with fierce censure and stopped talking.

I descended from the lorry with my face and clothes soiled by the red dust of the road. At the station in El Alaâ, a "service" taxi was waiting for one more passenger. Once this taxi departed, I realized that the driver had studied with me at the institute in Haffouz. I remembered that he had been lazy, mean, and quarrelsome and liked to add dirty words to every sentence. On account of his bad behavior, he had been expelled from the institute. Since that time, I had never encountered him. On our way to Kairouan I noticed that he recognized me too but hadn't mentioned it. The five other passengers smoked silently all the way, as distracted and downcast as if they were being taken to the gallows! Once we were beyond Haffouz, the driver started the tape player, and a band called Nass El-Ghiwane started wailing over the barren plains: "*Fine ghadi biya khouya, fine ghadi biya*: Where are you taking me, Brother?"

Aziz

Another rainy day . . . I went to the market to buy vegetables and some veal. I returned to the apartment after also purchasing six beers and two bottles of red Magon wine at Monoprix. Then I sat in the kitchen sipping my coffee and listening to the news:

- In the city of Sfax, two hundred attorneys lodged a complaint against the imam of Al-Lakhmi Mosque, charging him with incitement to jihad and violence in his Friday sermon. In El-Khadra neighborhood in the capital, the imam of the mosque of Al-Rahma protested that extremist Salafi Muslims attacked him with rabid violence and evicted him from the house where he has lived for years with his family.
- In Sidi Bouzid, approximately twenty Jihadi Salafis attacked a hotel, destroying chairs and tables, and beat the hotel's proprietor and several guests at the hotel, including two Dutch tourists and a female correspondent for a French news agency. In Sidi Bouzid as well, Salafis attacked a residential neighborhood at 10 p.m. and kidnapped a married citizen who is the father of four children, accusing him of being "a drunken libertine." The police found him early the next morning, in critical condition, by the side of the road linking Sidi Bouzid to Sfax.
- The leader of the Nahda Movement advised supporters they needed to agitate to prohibit the sale of alcoholic beverages in large commercial outlets, restaurants, and bars and to punish businessmen who oppose this.

- During the last months and weeks, violent acts have pro-
  liferated in several educational institutes and faculties in
  the capital, and in the state capitals. In Kairouan, first-year
  students in the Institute of Fine Arts boycotted the classes of
  a female instructor who refused to wear hijab and insisted on
  wearing inappropriate trousers and blouses. In the Literature
  Faculty in Manouba, a Salafi student lowered the national flag
  and raised the black flag in its place. When a student named
  Khwaleh al-Rasheedi tried to stop him, he attacked and beat
  her, sparking a fight between Salafis and their opponents. The
  battle left five injured.

I turned off the radio. I'm not obliged to listen to such dreadful
news! I feel our country will not survive this "Spring" that people
are talking about. Instead, it may plunge into violence and anarchy.
Perhaps a lot of blood will flow, and people will fight each other in
the streets, as brother turns against brother. Yes . . . my mind and
heart have been warning me since I woke that our condition will
degenerate and deteriorate and that what's happening now is worse
and more frightening than anything I have experienced during my
entire life!

First came the War of Liberation. Ahhh . . ." War of Liberation:
Harb al-Jala'." How long ago was it? More than half a century—
isn't that right? Yes, more than half a century, even though its events
remain clearly etched in my memory even now.

I was ten at the time but felt adult enough to earn my daily bread
and buy my school supplies with the sweat of my brow. After my
mother died, my uncle's wife unleashed dreadful punishments on me
and neglected me, forcing me to live on the street, go hungry, and
field her daily insults. She even begrudged me my cousins' leftover
food and clothes. When my uncle returned from the high seas, she
would stand before him, like an owl of misfortune, and recite, with
a straight face, many lies she had fabricated about me. "Your sister's
boy is nasty and evil. It won't be long, I think, till he becomes a thief
or a dangerous criminal. I'm sure of what I am saying. This is why

you must separate him from your sons as soon as possible, because I'm afraid his evil may infect them. If you don't, I'll take care of that myself. Do you hear me?"

"Yes, I hear you," my uncle replied.

"If you really hear me, why don't you say even one word?"

My uncle stood up stiffly and pretended to slap me . . . but without hurting me!

Her blood boiled, and she shouted at him: "You didn't really hit him! You were playacting!"

Then my uncle, trembling with anger, screamed at her, "Listen, Woman: I didn't return to my house, after weeks away, to hear you yell. I came home to rest."

Having said that, he rushed out the door and disappeared down the narrow street. He didn't return until late that night.

I was saying . . . what was I saying? Ahhh . . . I was saying that after my mother's death, I grew up fast and had to earn my daily bread and buy school supplies by the sweat of my brow. I utilized my school holidays, short or long, to do various jobs. I would sell cigarettes, newspapers, stewed beans, and hardboiled eggs in bars. During the summer, I would spend the day on the beach selling soft drinks. At night, I devoted many hours to circulating through bars, coffeehouses, and restaurants selling garlands of jasmine blossoms. To keep my uncle's wife from confiscating the money I made from my various projects, as she had initially, I kept my savings with a good-hearted old woman who had been fond of my mother and treated her like her favorite daughter.

That summer—the summer of 1961—I started the initiatives I've mentioned. Then, one morning, I left the wretched room that still harbored some of my mother's fragrance—as if she wanted to remain in my memory forever—and headed to the Corniche. When I reached the city's center, I noticed that the coffeehouses and commercial establishments were closed. In the streets and squares, hundreds of unarmed strangers were pumping their fists in the air and shouting, "Arms! Weapons! Liberation! Independence!" Their shouts were accompanied by the singer Oulaya's voice, broadcast by the national station:

Sons of my nation, *luyuth* of confrontation, army of freedom,
From war, we desire peace and resistance to oppression.

I didn't understand the word *luyuth* in the song. So I headed to al-Ma'arif Bookstore, which was run by a distinguished shaykh, a man recognized as an unrivaled scholar of the secrets of the Arabic language by everyone in the city. I found him seated behind the counter, reading *Al-Sabah* newspaper. Once he sensed my presence, his gray head looked down at me from between the pages of his paper, and he asked with his typical courtesy, "Is there something you want?"

"I want to ask you the meaning of a word."

"What word?"

"*Luyuth* . . ."

The shaykh smiled and told me, "Ahhh . . . you heard that in Oulaya's anthem."

"Yes."

"*Luyuth* are lions."

"Lions?"

"Yes . . . lions!"

"Thanks," I said. Then I returned to the street, to the strangers who were chanting and pumping their fists in the air, trying to discern which one of them had the power or brutality of lions. But their scrawny bodies, which summer had scorched, their parched visages, and their downward gaze gave me the impression that they were, instead, victims of a perennial famine. Suddenly, tanks and other military vehicles appeared, and French soldiers started firing freely in all directions.

People were terrified, and those strangers began running every which way in search of shelter. I also ran, in my case toward the Medina. On the way, I saw corpses here and there and wounded people groaning and begging for assistance. Blood spattered the sidewalks. By the time I reached my wretched room, my heart was ready to leap from my chest.

Gunfire reverberated all day long. That day too, helicopters kept circling low. From time to time, violent explosions rocked the city, and the sirens of ambulances blended with the screams and groans of the afflicted and wounded. That night I made my way surreptitiously to the house of that fine old woman. I found her talking to a neighbor woman about French paratroopers attacking some neighborhoods and raping women as their husbands watched. She also informed the other woman that Makhlouf, the neighborhood idiot, had been killed by a stray bullet at the entrance to the Medina. When I started to return to the wretched room, the fine old woman pressed me to her chest the way my mother had and advised me not to leave my room—so I wouldn't die like Makhlouf—and I obeyed her.

A few days later, I don't remember whether three or four, news spread through our neighborhood that the war had ended. I ran to the center of the city and found French soldiers on the roofs of apartment buildings with their fingers on their triggers. In the streets and squares, corpses in different poses rotted beneath the blazing sun as determined flies swarmed over them. Because of the dreadful stench, passersby were covering their noses with their hands. Carts drawn by horses and donkeys transported the bodies of victims to the El Ayn Cemetery, west of the city, for burial in mass graves. I saw men and women I knew, and others I did not, weeping bitterly for their dead. Streets and sidewalks were soiled as bloody pools dried to become brown stains. Over the entire city hung the desolation of the calamities that had afflicted it.

For two entire days, I made my way through the city, searching for my father, without finding any trace of him—not among the living or the dead. The third day, I went to his house in the western district. I knocked on the door many times, but it didn't open. Then I returned to the wretched room with tired, swollen feet. I feared that my father might have been among the slain whose bodies had been taken to El Ayn Cemetery in carts or the people whose corpses were piled on top of each other, blocking the narrow street we called Al-Manubiya Alley. At noon the next day, I found him drinking and smoking absentmindedly in a filthy bar near the harbor—a place frequented by porters. When I stationed myself before him, he raised his head. Then he began to look at me silently and blankly, because he was drunk.

Finally, he asked me, "Who are you?"

"I'm your son!"

"My son?"

"Yes, your son Aziz."

"Ohhh . . . I remember. Do you want something?"

"I do not want anything."

He put his hand in a pocket of his shorts and held out a dinar.

"I told you: I don't want anything."

"Then why did you come?"

"I just came to assure myself you're okay."

He studied my face for a long time. Then he asked, "Do you love me?"

I did not reply.

"Ohhhh! So you hate me?"

I remained silent.

"You definitely hate me!"

Finally I summoned all my courage and told him, "I don't hate you . . . and I don't love you."

My answer delighted him. He smiled and said, "You seem to be a clever boy!"

When I left the bar, I started weeping. I sobbed all the way back to that wretched room.

Yes . . . more than half a century has passed since the "War of Liberation," but I am certain that people who lived through its events will never forget the disaster of that bloody summer!

Is my telephone ringing? Yes, it really is . . . It's Murad.

"Hello, Murad . . . How are you?"

"I don't know how to describe my condition."

"How is your brother's son?"

"His condition is still extremely serious."

"Greet him for me . . . and tell him I'll visit him soon."

"I'll do that. How is Saleem?"

"He no longer speaks to me, but I don't know why!"

"Same with me. I ran into him a week ago near Martyrs Square and wanted to say hello, but he hurried away."

"He may be having some problems . . ."

"What problems?"

"Psychological problems, perhaps."

"Did they attack him the way they attacked my nephew?"

"No . . . but . . . as a matter of fact, I still can't fathom his situation."

"Me too."

"I miss you a lot."

"Me too."

"When shall we meet?"

"I don't know. Let me get my affairs in order. I'll call and set up a meeting as soon as possible."

"See you!"

The one beautiful memory I still retain from that bitter summer, the summer of the "War of Liberation," was of making peace with Murad, who became my dearest friend after he had once been my implacable foe. We had previously argued and quarreled more than once, since each of us believed he was competing with the other boy to earn his living, because we both selected the same sequence of jobs for the different seasons of the year. When we ran into each other, we would glare furiously and begin to exchange insults. If these insults didn't assuage our anger, we would trade punches. Most often our verbal or physical struggles ended in a draw. I would always pray that he met the worst possible fate, like falling asleep and then waking to find he was blind or disabled, or that he would fall asleep and never wake up, so I would never see his revolting mug again. When we made peace, he told me had been doing the same thing, imploring God morning and evening to strike me with some catastrophe that would keep me out of his sight forever.

A week after the "War of Liberation," I went to the beach and found no one there. I stretched out on the sand, closed my eyes, and listened to the music of the waves as they rolled in and then swept back out to sea. At some moment I thought about that boy who was competing with me to earn a living and hoped he was one of the victims of that filthy war! When I opened my eyes, I spotted him a few meters away, looking at me rather fondly and affectionately. After some moments of silence, he walked toward me and said, "I've been searching for you."

"Why?"

"I was afraid you might have been injured in the war!"

I lied to him and told him, "I was afraid for you, too!"

He smiled and sat down beside me. He told me as affectionately as one brother to another after a long separation: "Believe me, I haven't worried about anyone the way I did for you!"

I lied again and said, "Me too. I prayed night and day that God would shield you from every harm!"

He smiled once more. "That shows what a pure heart and fine soul you have!"

After remaining silent for some moments, he asked, "What's your name?"

"Aziz . . . and yours?"

"Murad."

I extended my hand to shake his and said, "From now on, we're friends, right?"

He pressed my hand firmly and replied, "Right . . . from now on, we're friends!"

Omran

As he watched rain drench the small garden, he ate breakfast: barley bread dipped in honey and olive oil, accompanied by orange juice. He had better postpone his walk until the evening. Perhaps now he could record some reflections and thoughts! That afternoon he would continue reading Montaigne's *Essays*. But what reflections and thoughts would he jot down?

When a pandemic harvested hundreds of men, women, and children and when people daily faced conflagrations and plundering raids, Montaigne's friend Étienne de la Boétie wrote: "What fate caused us to be born in this era?" Omran might also consider this thorny question, because—from the start—he had found himself embedded in an age fraught with disturbances, injustices, bitter defeats, and frightening nightmares. All the same, he had remained hopeful, even in the most stressful and difficult times and circumstances. Perhaps books had played an important role in guiding and directing him—yes, the books on which he had relied since he was a student at Ez-Zitouna University. He had sought refuge with them from the annoyance of sitting cross-legged for long periods on frayed mats while listening to lectures weighed down by eloquence larded with indigestible expressions and long-dead words, delivered by tiresome shaykhs who had scowling faces and dwelled in some other era, sheltering there in fraudulent glories while obsessed by phantasms devised by their own sick minds. They relied on jaundiced jurisprudence and excelled at embellishing fatwas that forbade, chastised, and terrorized. They imagined that these legal dicta guaranteed man's salvation on earth and opened the door of paradise for him in the hereafter.

Al-Ayyam by Taha Hussein was the first tome to introduce him to the astonishing and amazing world of books. Knowledge then became enchanting, magical, and enlightening for his heart, spirit, and intellect. He remembered in detail the day he discovered this book—a cold day in December 1947. That morning, for three hours, his nasal voice stretching out consonants and words, the shaykh, who delighted in tormenting them with his vapid eloquence and fatwas that landed on their heads like iron cudgels, had discussed those whose destiny and lodging in the next world will be hell where they will burn nonstop in fire. Once their skins are scorched, they acquire new pelts so they can suffer again. In the continuously and eternally flaming fire, they crackle and whine. They are fettered together, wearing garments made of tar, while scalding water pours over their heads. They are struck by metal pellets from catapults every time they want to escape that grief and sent back. They eat only fruit from the infernal Zaqqum tree, which grows from the pit of hell.[21] Its branches resemble heads of demons, and its fruit, which is reminiscent of rotting flesh, boils in sinners' bellies, and so on.

When the lecture ended, he went for a walk through the alleys of the Medina, imagining that fire was burning his bones, intestines, and hair and that his body was festering and rotting as black maggots crawled out of it. Trying to escape from those terrifying images, he stopped in front of a bookstore that carried books and magazines imported from Egypt and Lebanon. The only book that attracted his attention was *Al-Ayyam* by Taha Hussein, whose name he had heard more than once. A glance at the first page inspired him to buy the book without any hesitation. He quickly returned to the dismal room he shared with his brother in their student hostel in the Bab El Suwayqa neighborhood. He slipped under the covers and started reading. He did not stop until he had finished the book. Now he no longer saw his dismal room and its dingy walls. He did not smell the stench of the backed-up toilets, hear the ruckus of students arguing and quarreling over petty issues, or worry about fleas sucking his blood or lice biting him while he slept. In fact, he even ignored his brother when he returned from his classes and did not feel like talking to him or answering his questions. He was swimming in another world and wanted to continue swimming there for a long time. In that world he discovered someone who would help free him from fear, anxiety, vacillation, rural insecurity, and his many other defects—by providing him a vitality and daring he had never experienced before. He felt then that he could become the master of his own destiny. He could dare raise his voice to challenge the scowling shaykhs, who never stopped threatening him with punishment in hell and a reckoning on the Day of Judgment. He would be able to mock their jaundiced fatwas, tedious lectures, and florid eloquence. He would be able to expose their superficiality and ignorance of their own age as well as how they clung to the distant past's ghosts and gloomy recesses, because they feared coming to terms with the present. Like the hero of *The Days*—a blind boy who came from the barren countryside of Upper Egypt—he would confront life's difficulties, pains, injustices, and obstacles with determination, force, and defiance. Yes, he would do that. He would wade into the adventure called freedom and persevere to the end. He would not hesitate, even if that cost him his life. What meaning was there to life if a living person could not seize liberty?

After *The Days*, he devoured all the other works of Taha Hussein and paid close attention to any information about him that appeared in newspapers and magazines, following the Egyptian author's critical and intellectual battles and struggles. He was so fixated on Taha Hussein that he told his brother and friends he wished he had been born blind too. Occasionally, he would wrap a cloth around his eyes and recite paragraphs from the works of Taha Hussein or stanzas of ancient Arabic poems. Emulating this Egyptian author, he read al-Ma'arri's *Saqt al-Zand*, or *The Tinder Spark*, to make his intellect his imam and guide. He memorized the most famous stanzas of al-Mutanabbi and the great ancient poets. Under his influence, he discovered al-Jahiz, al-Tawhidi, and Abu al-Faraj al-Isfahani. He studied Ibn Khaldun's *Muqaddimah* thoroughly, and it became one of the works he cited and relied on in his many debates inside and outside the university. Taha Hussein's short book *Qadat al-Fikr*

(Intellectual Leaders) led him to the great poets and philosophers of ancient Greece. Thus, his horizons expanded until knowledge became a vast labyrinth where he liked to lose himself and wander.

Whether trying to mimic Taha Hussein or not, he deliberately started enraging the "distinguished" shaykhs. To show his lack of respect for their sermons and lectures, he would lean back against the wall at times and close his eyes, pretending to be asleep. On other occasions, he would succeed in embarrassing them by drawing them into a discussion of tricky cases, inspired by his reading of books or ideas with which they weren't familiar. Then they would become disconcerted, blush, look upset, and their mouths would run dry. Finally, they would explode with anger and order him to leave the lecture hall immediately.

When a rotund shaykh, who breathed heavily and was known for his rigidity and ruthlessness, was explaining an issue of Islamic jurisprudence, Omran stopped him by asking, "Your Eminence, will you allow me to ask a question?"

The shaykh hesitated before replying; then he inquired, "What question?"

"Your Eminence the Shaykh, what does this dictum mean: 'I think, therefore I am?'"

The shaykh's expression changed, and his face turned gray. With a quavering voice, he inquired, "Who said this 'dictum'?"

"Descartes."

"Who might this Descartes be?"

"A famous French philosopher!"

With spittle on lips, the shaykh exploded with anger and shouted at Omran: "Listen, Jerk, I think you have tested the limits more than once. I need to inform you that your reliance on dicta unrelated to the Book and the Sunnah gives me the right to ban you immediately from this sacred space!"

In Arabic language and literature courses, the shaykhs avoided mentioning any poets or writers suspected of libertinage, depravity, rebellion against sacred truths, or violation of societal norms. They restricted their scholastic canon to works by poets and authors of ages of decline. They were men who had bowed to political and religious authorities and never deviated from **their** goals and interests. Early one autumn morning, when flies and dust were abundant, an eminent, dignified shaykh interrupted his own exegesis of an ode larded with sermons and prayers to ask, "You, young man, why do you yawn all the time?"

He replied calmly, "Your Eminence the Shaykh, allow me to tell you that the ode you are discussing is weak and tedious. There is nothing poetic about it!"

Caught off guard by what he heard, the shaykh fidgeted inside his vast jubbah. He glared silently at his student for some time and then shouted, "Who are you to allow yourself to utter such obscenities?"

"Excuse me, Your Eminence the Shaykh. I was not uttering obscenities. I was merely expressing my opinion."

"What is your opinion?"

"My opinion, Your Eminence the Shaykh, is that you all repeat continually that the Arabs are the people of poetry but discuss only poets whose style and subject matter are worthless!"

Forgetting his prestige and dignity, the shaykh started shouting, while spreading saliva aerosol through the room: "You are a stupid and conceited young man! You must leave the lecture hall immediately!"

Accused of "insolence" and a "lack of respect for his eminent shaykhs," he was subjected to numerous harsh punishments. All the same, he persisted in his daring struggles, without ever halting his own reading and research. When he lacked the money to buy a book or a fancy journal, he would stand at the door of the bookstore—oblivious to the heat or the cold and any other distraction—and read it there!

In hopes of emulating Taha Hussein one day, he enrolled in a private school to learn French, which wasn't taught at Ez-Zitouna University. In coffeehouses and social clubs, he mingled with students from Sadiqi College and heard their entertaining debates about French culture, poets, authors, and philosophers. After just two years, he was able to read, in their mother tongue, Molière, Victor Hugo,

Baudelaire, Balzac, and Zola as well as the Rationalist and Enlightenment philosophers who paved the way for the French Revolution.

Once he realized that there was more to authentic culture than
reading books, he started going to theaters, cinemas, and concerts,
either alone or with his brother. These changes were all reflected
in his conduct and personal relationships. He could no longer bear
to fraternize with lethargic, befuddled students who sought physical
and mental security with the herd and avoided surprises that might
cause them to leave "The Strait Path" prescribed for them by their
"Eminent Shaykhs." For this reason, he fled whenever one of them
attempted to approach or converse with him. Once he realized that
the Medina could no longer harbor his ideas or dreams, he began
to search the modern city of Tunis with its French, Italian, Maltese, and Jewish neighborhoods for spaces that would allow him to
become acquainted with hidden aspects of the lives of their inhabitants and their customs and traditions. One fine spring evening he
saw the film *The Bicycle Thief* by the Italian director Vittorio de
Sica. After that he sat in the Canigou Café in the Lafayette neighborhood where there were many Frenchmen. He sipped his coffee while
listening to witty remarks and jokes exchanged by poets and artists
who were famous in the city for their crazy joie de vivre and defiance
of received norms. His "Eminent Shaykhs" accused these people of
depravity, licentiousness, and attacks on decency. **They** could have
cared less. Indeed, they just became more daring and impudent.

That evening, a youth from his same year at the university entered
the café, although neither of them knew the other. This young man
was slim, always distracted, eccentric, and extremely secretive about
his private life. He was silent when he arrived for a lecture and still
silent when he left. His only companion was his bag, which was
stuffed with notebooks and books whose titles nobody else knew.
The young man might miss lectures for days or weeks and then
return pale-faced, his gaze darting about, his steps stumbling, as if
he had just been released from prison or some other affliction. When
they realized he had arrived, the group of poets and artists rose to
embrace him warmly.

"We've missed you, damn Diogenes!"

"Me too!"

"Where were you?"

"In my hometown."

"How could you stand to spend two weeks in that desolate wilderness?"

"My mother is very ill!"

"May God heal her."

"Thank you."

"How is she now?"

"I can't say."

Frowning, he added, "In any case . . . her passing will hit me hard!"

"Sorry . . . life can be like this."

The group fell silent for some moments. Then more questions rained down on the youth, especially: "What new poetry have you written?"

The fact of the matter was that his visit to his village had been very productive. At first, the condition of his mother, who was in pain day and night, had paralyzed his thinking and ability to focus. Gradually, though, his vitality had returned, and he had begun to write feverishly.

Would he read them something he had written?

He could not . . . He needed to revise his new compositions.

Ah . . . so he was a poet, and his name was Diogenes. But that was clearly a pen name. The real Diogenes was a Greek philosopher Taha Hussein discussed in *Pioneers of Thought*, reporting that Diogenes said true liberty could be acquired only through rebellion and a revolt against the prevailing values and ethical systems that shackle a person. He had rejected everything that interfered with his personal liberty, preferring to sleep in a ceramic drum in the center of Athens. He allowed himself to urinate in the street and masturbate in public. Occasionally he would roam the streets barefoot, in daylight, carrying a lamp. If someone asked, "Why are you carrying a burning lamp in broad daylight?" he would reply, "I'm searching for a true man. I see a lot of people but don't see a true man!" Diogenes was also a scold who did not fear celebrities—whether they were intellectuals or influential, powerful men! He continually ridiculed Plato, who was his contemporary, and mocked his ideas, lessons, and conceptions of the gods and mankind. When Alexander the Great was on his way east, he saw Diogenes in his barrel and asked if he would like something. Diogenes, ever the calm sage, asked the emperor to step back, because he was blocking the sunlight!

Eventually, the young poet noticed Omran, smiled, and gestured for him to join the group. That made him very happy. Once he took a seat with them, the youth addressed his friends: "I am delighted to introduce to you the brightest student in my year and possibly in all of Ez-Zitouna University. I think his name is Omran. Is that right?"

"Yes, my name's Omran."

The young man continued, "My friends, this fellow, Omran, will be something. Yes, I'm sure of that. He is daring and silences the shaykhs with his arguments, infuriating them with his incendiary ideas. He exposes their vapidity and ignorance. For this reason, they can't bear to have him in their class."

"You're exaggerating!"

"Not at all. I'm not flattering you. I'm simply stating the truth. You amaze me, Omran, and my admiration only increases every time you wipe the floor with the dignity of our eminent shaykhs. Hahhhhhh!"

"Thank you!"

He wanted to order another coffee, but Diogenes interjected, "Listen, my friend . . . coffee doesn't suit our soirées!"

"What should I drink then?"

"I will offer you a cold beer!"

It would have been hard for him to reject this invitation, and that beer deflowered his rural virginity, admitting him to a world he had craved since he had decided to rebel against all his culture's prohibitions and received opinions and to liberate himself from all bonds that shackled his body and thought.

At ten that night, when the group left the Canigou Café, Diogenes suggested the two of them go for a walk, since the streets had started to clear of vehicles and passersby. At first they walked along in silence, listening to a nocturnal calm settle over the city. When they neared Bab el Bhar, Diogenes said, "Omran, I won't conceal from you that I've always wanted to speak with you. Now that chance has come to my aid, I ask that our relationship at the university continue unchanged. In other words, we should treat each other as though we haven't met."

"Why?"

"Because I don't want to have any relationships at the university. I don't want the shaykhs and students to know who I really am, what I do, or how I live and think."

"Why do you attend this university then?"

"The truth is that the shaykhs' chattering thoroughly amuses me. Moreover, I've found that even bad, obsolete ideas can help perfect excellent, vital ideas. Weren't Echebbi[22] and al-Tahir al-Haddad students at Ez-Zitouna?"

"That's true . . . but I would like to know why you chose the name Diogenes!"

"That wasn't my choice. My friends at the Canigou Café chose it for me. I think they chose well, because I'm fascinated by this philosopher and his ideas. Besides, it's a name that helps me conceal my identity. I append it to my poems and texts."

"Have you published them?"

"No . . ."

"Why not?"

"Because I hate haste."

"Would you share some with me?"

"Yes, I will, because, as of tonight, you are a true friend!"

He returned to his dismal room, where he began reading poems by Diogenes in the meager lamplight while his brother slept soundly, snoring. He finished reading that set of poems as he heard the dawn call to prayer. He stretched out, hoping to fall asleep, but soon found himself back on the street, which was humming with the day's commotion. He took a seat in a coffeehouse that had just opened and ordered a cup of coffee. Then he started watching what was happening on the street as his head vibrated with the moods of Diogenes' poems, which were filled with fury, rebellion, and revolution against an old world that cast its shadow over life, language, and received patterns of thought. Some of his poems reflected the influences of Arab Romantic poets, especially Gibran Khalil Gibran and Echebbi, but Diogenes' own personality was evident too. For this reason, he felt confident that Diogenes would be a poet of the future, someone capable of devising a new language liberated from the rust of the past and the spiderwebs of dead eloquence.

Yes, Diogenes would be a poet of the future; there was no doubt about that. And Omran would be his friend and supporter!

Saleem

My fiftieth birthday: terrible weather, cloudy sky, stormy sea. The radio reports that Salafis have torched numerous tombs of saints in the capital and in some cities in the interior. They are threatening to set fire to and destroy the most important Roman monuments in Carthage, El Jem, El Kef, and Jendouba. I arrived at work with a troubled heart, because my wife did not deign to recognize my birthday—not even with a few cold, neutral words—and prevented me from kissing my daughter! I also must acknowledge that I now fear going to work, because my colleagues have stopped greeting me fondly and affectionately, as they used to. If I request an explanation from one of them or ask a question, the fellow will mumble some murky words and hastily flee. More than once I've tried to kid around with them, recounting anecdotes or jokes, but that just made them frown more and whisper to one another, exchanging looks as if I had committed some heinous offense. When they hear my footsteps, they stop laughing or chatting. Every effort I make to restore my relationship with them seems doomed to abject failure.

When I entered the office, the phone rang. I lifted the receiver, trembling with fear, but didn't know why. The flirtatious secretary, Siham, whom all the men dream of screwing, said in a severe voice that my boss wanted to speak with me in a half an hour. Once I replaced the receiver and started flipping through the file before me, my entire body began to shake. Even though I attempted to convince myself that this would be just an ordinary meeting and that a promotion might await me, I was gripped by fear and even started to feel I was being strangled by a stout rope!

Floundering in this extremely bad situation, I climbed to the third floor with shaky steps. The tepid greeting that Siham, the secretary, granted me, while she avoided looking my way, upset me all the more. My boss received me almost fondly and ordered coffee for me. Then he asked how I and my little family were. I replied to his queries very tersely. After that, he examined me for a time. Then he said, sounding serious and stern, the way he did on official occasions and in meetings: "Mr. Saleem . . . you've changed a lot recently. Isn't that so?"

I didn't understand what he was getting at! So, I remained silent and stared at him the way a defendant on trial reacts when posed a question that scatters his thoughts and leaves him uncertain how to respond.

As his expression became increasingly serious and stern, he added, "Yes, Mr. Saleem, you have changed a lot. I won't conceal from you that all the reports that have reached me agree that your work output has become awful. These accounts also indicate that you spend a lot of time trimming your fingernails while mumbling and muttering. Indeed, you occasionally babble so incoherently that none of your colleagues can understand you. In a single week, you were late for work four days in a row. You have also left work early without obtaining permission from anyone."

He sat back in his chair. For some moments he scrutinized me. Then, almost fondly, he asked me, "Is something troubling you, Mr. Saleem?"

His question frightened me, and I was unable to utter a single word.

His expression relaxed then, and I heard him say gently and graciously, "Mr. Saleem. You used to be an exemplary employee. For the ten years I've been here, all your work has been satisfactory and praiseworthy. You know full well that I have praised your work ethic and diligence repeatedly—not just to myself but to your face and in front of your colleagues. This time, though, I think I must warn you before it is too late!"

I summoned all my forces, focused entirely on defending myself, and told my boss, "Sir . . . I apologize. But I think the reports have not been at all accurate. I work as seriously as ever and as earnestly as in the past. I have never arrived late to the office. I have never left work before six. Therefore, I can say that those statements in the reports were merely biased rumors . . ."

Looking serious and stern again, the director replied, "You know, Mr. Saleem, that I ignore slander and gossip. This is a principle I have adhered to here since I became head of this agency. I will continue my dedication to this principle to the end. Put simply, I advise you, Mr. Saleem, to take my warning seriously. What I hope is that you will return to your previous condition!"

The director rose. He shook my hand warmly. I returned to the office. As I entered, my colleagues immediately stopped talking and resumed their sullen silence. I buried my head in the folders piled on my desk and set to work.

At 6 p.m. I left work, determined to visit Omran. I was walking down rue d'Espagne, which was crowded with people, as it usually is at transitions between day and night, when I heard someone shout churlishly: "Keep your eyes to yourself, Shithead!"

I turned to find myself confronted by a youth with a shaved head and bulging biceps. The tattoo on his chest was covered by hair, and his eyes flashed angrily. He advanced toward me, thrusting his index finger toward my eyes.

"Do you want us to poke out your eyes, Bastard . . ."

"What have I done?"

"Ohhh . . . don't you know what you did?"

"No . . ."

Some pedestrians began to gather and formed a small circle around us. The young man grew angrier and more excited. "Do you want us to crush you, Idiot?"

"For what?"

"You don't know?"

"No!"

"Take this, so you won't forget!"

The first blow almost felled me, but I was able to keep upright! I waited for the onlookers to intervene, but they all seemed eager for more thrills and excitement. I moved, trying to save myself, and the young man landed a blow that toppled me. He didn't stop at that; he began kicking me with his military boots until I almost passed out. When he left, I was groaning with pain. Then the onlookers left. I rose with difficulty and continued on my way. I stopped in front of a shop window, and what I saw in the reflection scared me. My face was entirely covered with scratches and bruises. There were black circles around my eyes. Oh, I couldn't visit Omran looking like this. Nor could I return home. I could not even go to The Corsairs. Or. . . . Uuuuf! What could I do? Should I spend the night with Aziz? Oooh . . . no, no, no. I had avoided meeting or talking with him for many months, for some reason I do not understand. To go to him in this terrible condition would be a grave mistake. But where would I spend the night? Where? So, what had I done? *What have I done?* Had I bumped into the youth? I don't remember. I really do **not** remember. What's certain is that those onlookers returned to their homes mocking my cowardice and stupidity. But what could I have done with a young guy who appeared to be a criminal who had escaped from prison when the regime fell? The news said there are thousands of them. Now they have spread throughout the country, wreaking havoc and causing destruction. They perpetrate dreadful crimes every day. Hundreds of them have jumped aboard deadly, unseaworthy boats, and those who escape drowning arrive at the far shore and congregate on the island of Lampedusa, hoping to occupy it.

Those passersby must be making fun of me now, entertaining their wives, children, and friends with my disgrace: "Do you know the insurance agent who frequents The Corsairs with that ugly old man Aziz?"

"Oh, the guy whose beautiful wife teaches English?"

"Yes, yes. That one."

"What about him?"

"He got a beating that almost killed him."

"Why?"

"He seems to have made fun of a young man—built like a Spanish bull—who had just escaped from prison."

"Amazing! But he seems to be a bright, decent man . . ."

"No, he's not bright or decent. It's better to cross a noisy river than traverse a silent wadi."

Ugh . . . What a dilemma! What shall I do? What can I do?

After nine o'clock that night, I was entirely outside the city, and all I could hear was the sound of my footsteps on the sidewalk. As I passed the Municipal Building, a police car stopped. When the officer saw the scrapes and bruises on my face, he asked me, "Did you get in a fight with someone?"

"A young guy attacked me on rue d'Espagne for no apparent reason!"

"Do you know the young man?"

"No."

"When did he attack you?"

"About three hours ago."

"Why haven't you returned home?"

I hesitated momentarily and then asked, "Could I return to my wife and little daughter looking like this?"

"But don't you know that walking around at this time of night has become very dangerous?"

"I know."

"Then, the best thing is for you to return home."

I walked toward our apartment building, taking one step forward and two steps back. The elevator hadn't worked for a week. On tiptoe, I climbed the four flights of stairs. I turned the key twice in the lock. The door opened. Then I found myself face-to-face with my wife. For some moments she stared at me in astonishment, her mouth hanging open from the terrible shock. Then she quickly entered her room without uttering a word!

Aziz

I did not sleep well last night and kept twisting and turning in my bed till day's pale light crept into the apartment. I was brooding about the events shaking the country and terrifying our souls. Every day—no, every hour—life grows more difficult and problematic. All the promises made by everyone who swarmed on the scene after the fall of the past regime have evaporated and become a mirage.

I woke at 10 a.m. and, after a quick glass of hot milk, stretched out on the sofa. Now it's 1 p.m., and I haven't moved. I thought of telephoning my friend Saleem more than once to wish him a happy fiftieth birthday but finally decided not to. He probably wouldn't have picked up. Or he might have screamed at me not to bother him again. Yes, he might well have. He might even have done worse than that. In any event, I'm sure he'll open his heart to me one day and share the secret of his psychological torment while we drink a cold beer or Magon wine at The Corsairs or walk along the beach the way we once did during happier times.

When was my birthday? Oh . . . it was exactly two months and one week ago, but I didn't celebrate it. I ignored it, paying no attention to it until the following day. That's what usually happens. Now that I'm older than sixty-six, I doubt I'll change my habits. As a matter of fact, it's occasionally hard to convince myself that I am this old. As a child and a young man, I believed I would die early. I was always brooding about death. That did not stop until I turned forty. Nowadays, it is all the same to me whether Azrael seizes my spirit today or tomorrow, since I believe I've lived long enough, or even too long. Moreover, I don't want to live so long that I turn into a creature that stirs sympathy or revulsion, someone who shits and pees in his breeches and must rely on other people to assist him with his simplest chores. In any case, I'm certain no one will rise to the occasion and help me when I become a crippled old coot who can barely hear or see. That's why I pray night and day that my end will be easy—that I fall asleep and wake the next morning to find myself in another world.

When I scrutinize my life, I feel some satisfaction and pride, because I rescued myself from falling into dangerous abysses, belying my aunt's predictions. She always asserted that I would become a petty criminal or dangerous thief, and I could well have been seduced into the world of deviant criminality like other sons of our impoverished neighborhood. Credit for my escape from the traps and land mines of being an impoverished orphan, however, belongs to Madame Rose-Marie and to books and the cinema!

Ah . . . how extraordinary and tender that Frenchwoman was! I learned a lot from her—especially how to keep my equilibrium. I learned how to retain the ability to laugh and hope even in rough and gloomy times!

A few weeks after the fires of the War of Liberation were extinguished, huge numbers of Frenchmen started to leave the city. Those of us who were adults, and children too, would stand on the quay at the port each morning and evening to watch them silently board steamships with tears in their eyes, weighed down by their personal effects and heavy suitcases. Within a few days, the city was free of them, and a heavy pall fell over it. Through its streets and squares stretched a disgust as lethal and hideous as a slain serpent. Then, suddenly, outsiders descended on the city to occupy the beautiful houses abandoned by the French, turning their extraordinary gardens into pens for goats and sheep and placing chicken coops there. No longer did the fragrances of roses, jasmine, and fascinating blonde women waft from them; instead, the air was sour with disgusting, foul stenches that made you want to vomit.

Of all the citizens of our city, I may have regretted the departure of the French the most, because they had been my best customers for every hustle I undertook during my school breaks, long or short. Unlike the inhabitants of our impoverished neighborhood, the French didn't show any revulsion toward my ugly appearance. They may even have sympathized with me on account of it and treated me more tenderly.

One oppressive morning, during the flaming heat of the end of summer, I went to the Grand Souq with faltering steps, feeling bitter. When I approached the entrance, I saw a French lady with short, gray hair. She wore a brightly colored dress and white sandals and advanced toward me grasping a basket laden with vegetables, fruit, and other purchases. I hurried toward her at once, wanting to assist her. When I stopped before her, she placed her basket on the ground and gazed at me for some moments with gray eyes, which had retained their magic.

Then she smiled and asked, in French, "What's your name?"

"Aziz!"

"*Tu es moche, mais tu parais gentil*: You're homely but seem sweet."

I picked up the heavy basket and followed her to her old, white Simca. After I placed the basket in the trunk of the car, she gestured for me to ride beside her. I climbed in without any hesitation.

The car left the market and crossed the bridge between the sea and the old harbor. Then I realized she was a resident of the posh Corniche neighborhood, which I had entered only once. Otherwise I had been satisfied, like other citizens of the city, to regard it from afar. During the vehicle's short trip, the French lady didn't say a thing. But, from time to time, when she glanced at me with a smile, the look in her gray eyes suggested a fondness and affection comparable to my mother's.

When we reached the Corniche neighborhood, the car turned right, and she stopped in front of a villa with a small, exquisite garden. On the far side, the murmur of gentle summer waves was audible. The French lady parked her car in the garage and opened the trunk. She asked me to carry the basket and follow her. After she had put the vegetables, provisions, meat, and fish in the refrigerator, she offered me a glass of cold lemonade. That refreshed me and dispelled the gloom that had been accumulating in my heart since I got up. Next I helped her clean the kitchen and the rest of the house. I thought she would ask me to leave then, but she insisted that I eat lunch with her. The grilled fish, fries, and green salad were delicious!

By the time we finished lunch, I had learned a lot about the life of this generous Frenchwoman. She was called Marie-Rose. Her husband, a high-ranking officer in the French army, had died of a heart attack two years earlier. She had no children and refused to leave our city, sensing that her life would fall apart if she returned to France. Despite some trepidation, she wished to complete her life in her lovely villa on the seashore.

In a few weeks, my relationship with Madame Rose-Marie was solidified, and I became her *moche petit* Aziz—her homely little Aziz. I would accompany her to the market and to the beach, where she liked to go early in the morning, even on cold winter days. I would assist her with household chores and massage her back when she was in the bathtub.

Eventually, that was not enough, and she started to ask me to massage her chest. Occasionally, she would take my hands and place them between her thighs as she closed her eyes. That might last for some minutes. Then she would sigh repeatedly and exclaim, "*Comme c'est délicieux, mon petit Aziz.*" I gradually began to enjoy her moans, which set my body on fire and made me want to embrace and kiss her. When she sensed that I was responding to her, she began to fondle my thing so tenderly that I almost lost control of myself. While she did that, she would tremble silently, with her eyes closed. Occasionally, she would pull it out of the opening of my pants. It would be erect, and she would kiss it and lick it with her crimson tongue. But once we left the bathroom, Madame Rose-Marie acted as if what we had experienced together belonged to a different world, a world of fantasies and dreams—not to the real world. Yes, this is how she conducted herself with me. The bathtub was the only venue where Madame Rose-Marie allowed herself to transgress the boundaries she had established between us. In the salon or kitchen, in her bedroom or on the street, I continued to be her "homely little Aziz," nothing more.

Madame Rose-Marie did not begrudge me anything. She bought me handsome clothes and shoes. My uncle's gray-haired wife seized some of these to award to one of her own sons. Every week Madame Rose-Marie paid me enough to watch films I loved in the cinemas with Murad. We spent so much time in cinemas that we became acquainted with all the international stars—male and female. We would choose one as our favorite star. After we watched *High Noon*, Gary Cooper became our idol, and we never missed a chance to see any film he starred in. We would really have liked to possess his broad-brimmed black hat, tall slender body, and mesmerizing good looks and to be able to walk the streets of the city shooting at anyone who upset us, disrespected us, shunned our homely looks, or cursed us for being orphans! Eventually, Gary Cooper's star dimmed, and Sidney Poitier's shone bright after we saw his film *The Defiant Ones* four times in a single week. We managed to learn the first stanza of the amazing, mournful song he sings at the end of the film while the sheriff stares incredulously at him and his white friend, who were both on the lam. During our treks along the beach or through the forest overlooking the sea to the north of the city, we liked to bind our hands with rope and sing that song! Once, a grown-up surprised us in the forest when we were doing that. He fled immediately . . . hahhhhhhh! He may have thought we had just escaped from a lunatic asylum!

The star Simone Signoret shone down on us like the planet Venus, the Morning Star, once we saw her in the film *Casque d'Or*. On the third anniversary of Tunisian Independence we saw the film *The Night of the Hunter*, and Robert Mitchum, who played the role of Harry Powell, a minister who kills widows, believing God wants him to, became one of our favorite stars, together with Kirk Douglas in the film *Paths of Glory*, Henry Fonda in the film *12 Angry Men*, Sofia Loren in *It Started in Naples* and *Heller in Pink Tights*, Paul Newman in *The Hustler*, Humphrey Bogart and Ingrid Bergman in *Casablanca*, and Anthony Quinn in *Zorba the Greek*. I remember that we watched that last film at noon one splendid spring day and then at sunset rushed to the beach to dance like Anthony Quinn till we collapsed breathless on the sand, our clothes soaked with sweat. We also loved the Egyptian film stars, especially Omar Sharif, Faten Hamama, Hind Rostom, Rushdy Abaza, Abdel Salam al-Nabulsi, and Tawfiq al-Daqan, whom we loved when he played a villain, drunkard, or thug.

All those films, which made us laugh or cry and stirred in us emotions and feelings, had an extraordinary impact on our lives, destiny, and thinking. Thanks to them, we no longer considered the status of impoverished orphans to be a curse. Instead, we started to feel good about this. We no longer grumbled or felt disgusted by our lot. We did not feel sorry for ourselves, because in most of these films we witnessed how many orphans as well as poor, dispossessed, and oppressed people were able to surmount their torments and misfortunes and achieve a tranquil and happy life. They might even become important, influential figures in their countries and societies! These films also taught us to shun anything that reeked of evil, treachery, cunning, betrayal, abasement, hypocrisy, brute force, depravity, and ugliness. For this reason, we started to avoid gangs and toughs or participating in any of their activities. They lived in a dark, rowdy, corrupt, frightening world, whereas—although our world had its headaches and problems—we accepted them and refused to betray or rebel against our world on any pretense or excuse.

Since Madame Marie-Rose spoke only French to me, in half a year I was able to converse with her and answer her questions in her language without stammering or feeling disconcerted, as I had at first. In school, I started to gain the respect of my teachers in French-language courses. My schoolmates, though, declared war on me. Some did not hesitate to curse and insult me, since—according to them—I was merely "the pathetic lapdog of that old Frenchwoman." But I ignored them and their curses, content with the sound bond of friendship that tied me to Murad and provided my life a perfume that dissipated all the stinky smells lobbed at me by souls sullied by hatred, vitriol, and envy.

When Madame Marie-Rose noticed that my command of French had improved, she began to encourage me to read. The first book she gave me was *The Little Prince* by Saint-Exupéry. That was at Christmas in 1963 when a violent cyclone shook the city with rain, thunder, and lightning. Trees howled in the wind, and high waves roared, colliding with boulders and the walls of houses. Madame Marie-Rose roasted a turkey in the oven. On the table she placed a large white candle, a bottle of red wine, and two glasses. She filled my glass and then hers, raised hers, smiling, and called out to me: "*A ta santé, mon cher petit Aziz!*"

I hesitated for a time; then I raised mine and said very cheerfully, "And to your health, dear Madame!"

For a few minutes, the wine made me feel dizzy. Then I felt the type of sweet relaxation afforded by stretching out on the sofa after taking a shower at noon during summer's heat. I ate my salad and a piece of turkey breast. Then I drank a second glass of wine. With the goat cheese I wanted a third glass, but Madame Marie-Rose cautioned me against that, saying: "Stop . . . One more glass for a novice like you might harm you, *mon cher petit Aziz.*"

Toward midnight, after the evening's celebration, Madame Marie-Rose gave me *The Little Prince* and told me about its author, whose plane had fallen into the Mediterranean Sea during World War II and whose body had never been found. She informed me that her late husband had also loved this author and, like her, had read all his books. Before we went to sleep, she asked me to write a one-page summary of the book after I finished reading it. She promised to give me more books if I succeeded in writing a précis that she liked of this one.

I finished reading the book the first day of the winter break. The next day I read it again. The third day I copied into my notebook some paragraphs I liked, hoping to memorize them.

Here are some:

I wonder . . . if the stars are lit up so that each of us can find his own, someday.[23]

    All grown-ups were children first. (But few of them remember it.)[24]

It's the time you spent on your rose that makes your rose so important,[25] the most beautiful and glorious.

I have learned that the world mirrors my soul. . . . When my soul is glad, the world will be happy. When the soul is worried, the world will be sad.

The world isn't sad or happy.

It simply is here.[26]

The book enchanted me, and I united myself with my soul, desiring to have no other companion. For this reason, I did my best to avoid running into Murad. I prowled the beach alone. I defied the cold and storms in the woods. The only thing in my mind was the little prince's spirit, which was chock-full of affection and love. What attracted my attention was that the little prince always sought to capture the affection and friendship of others. From a mountaintop he shouts: "Let's be friends . . . I'm lonely!"[27] He doesn't just love human beings; he loves animals too. For this reason, he approaches a snake and asks him to play, because he is "sad and alone." He celebrates the flower's beauty and everything that appears before him, because he does not want to live alone, sad, and deprived of love. According to him, someone who doesn't love isn't a person and can't be a person. Anyone who sniffs a flower and does not look with amazement at a star twinkling in the sky, who does not love another person and has never done anything to make others happy, cannot be a person. He is just an inanimate object.

On the sixth day of the school holiday, I walked to Madame Marie-Rose's house. She read my summary. Without saying a single word, she kissed me on my mouth, once, offered me a beer, and invited me to eat lunch with her. Before I left that afternoon, she gave me a collection of tales, saying they were by a famous Scandinavian author named Andersen.

Late that evening I ran into Murad near the harbor. He shouted angrily at me, "Where have you been, Scoundrel?"

"I've been with the little prince."

"What little prince?"

"Come."

"Where?"

"To the shore."

"When it's this cold?"

"I'll tell you a story that will make you forget the cold."

"What's happened to you? Have you gone mad since I last saw you?"

"Come. You won't regret it."

We walked along the beach, silently at first. Then I began recounting the story of the little prince, complete with all its details, reciting by heart the exceptional passages I had recorded in my notebook. Once I finished, Murad placed his hands on my shoulders and stopped me. He asked me as he stared at me in astonishment, "Where did you find that amazing story?"

"I read it in a book."

"What book?"

"A book Madame Marie-Rose gave me!"

"May I read it?"

"Your French may not be strong enough."

"I'll borrow a dictionary!"

I drew the book out of my small sack and presented it to him.

"Thanks, Aziz!"

Murad left me there on the shore and ran home.

Three days later, early in the morning, when I was only half awake, I heard loud knocking on the door of my wretched room.

"Who's there?"

"Open up, Scoundrel!"

I opened the door, and Murad threw himself into my arms. "Scoundrel, there can't be another demon like you in this city!"

"Have you read the book?"

"Of course! I've read it twice!"

"Did you like it?"

"Ahhh! Let's get out of this wretched room. Then you'll learn my opinion."

From that time, our love of the cinema was matched by our love of books. We read everything we could lay hands on—me in French and Murad in Arabic. Each of us would summarize for the other every book he read. As films had, books carried us off to strange and amazing worlds, allowing us to forget our miserable, monotonous lives and their vexations, pains, and sorrows. Those books moved us ever farther from the gangs who feared the sea and open spaces, preferring to congregate in deserted cemeteries and dark basements.

We walked with young Gerda in Andersen's story, searching for her dear friend Kay, who had suddenly disappeared after being enchanted by a demon. On her way to the Snow Queen far in the North, where fog, darkness, and scary desolation converge, Gerda meets robbers, talking animals, and a sorceress with an extraordinary garden. We accompanied Agatha Christie's characters abroad the Orient Express traveling across Europe. We experienced one adventure after another as one new surprise supplanted another. The historical romances of Jurji Zaydan transported us to the distant past through stories of romance and passion experienced by Arabs in Andalusia or Baghdad in the Golden Age. With Sherlock Holmes and Arsène Lupin we pursued criminals, thieves, and murderers. In the story by Maupassant, we sympathized with the prostitute Elizabeth Rousset, known as "Boule de Suif," when she offers her voluptuous, plump body to a Prussian officer to save the lives of aristocrats, gentry, and men of the cloth, even though they demean and mock her. With American Mark Twain's character Tom Sawyer, we fled from his stern grandmother and the stifling, monotonous life of their small town to sail the Mississippi and explore the world of pirates, violence, and terrifying crimes!

In short, Murad and I started a new chapter of our lives.

Omran

He received Sophie's letter before noon but did not open it until seven that evening, after he finished recording his ideas and reflections.

My Dear Teacher,
Your brief letter, in which you affirmed once more that you never lose your hope or your resolve in confronting difficulties, made me very happy. It also reassured me about your health and morale. But I won't conceal from you that I yearn for you a lot from time to time. I miss your sweet spirit and calm, sober voice when you discuss books, present ideas, and narrate historical events.

As for me, I can say that I am better, that perhaps I have emerged from the tunnel, because I feel a calm and serenity I never experienced during my years of loss, upset, and self-searching.

Last week I went by train to Zurich to visit a dear friend whom I met during my first year at the university. She had come to Paris to study for a certificate in the French language, since her mother tongue is German. She is now writing a dissertation about a major Swiss author named Robert Walser and for this reason can hardly stop talking about him. I think I'll buy some of his books soon. My motivation for this is not merely my friend's enthusiasm for him; he was eccentric and spent the greater part of his life in a sanatorium. Toward the end of 1956, on Christmas Day, to be specific, he left the mental hospital and walked through snowy fields before he lay down and died. Thus ended the life of one of "the greatest authors of the language of Goethe," according to my friend.

Do you know his work? I feel certain you do, because I've noticed you pay special attention to highly gifted authors who live in obscurity, out of the limelight, and finally pass to the other world without obtaining the fame they deserve.

My one excursion in Zurich was to the Carl Jung house, part of which has been turned into a museum. While I walked through the snow-covered garden one bitterly cold afternoon, I remembered a passage from his autobiography. He wrote:

"My family . . . and the knowledge: I have a medical diploma from a Swiss university, I must help my patients, I have a wife and five children, I live at 228 Seestrasse in Küsnacht— these . . . actualities . . . made demands on me and proved to me . . . that I really existed, that I was not merely a blank page whirling about in the winds. . . ."[28]

I also visited the Fluntern Cemetery, where James Joyce and Elias Canetti lie side by side, and placed a small bouquet on each grave. Truth be told, I still haven't read much by either author, even though I am convinced they were two of the greatest writers of the twentieth century—perhaps of any century.

On the train back to Paris I read a book by Stefan Zweig titled *The Right to Heresy: Castellio against Calvin*. In it the author relates the life story of Sebastian Castellio, who lived in a rigidly puritanical age but retained his nobility and humanity, denouncing—with rare courage and daring—the massacres that were being committed in the name of God and religion. He did this by himself, deprived of any weapon save reason and a profound consciousness of the authentic meaning of life . . . even though he knew he would pay a very high price. Castellio refused to yield and submit to his inveterate foe, Calvin, who repeated, as Muslim fundamentalists do today, that his sermons came straight from God and that God had ordered him to show people what was good and what was evil. Stefan Zweig says that Calvin considered all his opponents to be "serpents hissing against him, dogs barking behind him, and demons desiring to destroy his life." For this reason, he did not hesitate to erect gallows for them and burn them alive just as Muslim fundamentalists today treat those they accuse of "being infidels, freethinkers and atheists." Castellio, on the other hand, would say that a search for the truth and disclosure of what we are thinking can under no circumstances be a criminal act. He also said, "Killing a man does not defend doctrine. It simply kills a man."[29]

While I was reading about this great man's life, you were never out of my thoughts, not even for a moment! When I left the train at Gare de l'Est, you appeared before me. I saw you walking to greet me, smiling. You wore your old gray overcoat and your gray hat, which you wear all the time, even when you're sleeping. Hahhhhhh! You embraced me warmly, and then we took the Metro to the Luxembourg stop. Afterward we sat on a wooden bench, as we often do, and plunged into an elaborate and enjoyable discussion of Sebastian Castellio.

Don't you agree that he resembles you a lot?

In any case, I don't think I'm exaggerating when I say you have no less courage, daring, force of argument, steadfastness, self-confidence, calm, and composure.

I wait for a letter from you and send you, my dear teacher, my sincere greetings and everlasting affection.

> Your spiritual daughter,
> Sophie

Wishing to respond immediately to her letter, he wrote:

My Dear Sophie,
I was delighted by your letter, which refreshed my spirit with the sweetness of your words, the truth of your emotions, and your love for books and life.

I will tell you candidly that your letter left me thinking that you have emerged from the tunnel and are opening a new page of your life. This reassures me about you and your future. So long as you retain your force of will, you have nothing to fear and won't despair. I also feel certain that you will always be able to overcome difficulties and withstand trials.

I would dearly have liked to be with you in Zurich, which I visited more than once in the 1960s, in other words back when I loved to travel and felt a strong urge to become acquainted with the cities and people of the "old continent." I remember that I also visited Jung's house but not the Fluntern Cemetery. I settled for a visit to the Café Odeon, which has been frequented by many of the most famous politicians, writers, and thinkers who lived in Zurich: people like Stefan Zweig, James Joyce, Einstein, and Lenin, who left it for Saint Petersburg to direct the Bolshevik Revolution in 1917. I think Solzhenitsyn described him best as he was during the year he spent in this city. He did that in a book I read years ago. It is called *Lenin in Zurich*. In this book he disclosed important sides of Lenin's personality and suggested that Lenin believed, when he was in Bern and then Zurich, that the socialist revolution he dreamt of could take place in Switzerland. Hahhhhhh! Then he changed his mind and began to think his revolution might see the light of day in Sweden. Hahhhhhh! Solzhenitsyn also reveals that Lenin's ideas grew increasingly extreme in Zurich. To his Bolshevik comrades he would say, "To make an omelet, you must break an egg." That means he thought violence would be needed for a revolution, which he likened to an omelet, to succeed. Hahhhhhh! Perhaps for this reason, he criticized the Paris Commune more than once for not nationalizing the banks and for being "too soft" on its enemies. He criticized the leaders and champions of the Commune for not employing armed force against the bourgeoisie and conservatives. Lenin left Zurich without seeing the commemorative plaque stating that the German author Georg Büchner lived in Zurich, where he wrote "Danton's Death," the famous play that showed how the French Revolution devoured its own children and founders, leaving behind only death and destruction. When Czarist rule collapsed in Russia, Lenin immediately began to implement his theory about the use of revolutionary violence, causing the death of thousands of victims. The Czar and his family were among the first. After Lenin's death, most leaders of Communist parties followed his example—especially Stalin and Mao Zedong, who said: "A revolution is not a dinner party. . . . A revolution is . . . an act of violence by which one class [the working class] overthrows another [the bourgeoisie]."[30]

My dear Sophie, the truth is that in my youth I believed in revolutionary violence, which I defended with zealous ferocity. I had to survive bitter experiments in various places before I realized that evils resulting from revolutions usually are greater than their benefits, because they destroy functional and vital expressions of a society, annihilating its best elements and opening the doors wide to extreme evil, wickedness, and peril. A revolution may cost a country its prosperity, thanks to cunning manipulators, occupying forces, drifters, and villains.

I thank you profusely for likening me to Sebastian Castellio, but I believe you are too kind. I know that in Christian history there were many victims of religious puritanism, rigidity, and extremism. But there have been many more victims of these tendencies in the Islamic Arab world. What one needs to emphasize is that trials and prosecution of writers and thinkers, their detention, imprisonment, and torture, the burning of their books, and their exile still exist in most Arab and Islamic countries, where tyrannical jurists continue to have free rein, terrorizing people with fatwas and sermons. In the Christian West, these tendencies have decreased and may even have totally disappeared.

Yes, you go too far in comparing me to Sebastian Castellio, because Arab Muslim history, both past and present, is filled with the names of authors, poets, and thinkers who confronted and challenged, with rare courage, the forces of darkness and fanaticism. For this reason, they paid dearly. Some had their books burned, some were slaughtered and had their heads hung on the gates of cities, and some were tortured to death. Can you imagine that a great writer like Abdallah Ibn al-Muqaffaʻ, who condemned injustice and Middle Eastern tyranny through the tongues of animals in a fable, had his limbs cut off and thrown into a furnace—after he was charged with using language that seemed ugly and disrespectful to the Caliph Mansur!

I will never forget the atrocious crime committed against Bashshar ibn Burd, who was born blind and poor. His own mother sold him as a boy to be rid of him. From an early age he showed poetic genius, excelling in lampoons and satires. This talent gained him many enemies among the ruling class and men of religion. This poet made no secret of his hostility to fanaticism and religious hypocrisy. To those who accused him of atheism, he replied, "I know only what I have personally inspected and comparable things." He is said to have raised the call to prayer at the wrong time when intoxicated; this annoyed jurisprudents even more. When he did not retract his satire, Caliph al-Mahdi ordered him lashed seventy times. While the guards were whipping him, Bashshar did not utter a word that suggested groveling or any request to God or the Caliph for forgiveness. After he breathed his last gasp, his body was tossed into a busy square in Basra, where he had lived. It is reported that his enemies congratulated each other when they saw his deformed corpse, spattered with blood, exposed to the sun.

Early in my youth, I became acquainted with a young man who chose to be called Diogenes—actually, his friends chose that name for him. He was a sensitive, gifted poet, a rebel, a dreamer, and a person who loved life to a degree that enraged his enemies. The two of us stuck together for many years, only rarely separating. I acknowledge that I learned a lot from him. I loved him more than any other friend during that period. We shared a single spirit. Our dreams knew no bounds. Once colonial rule ended, we thought our dreams would be real-ized. Our shock, though, was painful and violent. Soon after

Tunisia became independent, my friend Diogenes was arrested because of a satirical poem about the political prevarication and self-aggrandizing, hollow slogans of our new rulers. He was tortured in prison in excruciating ways and treated terribly. He left prison totally broken and shattered. His equilibrium was destroyed, and he sank into a dark night of insanity. Until his death, he walked the capital's streets night and day, raving incoherently.

Does this suffice?

You say your friend is writing a dissertation on Robert Walser and that you would like to read his works. This is commendable and excellent. I read some of them when I was in my forties, especially during a period when I sensed I was beginning to change and shed ideas to which I had previously been firmly wed. What I remember is that this writer's nihilism astonished me. While he lived and wrote, his genuine talent was unrecognized. Indeed, he may have wanted to be merely what the Spanish critic Enrique Vila-Matas said of him: "A zero to the left and a zero to the right." Therefore no one paid attention to him either during his lifetime or after his death. He was never credited with the glory or renown of a rare and original writer.

With regard to my condition, I can say I'm fine: I persevere in recording my ideas and thoughts almost every day. Keeping company with Montaigne, I live, think, and dream.

I have two friends in this coastal city. The first is named Saleem. He is a cultured man and extremely affable. I find it especially agreeable to discuss American literature with him. Since I first arrived in this city, he has visited me twice. The first time he appeared to be somewhat rattled and nervous. During his second visit, I noticed he was not in good shape. Fear was clearly visible in his eyes. The events this country is experiencing may be responsible for his alarm and upset. According to explanations in the newspapers and on the radio, many people suffer during this period, like him, from agitation and severe psychological crises. Perhaps for this reason there has been an increase in the number of incidents of violence and suicide—especially among young men!

I met my second friend through Saleem—a man named Aziz. He is homely looking and old, but bright, witty, and light-spirited; he has an extraordinary gift for black humor. He could easily walk onto the stage in a play by Molière. He is also a perceptive reader with a deep knowledge of literature, even though he quit school without attempting the *Baccalauréat* and was content with a career as a clerk in the postal service. This friend has visited me once. Then he bombarded me with a series of questions about the "Revolution" and "Arab Spring," even though I replied to his inquiries tersely and did not answer some at all, since I am wary of drawing overly hasty and swift conclusions.

It is almost nine now . . .

I will drink a glass of warm milk, read some pages of Montaigne's *Essais* . . . and then go to bed.

Goodnight, Sophie, my dear.

Saleem

I walked down narrow streets empty of people and anything else save heaps of rubbish. Occasionally huge, ugly rats would suddenly leap in front of me. Then, dressed in Afghan jellabiyas, men with shaggy beards, large, shaved heads, and black calluses on their foreheads attacked me. They stripped me naked in a dark corner and abused me in such a nasty way that I would never dare relate the details. Nor could I describe its psychological effects on me with the necessary accuracy. They did that to me while I was sleeping beside my beautiful wife, for whom my colleagues at work envy me. I know this from their glances, gestures, and whispers when she occasionally waits for me in front of the place where I work. When I woke from this alarming nightmare, I found myself pressed against her. She was as hot as a burning ember, the bottom half of her body was naked, and my penis was touching her buttocks. She was fidgeting for me to enter forcefully, emitting the moan I like to hear before copulation. But my penis had shrunk and contracted, and I could not rouse it at all. The next morning, my wife didn't kiss me the way she normally did and avoided any eye contact until she left the apartment.

My young daughter, Sana', no longer rushes happily to kiss me when she wakes and no longer throws herself into my arms when I return from work in the evening. She has begun to refuse my offer categorically when I want to tell her a Middle Eastern story before she goes to sleep. She won't let me take her to school or to the zoo in the capital or allow me to touch her, not even a gentle pat. Just the sight of me causes her to flee, as if I were a beast in a horror film. At other times, she stands at a distance from me and stares at

119

me suspiciously and cautiously, as if I were a strange intruder. If I try to approach or speak to her, she screams so loudly with terror that I am forced to stop immediately and distance myself from her as far as possible. Thus, I remain alone until a late hour in the sitting room, where I don't turn on the TV for fear of seeing jihadis march across deserts, raise black flags, shout "La ilah ila Allah" and "Allahu Akbar," and issue fatwas to kill and destroy, plunder, and enslave, wherever they pass. I have gone to great efforts to ban them from my brain and memory but have failed miserably. The jihadis are always in front of me and behind me, to my right and my left, as if they were my inevitable shadow.

These nightmares torment me whether I'm awake or asleep.

I see them forge ahead, covered with thick dust. They advance like a tremendous sandstorm. Everywhere they go, they plunder, set fires, kill all the men and enslave and rape the women, while holding aloft their black flags and brandishing their blood-splattered swords. They advance, leaving behind them battlefields red with the blood of their victims and strewn with severed heads and limbs, bellies that have been split open, and rotting corpses that vultures and stray dogs devour.

They are always advancing.

They advance with scowling countenances and dusty, ill-kempt beards, reciting God's praises, constantly pursuing me. They never allow me any peace of mind. They are with me in empty and crowded streets, in public gardens, in the jam-packed stores where I occasionally shop. They are beside me or in front of me, sitting in the gray, depressing office at the insurance agency where I work. Even when I go to relax on the beach in the evening and inhale the healthy, fresh air, I see them pursuing me persistently, determinedly, and stubbornly, till I am obliged to return home quickly, breathless, with troubled steps, my soul weighed down by dark thoughts and terrifying worries.

At night, they make it impossible for me to sleep, like bedbugs and mosquitoes during the fiery summer months. Then I keep rolling around on a bed of thorns until sunrise without getting a wink of sleep, while they gnaw on my flesh and drink my blood.

My nightmares have turned into horror films that show me black-clad men raiding our coastal city; closing its markets, cafés, and restaurants; prohibiting children from attending school and men from going to work; and draping black cloth around its squares, streets, and public gardens. They spread along the shoreline until they obscure the horizon. Finally, they evict women who express their emotions by slapping themselves and weeping for their husbands, sons, fathers, and kinsmen.

Yes . . . I saw all of this like a succession of terrifying images projected on a large screen. I might also see mountains moving, hills dancing together, the sky pelting our city with the bones of the dead, and the earth cracking open to release rotting corpses. I also saw severed heads and locusts attacking like black clouds to decimate crops and trees until the earth became a dry desert devoid of people and animals. I would repeatedly hear an enormous shriek and awake with a dry mouth, my body flaming hot. Naturally, my screams of terror wake my wife and daughter and make me feel as humiliated in their eyes as if I had committed some hideous sin that could never be forgiven. Eventually, my wife could no longer stand all this and indicated to me with glacial silence that life with me was no longer supportable.

A few days ago, I left the office and walked off, heading in no particular direction. The cold was bitter, the congestion was severe, automobiles squawked loudly, and the chaos was unbearable. Fleeing from all of this, I hurried to The Corsairs, wanting to drink a glass that might dull my tension and anxiety. The frowning bartender Charley, without responding to my greeting, asked me dryly and decisively to leave at once, without offering any explanation. I obeyed his demand and left, humiliated, my head between my shoulders, like a bird clinging to a branch in a storm. What's happened, I wonder? My life is ruined, rotting. My enemies are proliferating. One day I will find myself alone with no support and nary a friend.

Perhaps I'll be unemployed and lack a place to shelter. What do you suppose has turned me into this hostile creature with a nasty disposition, someone who is hard to get along with and has a foul tongue? I have pressed myself to answer this question repeatedly and failed miserably. Perhaps I have been predestined for catastrophic failure. Every day the number of my enemies increases, and they become even more powerful, ferocious, and violent.

Pedestrian and vehicular traffic in the city decreased that evening. Stores closed their doors. The cold grew increasingly bitter. I entered a bar called "Happiness" and found it packed with patrons. They were all drinking, smoking voraciously, and discussing what was happening in the country, creating a tremendous racket. I ordered a beer and began to drink it at the bar while I studied faces that rippled before me like waves. I don't know what happened after that. The next thing I remember is being interrogated by three policemen in a police station about my alleged incitement to riot at al-Sa'ada Bar. They mentioned that I had insulted the bartender, broken glasses, cursed the patrons, and spat at one of them. I had even insulted the Head of State and uttered obscenities.

"I apologize, Gentlemen . . . but I don't remember any of that!"

Each officer thrust his head toward me, and then they asked in unison: "Would we lie to you?"

"No, no, no! I don't mean that . . . Just believe me when I say I really do not remember doing any of that!"

They exchanged glances. The officer who seemed to be in charge told me, "I know you very well, Mr. Saleem. I know you are a charming man who hasn't caused any trouble in the past. This is why I find it odd that you would perpetrate actions like these!"

"Honorable Gentlemen, I apologize to you again for my conduct and affirm it will not happen again!"

"You admit then to performing these riotous actions. Isn't that so?"

"I apologize, Gentlemen!"

They looked at each other once more. Then the commanding officer told me, "Okay, Mr. Saleem. We accept your apology. Now you may return home. We strongly advise you not to visit any bar in the future!"

"Thanks, Honorable Gentlemen!"

I returned home at 1 a.m. When I woke up, I found myself stretched out fully clothed on the sofa. A few meters from me stood my wife and my daughter Sana'. They were glaring at me disgustedly—as if I were a stinky stray dog that had snuck into the apartment when they weren't looking!

Aziz

A dreary morning: the city has been yawning irritably since sunrise. That's why I cut short my planned walk and hurried back to my apartment. Now I'm sitting in its little kitchen with a cup of coffee, trying to devise a plan for the rest of the day. Should I phone Murad? But he is preoccupied by his nephew's situation and visits him daily in the hospital. Should I call on Omran? No, no, no, I won't do that while I'm feeling out of sorts. The best thing will be to stretch out on the sofa and sift through my memories, because nothing is sweeter for an old man like me, who has no novel experiences to expect from life, than to recall memories of the distant past—especially memories of my years with Madame Marie-Rose.

Candlelight on a winter night reminds me of Christmas and New Year's celebrations in her house where we listened to the songs of Edith Piaf, Dalida, Jacques Brel, and the American king of jazz, Louis Armstrong.

The roar of the waves when I roam the beach on a cold night reminds me of serene evenings when she would tell me about American detective novels, scary Hitchcock films, her childhood and adolescence in Marseille, and the first time she met the handsome young man who became her husband a month before World War II started.

The aroma of grilled fish in a working-class restaurant on the quay of the old harbor carries me back to the first day I met her. The film *La vie devant soi*, which won an Oscar in Hollywood, always inspires memories of the years I spent with her. Simone Signoret playing Madame Rosa in this film seems as affectionate and sensitive as Madame Marie-Rose. Back then I resembled the Amazigh boy

Momo whom Madame Rosa rescues from hard times, when he was a neglected orphan, before dying in his arms!

Meryl Streep's tears in *The Bridges of Madison County* allow me to relive moments of my painful farewell to her on June 6, 1967, the day of the bitter Arab defeat.

What I remember is that this swift war, which some say lasted six days but others claim only a few hours, during which Israel was able to destroy the military arsenals of Egypt, Syria, and Jordan, surprised us as much as Tunisia's War of Liberation. Yes, it surprised us in the worst possible way. The inhabitants of our city were promising themselves a relaxing summer, during which they would enjoy swimming, the weddings that are common during this season, and soirées that last until late at night or even till dawn in the restaurants and cafés distributed the length of the shore. As she typically did, Madame Marie-Rose had repainted her house, including its window frames and doors, and put away anything that would remind her of winter. She wore brightly colored, lightweight summer frocks when she went to the market or strolled the city's streets. She was keen to reach the beach early in the day before vacationers invaded it. As for me, I had found work in a restaurant called The Beautiful Shore in the Corniche neighborhood, not too far from Madame Marie-Rose's house. My job involved washing plates and cutlery and cleaning the dining room, before patrons arrived, and the kitchen after the restaurant closed.

On the night of June 5th, I finished work at the restaurant at 1:30 the next morning and returned on foot to my wretched room. I fell into a sound sleep from which pounding on the door snatched me. Before I could rise to open it, I heard Murad shout, "Get up, Scoundrel! The East is burning!"

I opened the door to find Murad with his face blackened with soot, as if he had spent the night selling coal!

"What's happened?"

"The East is burning!"

"What East?"

"Egypt, Syria, Jordan, and Lebanon!"

"I don't understand!"

"A fiery war has started there!"

"War?"

"Yes, a war . . . a war between the Arabs and Israel!"

"When?"

"Yesterday."

"What did the news say?"

"I don't know. Come: let's roam the city to learn what has happened and will happen!"

We toured the city, which seemed to be in mourning, from north to south and east to west. The voices of radio announcers blasted from cafés, shops, stores, houses, and apartment buildings, providing details of battles taking place in Sinai, the Golan Heights, outside Jerusalem, and elsewhere. People listened to these reports glumly, pale-faced, their eyes wandering, rarely saying a word. Everyone seemed preoccupied by what was happening over there, far to the east, much more than to what or who was around them.

In a small bar, near the port, my father was the sole customer. He was smoking disconsolately, with five empty beer bottles before him. I approached and held out my hand. He looked at me with clouded eyes and asked, "What do you want?"

"I want to shake your hand!"

"Why?"

"Have you forgotten me?"

"Who are you?"

"I'm your son, Aziz!"

He scrutinized me for a long time and finally said, "You've grown up fast!"

"Do you want a beer?"

"Do you have enough money to pay for it?"

"Yes!"

"That's great!"

The waiter placed a beer in front of him, and I gestured for Murad to join us. When he did, my father asked me, "Who is this young man?"

"He's my friend!"

My father offered no comment on that reply. He started smoking and drinking silently, oblivious to our presence.

I ordered two more beers. When the waiter placed them in front of us, my father asked him somewhat irritably, "Who is this beer for?"

The waiter replied, "For the fellow who says he's your son and his friend."

My father began scrutinizing me again and then whispered, "You really have grown up. You can do whatever you want!"

Murad drank his beer and then asked my father, "Have you heard about the war?"

My father said nothing for a time and then asked, "What war?"

"The war between Israel and the Arabs!"

"When did that happen?"

"Yesterday!"

"Is it over now?"

"No."

My father was silent for a time. Then he said, "I'm not interested in that. Let me drink my beer in peace."

We caught his drift. So, we drained our glasses quickly and left that little bar without saying good-bye.

We returned to patrolling the streets . . . The city was quiet. People were as silent as if they were attending a giant funeral. There was no clear news about the distant war. Murad and I parted at five that evening.

On my way to work, I passed by Madame Marie-Rose's house. She would not open the door until she was certain that I was "her homely Aziz." I found her trembling with fright, and the beauty of her gray eyes had faded. Her face was the pallid color of a sick or dying person.

What had happened?

That morning she had gone to the market as usual. People had confronted her with angry faces and hate-filled looks—as if she had committed some grave sin. The fishmonger displayed a coarseness totally untypical of him or of those vendors as a whole and only grudgingly complied with her requests, leaving her with the impression that she had better not return to the market in the future. As she left the market and headed to her car, she heard someone threaten her, calling out, *"On va vous tuer, Sale Juive!"* (*We'll kill you, filthy Jew!*).

She collapsed on the sofa and started to gasp as she wept. She said that she wasn't Jewish and that she loved the city and its people. She didn't want to leave. She had thought she had friends here. But this morning she had realized she was a foreigner and no longer welcome. Now she was afraid . . . very fearful. She did not know how she would fare in the coming days. I tried to calm her. Without ever ceasing to weep, she said, *"Mon cher Aziz, la haine provoquée par les guerres est la pire!"* (Hatred spawned by war is the very worst kind!).

The next day news spread that the capital was ablaze and that thousands of irate demonstrators had set fire to embassies and foreign cultural centers. They torched Jewish neighborhoods, shops, restaurants, and cafés. People returning from the capital affirmed that you could smell the smoke from twenty kilometers away.

I left my wretched room and headed to work. I saw Murad racing toward me. He stopped a few feet away. As his chest heaved, he told me, "They've attacked Madame Marie-Rose's house!"

"Who?"

"I don't know."

"Is Madame Marie-Rose okay?"

"I don't know."

We found Madame Marie-Rose's house surrounded by policemen. Through the open door and windows, I could see that all the furniture had disappeared. The kitchen was also empty. I noticed too that not a single flower plant or shrub remained in the garden! It looked as if a cyclone had stormed through, causing frightful damage!

I approached a young policeman and asked, "Where is Madame Marie-Rose?"

He looked me up and down, twice. Then he replied, "Why are you asking about her?"

"She is my friend!"

"Your friend?"

"Yes, my friend. I worked for her."

"Come!"

He led me to a police car beside which stood an officer with two stars on his uniform. He told the officer, "This boy says he's a friend of the Frenchwoman!"

"Ah . . . I know him," the officer said. "He really did work for her. He always accompanied her to the market."

The young policeman left, and the officer asked, "When did you last see Madame Marie-Rose?"

"After noon, the day before yesterday, on my way to work at Al-Shati' al-Jamil Restaurant."

"How was she then?"

"She was frightened and wept a lot."

He thought a little and then told me, "We are currently searching for her."

"Has she disappeared?"

"Yes, she disappeared, and we still haven't found any trace of her!"

Distressed, I told him, "They may have killed her!"

"I don't think so. She may have fled to the capital."

"So far as I know, she doesn't have any friends there!"

"In any case, we'll continue our search. I hope we'll find her soon."

Early on the morning of the war's sixth day, after a night during which I didn't sleep a wink, I went to the city, feeling I was wandering through a cemetery where ghosts prowled. I drank coffee on the quay of the old harbor. Then I headed to the police station, hoping for news of Madame Marie-Rose's fate. After I waited for more than half an hour, the officer with two stars received me.

"Thank God, your friend has been found!"

"Where?"

"In the woods!"

"What do you mean, in the woods?"

"We didn't find her. The forest ranger did. The poor woman apparently fled from her house half-naked when they attacked it and spent three days and nights in the forest. She might easily have been eaten by wolves or killed by wild boars! Fortunately, she was able to escape from all those dangers."

"Where is she now?"

"Here, in the station."

"May I speak to her?"

"Yes . . . you may. But only briefly. Because we're transporting her to her country's embassy in less than half an hour."

"Thank you!"

In the empty gray office where the only piece of furniture was the chair on which she sat, I found Madame Marie-Rose. She was trembling as if she were naked in the winter's ice. The days and nights she had spent in the woods had aged her considerably. She looked as miserable as the neglected widows in our impoverished neighborhood. Once she caught sight of me, she started weeping silently, making me feel so awful I couldn't utter a single word. Her weeping made me feel complicit in the tragedy she had suffered. As I started to leave the gray office, Madame Marie-Rose threw herself on me and hugged me forcefully. In a voice partially muffled by tears, she whispered to me, *"Je ne t'oublierai jamais, mon cher petit Aziz"* (I'll never forget you, my dear little Aziz).

I left the police station a different person than when I entered. I was someone who had aged and grown old, a man whose heart was shattered, whose spirit was festering, who had no desire to live any longer. The people around me were groaning under the painful weight of the defeat. They floundered about as if they had lost their minds, memory, and consciousness of living on the face of the earth. Behind the doors in the Medina's neighborhoods, women lamented the loss of Jerusalem and of Arab honor.

Omran

He woke at dawn, turned on the light, and opened the *Essais* of Montaigne. His daily reading of these essays made him feel as if his spirit and intellect were communicating with the author's. All the boundaries and distances between them had faded until Omran felt he wasn't grasping a set of literary and philosophic essays but listening to valuable advice from Montaigne, who, in a soft voice, was telling Omran about the fragility of human life, the inability of the human intellect to comprehend the secrets of the universe or to grasp the mysteries of existence, and the insignificance of rulers, their arrogance and insane love for power and glory, while also discussing lies, deception, conceit, depravity, death, egotism, zealotry, and lethal creeds.

Montaigne was telling him what Stefan Zweig had said:

> The events of your age will be unable to violate you and grab hold of you so long as you are careful not to plunge into them and preserve your purity of mind. You will not feel your regrettable adventures and fate's harsh blows, unless you bend before them, because you are the only one who can grant things value and weight, joy and pain.

Omran believed Stefan Zweig was right when he said that only a person capable of liberating himself from everyone and everything can deepen the concept of liberty and safeguard it on earth, even in eras and situations devoid of all human principles and values.

This morning he would read the essay in which Montaigne praises the traits of friendship. Omran was sure this chapter had been influenced by Montaigne's platonic relationship with Étienne de La Boétie, that genius who succumbed to the plague when he was only thirty-two, leaving behind him one work: his *Discourse on Voluntary Servitude*. He recalls that this book, which is small in size but vast in ideas and thoughts, powerfully influenced him and forced him to revisit everything he had considered certain truths, which could not be doubted on any grounds.

Even though La Boétie had not lived in the Middle East, what he said was relevant to characteristic traits of Middle Eastern rulers and their subjects. Like the Romans who wept when Nero—the tyrant who torched Rome—died, Middle Eastern peoples have persistently wept for the tyrants and dictators who mistreat them, ruin their lives, and turn their nations into dreadful prisons where screams resound. A distinguishing characteristic of Middle Eastern despots, in ancient and modern times, is their supreme ability to narcotize their subjects and rob them of the ability and will to protest, rebel, and revolt. These tyrants have used various means, all of which harbored elements of violence, obstruction, and intimidation. Thanks to La Boétie, Omran no longer believed—as he had in his youth—that the peoples of the Middle East were not complicit in the subjugation, violence, and terrible outrages visited upon them. Instead, responsibility for this might be attributed to their own servility, cowardice, limited freedom of thought, and lingering subservience to received notions, lies, and fantasies. Indeed, they neglect their own rights and submit to strongmen and tyrants, whom they allow to strip them of everything, including their lives.

Montaigne and La Boétie met for the first time at a celebration held in the city of Bordeaux in 1559. Each man was immediately drawn to the other, and over the next four years a strong platonic friendship developed between them—like that between Socrates and Alcibiades or Goethe and Schiller. Montaigne wrote of their friendship: "If anyone insists on asking why I loved him, my only reply is: 'Because it was he, because it was I.'"[31] Montaigne also wrote that no enjoyment had any savor unless La Boétie shared it with him.

During the exhausting and bitter days when La Boétie was dying, Montaigne was keen to be at his friend's bedside and stayed with him until he breathed his last, at four in the morning on Wednesday,

August 18, 1563. Sixteen years later Montaigne wrote: "Were I to compare the remainder of my life, indeed my entire life, with the four years granted to me for the enjoyment of affectionate companionship with that forceful personality, I can say that all the rest was smoke and a dark, exhausting night. Since his demise, all I do is hang around indecisively, weakly, and no enjoyment afforded me consoles me; it merely intensifies my sorrow at his loss."

Omran too had learned the meaning of friendship in its most beautiful and noblest form with Diogenes during their youth, which was replete with hopes, dreams, grand aspirations, and stimulation for the ego to rid itself of anything that might decrease its freedom and the affirmation of its existence. They met daily to exchange ideas and discuss literary, intellectual, and political issues raised by books and periodicals that came from Cairo, Beirut, or Paris. After each meeting, he felt more self-confident and prouder of his friend, who possessed an extraordinary ability to beget brilliant ideas and liberate language from the defects of the dead, pedestrian "eloquence" of their shaykhs.

One afternoon, on a day perfumed by the fragrance of spring flowers, he had strolled with Diogenes through the Belvedere Garden, and they had not parted until sunset. Feeling tired, Omran had returned to the hostel to go to bed early. While he slept, he dreamt he was seated at a table with nothing on it. His father suddenly emerged from a light fog, clad, as for an Eid or other holiday, in a white jubba, with a red chechia on his head. Smiling, he approached his son, placed a piece of white paper and a pen on the table before him, and whispered: "Write, Son!"

"What shall I write?"

"Write!"

"I'm not a writer."

"You will be a writer, son!"

His father disappeared, and Omran woke with a dry mouth, sweat dripping copiously from him.

He drank half a bottle of water and then sat down at the table. For approximately thirty minutes he was lost in thought. Finally, he took a white piece of paper and a pen and began writing a text he entitled "Extolling Liberty." In it he summarized the thoughts and actions on this topic of philosophers, poets, and authors who had discussed freedom. Some had sacrificed their life defending it or been sent to prison or exiled. Some of their books had been burned because of their defense and glorification of liberty. First among these was Socrates, who had been forced to drink poison after being charged with "corrupting the youth of Athens." Words fell on the white page like calm, slow drops of rain.

At dawn he ended his text with the final stanzas of a poem by the French poet Éluard:

> On every available body
> On my friends' foreheads
> On every proffered hand
> I write your name.
> On every display of surprises
> On alert lips
> Atop silence
> I write your name.
> On my devastated sanctuaries
> On my demolished lighthouses
> On the walls of my ennui
> I write your name.
> On an absence without desire
> On naked solitude
> On the thresholds of death
> I write your name.
> On health regained
> On danger eliminated
> On hope devoid of memory
> I write your name.
> On the authority of a single word
> I start my life afresh
> I was born to know you
> To name you
> Liberty.[32]

He left the five pages of the text on the table and went outside to enjoy the fresh morning air and the extraordinary quiet that precedes the feverish beginning of daytime in the big city. After drinking coffee, he went back to sleep and did not wake until noon. At six he arrived at the Canigou Café, where he found Diogenes smoking and drinking alone. Omran placed the four pages before him and asked, "Would you mind reading this text?"

"Who wrote it?"

"I did."

"Sit far away, and I'll read it now."

Once he finished reading the four pages, Diogenes leaped to his feet and embraced Omran warmly. Then he asked, "When did you write this?"

"Last night. Do you like it?"

"It's the most beautiful text I've read by a living author from our country!"

"You're exaggerating!"

"No, I'm not exaggerating or flattering you. I just speak the truth. Now, let's go!"

"Where?"

"To the headquarters of the newspaper *Al-Sabah*!"

"Why?"

"One of my friends edits the culture page. I'll ask him to publish this text to inform people who care about culture that there is a writer who will become very important in this land!"

The culture editor received them hospitably and offered them a cup of coffee. Diogenes handed him the pages and said, "If you like this text, please publish it as soon as possible!"

Three days later, the entire text was published in the newspaper *Al-Sabah*. As Omran walked through the city, he was congratulated and heard expressions of admiration pour over him from other students, culturally savvy people, shopkeepers, affluent folks, and political operatives. He was praised by Shaykh Larbi al-Kabadi, who composed sad love songs for the famous singer Sulayha and knew by heart and recited, in his soirées at clubs and coffeehouse in the Medina, thousands of stanzas of ancient poetry and texts from al-Jahiz, al-Tawhidi, and Ibn al-Muqaffa' as well as stories from *The Thousand and One Nights.*

Al-Kabadi said: "I am sure he will be for our nation a writer like Taha Hussein or al-'Aqqad!"

His professor of Arabic literature ignored him for a week. Then at the end of the morning class, he remarked, "The text you published in *Al-Sabah* reflects your distorted views, which will lead you to a miserable end!"

Early in 1952, life in the country became turbulent, and resistance fighters retired to the mountains, where they announced the beginning of their armed struggle. In response, French colonial authorities arrested the major nationalist leaders, sending Bourguiba to La Galite Island, which was uninhabited. Toward the end of that gloomy year—to be precise, on December 5—a French terrorist group that called itself "La Main Rouge," assassinated the Tunisian labor leader Farhat Hached, and the entire country exploded. Huge crowds of protesters went out to demonstrate in the capital, challenging heavily armed French troops. Accompanied by Diogenes, Omran marched in the vanguard of the protesters. They distributed leaflets in the Medina to encourage people to rebel and revolt. The pair also published in *Al-Sabah* fiery essays that angered the colonial authorities. On a cold, rainy evening, when Omran was returning to the hostel with leaflets he planned to distribute late that night, gendarmes arrested him. After handcuffing and blindfolding him, they led him somewhere—he didn't know where. Once they removed the blindfold, he found himself in something like a huge warehouse with hundreds of men: graybeards, adults, and youths. He later learned that this "warehouse" was the remnants of a fine palace Ahmet Bey had built near al-Mohamedia, southwest of the capital, after a trip he took to Paris in 1846, because he wanted to replicate the Palais du Versailles. After his death, the palace was neglected and, over the course of years, became a ruin inhabited by mice and snakes. Owls also nested there.

He spent two whole months in this warehouse, tormented by lice, the cold, hunger, humiliations, foul odors, and the daily injustices meted out to prisoners by guards and soldiers. When he was released, he had to walk more than twenty kilometers in the rain from the outskirts of Mohamedia back to the capital. Once he reached the hostel, his brother threw himself into his arms, sobbing bitterly, because he thought Omran had been killed. As for his mother, she hadn't stopped weeping since the day Omran disappeared. In their village, people had flocked to her daily to try to console her. They felt almost certain that he had been killed in one of the many demonstrations during those dark, rough days, which were marked by violence, fear, and the breakdown of safety and security. He spent four days in bed, trying to recover his strength.

At the Canigou Café he learned that Diogenes had also been arrested and spent a month and a half in Borj El Roumi prison in Bizerte. On **his** release, Diogenes returned to his village in the South to check on his mother's health. When Omran returned to the Canigou Café, at the end of the week, he found a letter waiting for him from Diogenes. It said in part:

A friend from my village returned from the capital yesterday and told me they had released you. This made me very happy. I would have dearly loved to have been there the day you regained your liberty. Then we would have gone to a bar, a club, or the Belvedere Garden to celebrate liberty and resume our discussions about the issues preoccupying us: all the literary, political, intellectual ones.

No doubt you also suffered what I did in Borj El Roumi prison, where I found myself among brazen criminals and thieves. I won't hide from you that I was appalled at first when I heard them discuss the hideous crimes they had committed. Gradually, though, I discovered among them some who sheltered a compassionate heart and good spirit. Throughout my stay there, they afforded me courtesy, respect, and affection, referring to me as "the professor." Some of them asked me to tell them about literature and politics. At times, I recited for them poems by al-Mutanabbi, Abu Nuwas, Abu Qasim Echebbi, al-Ma'arri, and other ancient and modern poets. They responded to these poems, even though I'm sure they did not understand much of them. They may have understood nothing, but this erased the barriers between us. I received only praise, compliments, and kind words from them, and, in this way, they lightened the burden of prison's torment, pains, cold, lice, and hunger, and the guards' brutality. The day I was released, they bade me farewell very emotionally. I saw tears in their eyes.

Once I was released from prison, I returned to my village to reassure myself about my mother's health and found it had deteriorated. I even thought she was about to die. But two days after I arrived in the village, she started to recover her strength. For this reason, I may return to the capital in a week or two, at the most. The fact is that the days I have spent here have proved fruitful. I have written new poems inspired by my prison experience. I have also read some outstanding books, including a great one about Greek philosophy. Every morning before sunrise and each evening before sunset, I roam through the oases to enjoy the stillness, calm, and beauty of the desert, which is magical and enchanting at times like these.

Your devoted friend,
Diogenes

Saleem

Everything suggests that I am sinking into mud or tar and will soon reach a bottomless pit. This country, which I love, now seems alien to me, and I also feel that my link to it is growing more tenuous day by day. With people of all sorts, my quarrels and enmities have multiplied. In view of my poor performance at work, my boss advised me to rest for two weeks, in hopes that my condition will improve and that I will return to work as energetic and lively as before.

I thanked him and departed. I wandered through the Medina, which is full of piles of rubbish, cats, and old women. Although the sun was shining, the day was bitter and even bone-chillingly cold. I asked myself more than once: What will I do during the next two weeks? Should I go to my village, which I haven't visited for a long time? No . . . no . . . I won't do that! I can no longer bear the incessant quarrels between my brothers. Their disputes generally break out for trivial reasons related to a cow, an olive tree, or even a hen! In every quarrel, they exchange curses in loud voices and wave cudgels in the air. I believe the true cause for all this is that the blood of ancient tribes, which used to battle and fight each other endlessly for flimsy reasons, courses through my brothers' veins. If I went to my village, they would suspect my motive and think that I had come because I wanted something. Then they would all unite against me to make me return whence I had ventured, as quickly as possible. Indeed, they might incite all the villagers against me and accuse me of being a traitor who abandoned his family, tribe, and roots—a man who married a woman who speaks a foreign language, scorns the countryside, and flees from rural people as if they were nasty, hateful vermin. Thus, they had to expel me immediately to my burrow in the northern city where I have chosen to live. No, no, no. I won't go to my village!

Should I go to the capital? That idea would have bad consequences too, especially during these turbulent days when struggles and confrontations have become more prevalent, as the bearded ones brandish swords, threatening to behead infidels and to teach bareheaded woman a lesson. The best thing will be to stay here, in this northern city, which I have grown fond of and where I have planted my roots. The important thing is to prepare an excellent plan that will fill my days and nights and keep me from feeling lonely, bored, or frustrated. It is also important that I do my utmost to restore my affectionate relationship with my wife and daughter. If I can't manage that, I will remain anxious and worried, and dark ghosts will continue to pursue me, ruining my life and increasing my worries and pains!

The Medina funneled me to the sea, and I found myself contemplating with enchantment and delight the magnificent views and the brilliant colors that shone before me as the sun set over the western hills. My soul was delighted, and light flooded my heart and spirit. For some moments I sensed that my days of bitter isolation had ended and that my terrifying phantoms had disappeared forever. In those rosy moments, I thought that a short trip outside the country might restore my lost equilibrium. But where would I go? The best place would be New Orleans. Yes, the African American jazz capital where people dance in the streets, day and night. Once I returned, I would tell my wife everything that had happened. She would hug me to her chest, and we would begin a new love story more beautiful and delightful than the first. But the costs of the trip would be exorbitant and a visa very difficult to obtain at a time when every Arab is considered a terrorist until he proves he isn't one. New Orleans would be difficult if not impossible. France then? No . . . no. I won't go to that country, where the faults of its Arab immigrants outstrip those of the original inhabitants. Italy? No, I would find in that country people who had fled there on boats like death traps. Where, then? Ah . . . I've found it. I have! I have! To Malta, yes—to that island where people speak a language derived from our colloquial Arabic, where there is a museum that displays important paintings of the Italian artist Caravaggio, whose work my wife and I love. For her thirtieth birthday I gave her a book containing reproductions of all his most famous paintings, including works he painted in Malta, which was one of the places where he fled after killing one of his enemies in Rome. These include *The Beheading of Saint John the Baptist* and *Saint Jerome Writing*. In these two works, as in his other paintings, Caravaggio highlighted life's brutality and death's ubiquity. Death stalks man at every moment and in every place—as it did in Caravaggio's own lifetime.

Yes, I will go to Malta. I feel certain that a trip there will pull me out of this gloom and lethal despair. At least that's what I thought. The next day I went to a travel agency and purchased a ticket to Valletta. On the day of the trip, I went to the Tunis-Carthage Airport, chirping like a bird at the start of spring. The woman checking luggage and carry-ons opened my passport. Then she asked me, "Where's your visa?"

"What visa?"

"Don't you know you can't travel to Malta without a visa?"

"Ooooh! What rotten luck!"

I left the airport feeling like a prisoner returned by the authorities to his cramped cell shortly after they released him. I took a taxi to the harbor area and sat in a café attempting to find a solution for the crisis in which I had landed myself. Finally, I decided to spend the night in a small hotel. The next morning, I would go to the Maltese Consulate to obtain a visa.

I spent the afternoon in the hotel and then went out to explore the quiet city. I entered a beachfront restaurant and ordered grilled fish with fries and a bottle of white wine. I spent almost two hours there. On my way back to the hotel, three toughs who wore sweaters and black leather jackets surrounded me. A few meters beyond them, my nephew, who lives in the capital, glared at me, gloating. I was amazed he was there. When I tried to approach him, the three men prevented me.

"What do you want from me?" I asked.

One of them squeezed so hard on my neck that I was almost strangled. Then he told me, "Listen, Loser . . . from now on you will do only what we order!"

The three men hustled me into the rear seat of a black SUV. One man sat on my right and a second to my left. The third sat next to the driver, who was none other than my nephew.

The car shot off at high speed in a direction I couldn't discern, because its lights were off and there were no other vehicles on the road. From time to time I caught sight of roaming ghosts, gutted apartment buildings with dense smoke rising from them, dead animals, and flaming trees. I ignored their warning and asked, "Would you tell me where we are and where we're going?"

The man to my right squeezed my neck hard again and replied, "To hell and a miserable fate!"

The face of the man to my left turned blue from anger, and he shouted, "If you open your filthy trap again, we'll slay you and throw your corpse to the stray dogs—and there are lots of them nowadays!"

The SUV continued rushing through the dark for a long time. Then, suddenly, day broke: mournful and gloomy. All my eyes could see was a desolate desert with scattered thorny bushes and boulders with such strange shapes they resembled petrified human beings or wild animals. The barren mountains swaying in a mirage in the distance reminded me of ranges I had seen in southwestern Tunisia during a visit there when I was studying at the university. Finally, the SUV stopped in a dry gulch. A moment later this vehicle disappeared with the three men and my nephew, leaving me alone in that wadi, where there were no signs of life.

I felt hungry and thirsty and an overwhelming desire for my wife and daughter. My tears flowed copiously. While I stood there, weeping and cursing my fate in that fearful wasteland and sensing that this would be the end of me, four men, clad in Afghan jellabiyas and sporting shaggy beards and dusty faces, appeared. When I examined them carefully, I realized that these were the same four men who had kidnapped me while wearing sweaters and black leather jackets. My nephew was still with them and dressed like them.

I headed south, at their command, with two of them on either side of me. When we passed out of the wadi, the desert plain before us was filled with groups of men, who were also clad in Afghan jellabiyas. Their dark faces expressed such terror and bewilderment that they seemed to have just risen from their graves—the way Surahs of the Qur'an describe people on Resurrection Day. Some were exhausted old men who edged forward like ants. There were also young men with stern faces and fixed stares as well as elderly women with bent backs. Those massive congregations advanced silently, as if they had been struck dumb for all eternity. The only sound was the harsh cawing of crows soaring overhead.

Those groups quickly multiplied in number as other congregations joined them. Many of these people rode donkeys, mules, or camels. These multitudes continued, with us among them, until a city resembling Kairouan—with its walls, great mosque, and the cemeteries that surround it on every side—appeared nearby. It seemed to be a city inhabited exclusively by the dead. Then, amid clouds of dust, black banners were raised, along with swords and daggers, as everyone started shouting *"La ilah ila Allah"* and *"Allahu Akbar!"* They also called out, "Death and destruction to infidels, libertines, and sinners!"

When we reached this city, which, as I mentioned, resembled Kairouan, the vast courtyard of its mosque swarmed with groups that constantly recited the Islamic creed, proclaimed the oneness of God, and prayed. Behind a long dais, on which were arrayed ancient copies of the Qur'an sat shaykhs with enormous turbans, bulging bellies, and Afghan jellabiyas. When the eldest of them rose, the crowds yelled: *"La ilah ila Allah"* and *"Allahu Akbar"* until I imagined that the earth was quaking beneath my feet. Then silence prevailed—as if those multitudes had suddenly frozen in place and lost the ability to move or speak. At this juncture, the senior shaykh started to deliver his sermon, which apparently these multitudes had swarmed from everywhere on Earth to hear. At the outset, he said, "All praise to God who taught us what we did not know, singled us out with His power and might, granted us victory over infidel nations, tyrants, and evildoers, and subdued for us those who raised their swords to obstruct us when we came to them with the religion of mercy, forgiveness, and wise counsel."

He paused his sermon briefly to allow everyone to voice their allegiance to God and glorify Him.

Then the shaykh continued his lengthy sermon, which he embroidered with Quranic verses that advocate jihad and threaten infidels and enemies of Islam with painful chastisement. These were interrupted by the crowd's chants of allegiance to God and praise glorifying Him. In conclusion, the shaykh said, "O Sincere Believers . . . O You who have endured the suffering of the journey to experience this memorable event, allow me to provide you glad tidings and inform you that Mujahideen for the sake of God and for the victory of our authentic religion have defeated the most obdurate of all our enemies in this land: George the Berber!" While the congregation celebrated and glorified God, a warrior advanced to the dais bearing a bloody head on the tip of his spear.

When the crowds calmed down again, the shaykh declared, "This is the jihadi who killed that enemy of God and His Messenger, the infidel Berber George. He will tell you how."

After the congregants celebrated and glorified God once more, the warrior declared, "Sincere Believers, I saw this infidel, whose head is on my spear, riding a packhorse, shaded with peacock feathers by two slave girls. I trailed him, without him or the two young women seeing me. Once he reached barren land, I attacked, stabbing him. The slave women threw themselves over him, attempting to shield him from the blows of my sword. I quickly sliced off the hand of one woman. Then I gave him a coup de grâce and chopped off his head, which I placed on my spear."

There was delighted jubilation and glorification of God at this decisive victory.

Then a second warrior stepped forward with the head of a woman with blood-spattered black braids on his spear. The shaykh declared, "This warrior slew the Sorceress, Viper of the Berber Mountains!"

The throngs delightedly glorified and exalted God for this decisive victory.

Lifting high his spear, the second warrior narrated the slaying of the Prophetess: "Sincere Believers: as I fought to the east and west, to spread the religion of God and to exalt the Word of His Prophet, I never encountered an adversary more stubborn than this Berber woman. Over the course of many years, she continued to combat us, blocking our attacks ferociously. When news reached us that the Berbers had dispersed, as they quarreled among themselves until there remained no discipline or single point of view among them, we attacked her army. She joined battle with us, beating her chest and spreading her hair to incite the Berbers to fight, and telling them: 'Fight or lose your entire realm when you all are wiped out.' Battle flared up between our opposing forces, and scores of them fell dead. Then their troops began to retreat in dismay. When she noticed that, she fled. I followed her—she on her mare and me on my stallion. In a gorge, I slew her brutally. Her head is on my spear, Sincere Believers!"

There was delighted jubilation and glorification of God at this decisive victory.

Then the shaykh announced the imposition of the Shariah on those who had opposed and attacked it. There was a loud clamor, for which there seemed to be no reason, and people began to surge toward the dais, shouting and moaning. When I noticed that my kidnappers were distracted by this, I raced off so fast my feet kicked almost as high as my head. Once I ascertained that I was a safe distance away, I looked back but saw no trace of that city, which resembled Kairouan, nor of the throngs that had packed the courtyard of its Grand Mosque. I took a deep breath and praised God for my safety. Then I headed to a scrawny tree, which was the only one in that desolate desert. I leaned my head against its trunk and closed my eyes, trying to erase from my memory the terrifying adventures I had just experienced. But the earth around me shook in no time at all with a resounding reverberation like thunder. I opened my eyes and saw that black SUV stop a few meters from me. The three men jumped from it, clad again in sweaters and black leather trousers. They also wore black sunglasses. They bound my arms and legs, threw me in the rear seat, and ordered the driver, who was my nephew, to drive off.

"Do you know where we are taking you, Stray Dog?" the man on my right asked me.

I shook my head no.

Applying pressure to my neck, he replied, "To your village, which you fled and denounced. Your family will give you the punishment you deserve!"

This time it was clear the SUV really was heading toward my village. I could discern this from landmarks along the route and the villages and police stations we passed. All these were deserted and forlorn. When we reached the entry to my village, one of the men untied my fetters and shoved me out of the vehicle, which immediately disappeared in a thick cloud of dust. I looked around at my village, which I hadn't visited for a quarter of a century, and nothing seemed to have changed. It was as still as a cemetery, with no trace of a person or animal in sight. As I glanced around anxiously with alarm at the deserted house, huge black dogs charged toward me from every direction, baring their fangs but not barking. I started to run, screaming like a man who knew these dogs would chomp down on his butt and tear his body apart. Then I stumbled over a rock and fell to the ground.

I opened my eyes: darkness! Someone was pounding on the door . . .

Where am I?

Am I in my apartment?

No, no, no. What I'm lying on isn't the sofa where I've slept since the beginning of my trials.

Where am I then?

Oh! I'm in the little hotel at the port.

The knocking on my door grew stronger. I rose with difficulty and opened it to find the hotel's proprietor facing me—looking bewildered and alarmed!

"What happened to you?" he asked me.

"Nothing!"

"How could it be nothing when you were screaming loudly enough to wake me and most of the patrons of the hotel!"

I did not reply and bowed my head, feeling at a total loss.

"Are you sick?"

"No!"

He scrutinized my face for some moments. Then he exclaimed, "There seems to be something wrong with you!"

"I'm fine!"

"I don't think so. I advise you to consult a doctor, today when medical offices open!"

I closed the door once he left and continued to toss and turn in bed until daybreak.

Aziz

I went to the cemetery yesterday morning and sat beside my mother's grave. We had this conversation:

"How are you, Dear Mother?"

"I'm decaying bones, my son. How are you?"

"I'm fine!"

"You seem to have grown old!"

"How can you tell?"

"Your voice is no longer that of the child I left in the physical world when he was a young boy!"

"Yes, I have aged a lot, Mother. I have become an old man—toothless, bald, and even uglier than I used to be. Children in my neighborhood flee when they see me."

"As bad as that?"

"Yes . . . that bad, unfortunately."

"Time there passes quickly. Here, everything is frozen and heavy!"

"Yes, Mother, time where I am passes as swiftly as the wind. I'll soon join you in the next world."

"I'll be happy to see you after our long separation!"

"Me too!"

"How is your father?"

"May God have mercy on his soul."

"Did drinking kill him?"

"Yes."

"I was sure it would. Have you married?"

"No!"

"Why not?"

"Because I realized that I'm, quite simply, not cut out for marriage."

"You may be right; nothing tormented me in life so much as my marriage!"

"I know."

"How's the country?"

"Really dreadful!"

"When I was alive, I felt it resembled me."

"How so?"

"Her luck's always been bad!"

"Yes . . . bad luck. You're right, Dear Mother!"

"Your visit has gladdened me, Son!"

"Mother, you're always in my heart!"

"You too, My Precious!"

"Good-bye, Dear Mother. Till we meet again . . . soon, I hope!"

"Stay safe, Dear Boy!"

I wiped away the two warm tears flowing down my cheek. Then I headed to my father's grave but stayed there only a few moments, because I imagined him squirming in his grave from discomfort at my visit. In the other world he may still be as much a loner as he was in this one. He died, at the age of sixty-eight, of cirrhosis of the liver, the night of January 25th, 1978. The day of his burial, there were violent confrontations between the regime and the labor unions. There were dozens of fatalities, and people were wounded in the capital and other cities. Our city, though, remained relatively calm. Even so, only a few people, mostly alcoholics, attended my father's funeral. After he was buried, Murad and I went to a small bar near the harbor to drink a beer in honor of his soul. We didn't leave the bar until nightfall.

Before I left the cemetery, I spent a long time by the grave of my friend Ahmad, who died of lung cancer when he was sixty-seven. Even though that was ten years ago, I still spot his ghost prowling the alleyways of the old city, the quay of the old harbor, the beach, through the forest, and other places, carrying the black leather bag he took everywhere. He referred to it as "my liberty" and stored in it books, beer cans, and packs of the cheap cigarettes to which he was addicted. Until he died, he was the city's lone wolf, shunning relationships, gatherings, bars, and restaurants. Before I became acquainted with him and approached him and his world, I had heard reports that his father was a sailor who went down with his ship in a storm when Ahmad was seven. Even though his mother was still a beautiful young woman at the time, she rejected all suitors so she could focus on raising her only child. To provide him with a good life, she worked as a maid in the homes of Frenchmen. He excelled in his studies and obtained a baccalaureate with honors. Then he moved to the capital to study philosophy. Before completing the first year, he returned suddenly to our coastal city and refused to provide any reason for dropping out. He was content to take a clerical job in an import-export firm. After his mother died, he sold the family house, which was in El Ksiba, facing the old port and the fortress the Spanish built when they conquered the city in the sixteenth century. He quit his job in the import-export firm to live like a homeless person, wearing a long black overcoat and military boots in winter and on cold days in spring and autumn. In the summer, he wore olive-colored shorts and a gray T-shirt bearing a picture of Bob Marley, whom he loved and whose songs he never tired of hearing. He liked at times to leave the miserable cramped house where he lived in the Medina, to sleep on the beach, in the woods, or other places, taking with him a portable radio so he could listen to the foreign songs he loved. During my rambles on the beach or in the forest, I surprised him more than once smoking cheap cigarettes, drinking beer, listening to music, or reading books, which I never managed to identify by title or author.

During the period when I was suffering from the bitter pangs of separation from Madame Marie-Rose, I spent my free time far from the hubbub of the city. I would sit on boulders to enjoy the calm and tranquillity, watch steamships go and come and travel with them in my imagination to those cities and ports to the north. One warm spring afternoon I was busy reading *The Stranger* by Albert Camus.

Madame Marie-Rose had given me that novel a week before her house was torched. Ahmad appeared before me then and cast a quick glance at the book's cover. I heard him ask, "Do you like that book?"

"I haven't finished it yet, but it seems to be a beautiful book!"

"It's a great book . . . I read it when I was sixteen."

He sat down near me, opened his bag, and extracted two cans of beer from it. He gave me one. Then he asked, "Do you smoke?"

"Occasionally."

He lit a cigarette and handed it to me.

"I like you," he said.

"Why?"

"I don't know!"

After remaining silent for some moments, he added, "Perhaps because you read excellent books!"

"How do you know that?"

"Because I've been spying on you for a long time!"

I laughed and asked, "Why have you been spying on me?"

He smiled but did not reply.

My spontaneous meetings with Ahmad continued. At each one, he opened a peephole into his private world.

Following his father's death, he had slipped out of his house every day to go to the harbor and watch sailors return from fishing trips, hoping to discover his father among them. He continued to do that for many years. In his dreams, he saw his father battling high waves in a cyclone. On stormy days he was tempted to go to the shore to watch the surging waves. In his imagination, he saw the sea spitting out his father the next moment. Then he would seize his father's hand, and they would return together to their house. Since his father's image was etched in his memory and imagination, he started to shun congregating with other people or conversing with them, for fear that image might become blurred and fade until he lost it forever, while the world surrounding him grew increasingly gloomy and savage.

By the age of ten, he began to seriously consider killing himself by casting himself into the sea on a stormy night. The idea of suicide haunted him for many months. Finally, he abandoned it, out of love for his mother, who struggled daily to make him happy and fill the frightening void left by his father.

During his adolescence, he fell in love with reading, which mitigated the intensity of his nightmares and daytime torments. At first, he read everything he could lay hands on. Then he started reading novels with anxious heroes who were silent and withdrawn, characters who rejected servility, humiliation, and acquiescence to the orders of those who considered themselves to be masters of the universe. Characters he admired eschewed anything that could corrupt their inner world or deprive them of their freedom of thought, motion, or action. He also read the work of poets who wove into their poems their own sufferings and bitter experiences; their rebellion against inertia, lethargy, and poverty; their anger at every instance of tyranny, domination, and subjugation; and their love for life and response to its delights. These poets fled, with the wind at their heels, from the prisons represented by families and societies, which conspired to domesticate them; instead, they embarked on one adventure after another. With each of those they would taste a new flavor of liberty while exploring dreams, thoughts, and emotions never experienced before, creating a language that would be that of "spirit addressing spirit by condensing everything: spirits, colors, and sounds."

When he was eighteen, he read Plato's *Apology* and was overwhelmed by a feeling of having finally stumbled upon a figure who could lead him to the true meaning of "liberty." Little by little, Socrates became a familiar figure for him, indeed a dear friend. Ahmad could almost feel his coarse cloak, which he wore in all seasons, and see his snub nose and homely appearance. Ahmad roamed the streets of Athens with Socrates, who went barefoot, even on cold and frigid days, attending assemblies in which debate became heated. He memorized Socrates' statement: "Athens is like sluggish horse, and I am the gadfly that stings and awakens it back to life."[33]

He dedicated spring break that year to Heraclitus, repeating, like sweet songs, his famous words: "Everything flows. Everything is in constant motion. Therefore, we never swim in the same river twice."[34]

From Diogenes he learned asceticism and renunciation of the world's pleasure. He perceived, like Diogenes, that people's suffering stems from wearing themselves out by living materially, believing that physical aspects of life can provide people the happiness they desire. Later, under the influence of Diogenes, Ahmad chose a life-style that made people regard him as a barbarian they either mocked or pitied—someone who had lost his mind and could no longer cope with life—bereft of family, job, and shelter. The truth was that he sold his family home not merely because he could not bear to live there with the ghosts of his parents haunting it all the time, but also because he wished to test his ability to enjoy liberty as it was understood by the philosophers and poets whom he considered his spiritual life coaches!

He did not understand much of Kant's philosophy but liked Kant's self-imposed discipline in his contacts with the world at large, and his punctuality, which allegedly allowed housewives in his small city to start heating broth on the fire when he walked past their homes.

From Spinoza he learned that man will not rejoice or acquire his true liberty until he acknowledges the existence of an eternal order for the cosmos. For a man to be truly free, he must reject emotions and unruly reactions, preconceived notions, and false beliefs. He must also accept life and its pleasures, enjoying everything that is beautiful on the face of the earth, whether a brilliant book, an amazing painting, or an enchanting scene in nature. To be happy and relaxed, all a man needs is to watch a flower open or awake to birds singing in the morning.

In Schopenhauer's pessimism he found answers to questions that had kept him awake at night and still did. Ahmad learned from him that unity gives man the ability to be with himself rather than with others and that man's life is nothing but a struggle to exist despite his certainty that defeat is inevitable in the end!

He had thought that his acquaintance with philosophy would expand and deepen at the university. Thus, his disappointment was bitter during his first weeks there, when he found himself confronted by instructors who presented doctrines, ideas, and philosophical concepts as if they were stale food that might cause mental and digestive colic and cramps, secondhand goods at discount prices, or packaged products that could be promoted with the least possible effort. They discussed philosophers as if they were anxious, hesitant creatures, lost in the fog of an abstract, obscure, ill-defined world unconnected to reality and history. The way these instructors presented philosophers, they absolutely did not seem to have derived their doctrines from their personal experiences or by agonizing over questions of being and nothingness. Instead, they were yawning in ivory towers. Once he felt certain that he would be afflicted with an incurable intellectual lassitude there, he left the university with no regrets and returned to his coastal city, preferring to live philosophy in the open air rather than hear about it in stuffy gray rooms. He was satisfied to live simply, free of beliefs, of lethal monotony, and of the lofty aspirations that had inflated most of his former classmates in the Philosophy Department.

Unlike those of his contemporaries who were fascinated by major revolutions, he did not feel drawn toward Marx or his followers like Lenin, Mao Zedong, or others, because he learned from his spiritual masters that people who claim they can change the world and make it better are fantasizing and creating fraudulent, phony legends. He also learned from them that the true goal of philosophy is to help a person live his daily life with safe reassurance and to enable him to obtain enough insight to grasp the world around him.

Despite what I thought was a friendly relationship, Ahmad allowed me to enter his house only once—for some reason I can't remember. Oh! . . . Sorry: I have remembered. He wanted to give me a book about the trial of Socrates. In his bedroom he had many books stacked on top of each other. Over his bed hung a photograph of his father and one of his mother. Beneath these pictures, he had written—in thick black letters—a verse he said was by an Iranian poet known as Hafez: "I will fly away, leaving only my dust!"

I won't deny that Ahmad's ideas influenced me a lot. Many of them have provided guidance for my life. Thus, I also ended my studies after I received my baccalaureate and was content to work as a

postal clerk, after ridding my mind, once and for all, of the plan
to marry and establish a family. My friend Murad, though, considered Ahmad's ideas "negative." When I asked if he thought he could
do something important in life, Murad answered decisively: "Yes, I
can!"

"What?"

"You'll learn that soon!"

He then started performing grueling physical exercises almost
every day. He would work out on the beach, in the woods, or on the
mountain. Occasionally, he would ask me to punch him in the belly,
hard. When I asked why, he replied, "I want my belly to become as
tight as a drum!"

I laughed out loud. "Why?"

"Because I want to become a fedayee!"

"A fedayee?"

"Yes. I'll become a fedayee and join the Palestinian Resistance!"

"You're crazy!"

"Not at all. I'm sure this will happen soon!"

"But your family needs you. Don't they?"

"The importance of everything else seems trivial, balanced
against a just cause!"

For years Murad was preoccupied by the Palestinian cause.
That was the only one that interested him. He followed events in
Palestine daily: its struggles and battles. He knew by heart all its
anthems, the poems by its poets, and the slogans of the movement's
best-known factions. He could tell you about all the major Palestinian leaders—as if he broke bread with them daily and attended their
secret meetings. He was fascinated by Wadie Haddad and boasted
proudly about every airplane hijacking he conducted. When Haddad
died in the spring of 1978, Murad wept more bitterly for him than
for anyone else. He mourned for forty days, letting his beard grow,
wearing black, and refusing to eat, drink, or talk with anyone but
me. I remember him telling me, "Israel has killed its true adversary:
Wadie Haddad was the only person capable of harming it anywhere
in the world."

My response to his claim was: "But the news says he died of leukemia!"

Murad flew into a rage and screamed at me: "People who believe news reports like that are idiots! I'm certain that Mossad killed him!"

Since I considered Murad to be one of those Arabs who think Israel is responsible for every disaster or catastrophe that afflicts them, I tried to change the subject. But he refused to let me, retorting quickly, "I'm certain that time will show the Mossad killed him!"

Some years later at The Corsairs, Murad brought me an article in a Lebanese newspaper. It contained information that Wadie Haddad's assassination by Mossad had been admitted by Israel itself. The author of the article explained that Wadie Haddad was known to love Belgian chocolates and that when Mossad agents caught wind of this, they sent one of their operatives to Baghdad, where Haddad was living, to present him with a box of chocolates, which killed him a few weeks later.

The summer of 1982 was just as bitter as the summer of our War of Independence and the summer of the Arab rout, because Israel attacked Lebanon and laid siege to the Palestinians in Beirut. Murad posted himself before a television to follow news of this war. Jittery, angry, and enraged, he cursed the "treacherous" Arab rulers who didn't rush to assist and support their besieged brethren. The filthy war did not end until the Palestinians agreed to leave Lebanon and relocate to Tunisia. The day the media announced that the ship carrying them would dock in the harbor of our city one morning toward the end of September, people of all ranks and ages turned out to greet them. Murad, though, appeared at my apartment before sunrise in a foul mood and told me, "I don't want to stay in the city today!"

"Why not?"

"I can't bear to see Palestinians defeated and expelled **one more time!**"

We bought cans of beer, sandwiches, and two bottles of mineral water, placed all these provisions in a cooler, and headed to the woods to spend the entire day there. We discussed many things, but neither of us referred—not even with one word—to the Palestinians whose arrival in our country constituted a major event here and throughout the world. When we left the forest, we were too drunk to walk straight, and I felt certain that my friend Murad had finally abandoned his dream of becoming a fedayee who hijacked airplanes and targeted Israel around the world.

Omran

At the end of the short letter that he had received two days earlier, Sophie asked: "How can you write during a time of upheavals and disturbances?"

This morning he replied to her letter:

My Dear Sophie,

Judging by your short letter, I think you have escaped from the spider's web, and this makes me very happy. In response to your question, I would like to say there is no best time to write. The history of world literature offers us many examples of great works that emerged from turbulent, painful periods of human existence. They excel in number and value those produced in calm, relaxed eras of peace and contentment. There are many examples of this from ancient Greece. Homer's masterpieces, *The Odyssey* and *The Iliad*, reflect the ordeals, catastrophes, struggles, and destructive wars that Greece experienced. Other works have painted superb representations of great adventurers who confronted challenges to achieve perhaps only a small bit of what they desired. The adventures of some may even have resulted in failure and defeat, death on a battlefield, or aimless wandering through a land they did not know and where they were unknown. Socrates drank poison rather than renounce his ideas, which his foes claimed were "corrupting" the youth of Athens!

Most of the great works of literature produced in Roman times dealt directly with the tragedy of a person searching on

the face of the earth for a happiness that seems impossible.
Ovid dreamt of life in the bosom of love and peace and of a
happiness that would envelop all humanity. Instead, he ran
afoul of tyranny and despotism and was forced to leave his
homeland and live the remainder of his days feeling homesick
for the places that he loved and where his talent had flourished,
albeit conscious that words might help him savor the bitter taste
of life. What he wrote in exile in Tomis, on the shores of the
Black Sea, while looking out on a harsh barren land with no
signs of spring or autumn or evidence of fields or grapes being
harvested, was extremely painful:

> These verses you read
> I did not compose in my gardens
> Nor while I lay stretched out on my bed
> As I once wrote.
> I penned them amid gales,
> By the light of a cloudy sky,
> While waves rocked me
> And splashed my pages.[35]

I think the wars and bloody conflict that tore Italy apart
in the dark Middle Ages inspired Dante to write *The Divine
Comedy*. Major Russian authors like Gogol, Dostoyevsky, Tol-
stoy, and Chekhov wrote in turbulent times of injustices, assassinations, and escalation of the twin demons of extremism and
blind violence.

From the twin disasters of the two world wars, which
drenched the earth with the blood of millions, emerged extraordinary masterpieces like *Journey to the End of the Night* by
Louis-Ferdinand Céline, *All Quiet on the Western Front* by
Erich Maria Remarque, *A Farewell to Arms* by Ernest Hemingway, as well as *And Quiet Flows the Don* by Sholokhov.

At the beginning of an essay entitled "Book of Disasters,"
Jorge Luis Borges posed the following questions: Why do we
always find ourselves drawn to endings? Why do so few people

praise the beauties of sunrise compared with the many who celebrate sunset and evanescence? In Dante's *The Divine Comedy*, why do we prefer "The Inferno" to "Paradise"? Why do we think about Waterloo as a defeat much more often than as a victory? Why did the fall of Constantinople constitute the end of an era? Why are people more interested in tragedy than comedy? Why do we think happy endings artificial and silly? Why do we cherish the memory of defeated soldiers more often than of victors? Borges considers the characters of authors like Henry James and Kafka to seem trained to fail. He considers *Ulysses* by James Joyce to be an epic about dissolution and evanescence, as he put it.

In a text entitled "Abbreviated Confession," Emil Cioran, the nihilist philosopher, says, "I have no desire to write except in an explosive situation, in a convulsive fever, or in a stupor verging on delirium and insanity, and in an atmosphere of settling scores where abusive words take the place of slaps and punches."[36]

I am rereading the *Essais* of Montaigne and draw light from them for the dark days my country is experiencing. These magnificent essays were the fruit of a difficult period of French history and of European history as a whole. Montaigne wished to devote the remainder of his life to what he considered the most important thing in the world, and by that he meant his liberty. Therefore, he sought refuge in a fortified chateau and avoided people in a profound spiritual experiment that ultimately had no goal beyond exploring the hidden areas of the self in search of the meaning of life and existence. Montaigne began writing these essays while religious wars daily harvested hundreds of human lives: "I live in an era when struggles of evil in unimaginable forms have spread, because of what our civil wars have sanctioned: we don't see in the deeds of the ancients anything worse and more atrocious than what we live through daily, thanks to the experience of living together."

Montaigne had not imagined that people would turn into beasts who excel in killing one another for no other reason than their enjoyment of the crime. They hone their minds to perfect the most hideous and violent forms of torture and murder. Indeed, they consider representations of murder and torture to be entertaining, playful amusements. They do not hesitate to laugh, boast, and brag while watching a man die from the blows of a whip or a sword!

I hope my answer to your question is persuasive and helpful. In any case, once we meet after my return to Paris, I will be able to explore this topic in greater depth.

I was also happy to hear that the books I recommended to you proved helpful for your dissertation and provided you with a link to what Nietzsche called "gay science," in other words "joyful wisdom": learning that allows us to cope with the burden of a changing world, which becomes ever more corrupt, spoiled, and hostile toward those with refined sensitivities and innocent souls.

Stay safe from every harm!

Saleem

Yesterday morning, before she left with my daughter, my wife placed an envelope on the little table next to the sofa where I sleep. Then she departed with a furrowed brow. I took a shower, shaved, and dressed. Before eating anything, I went to a café overlooking the sea and ordered café au lait and a croissant. I opened the envelope and found my wife's note asking me to find other accommodation in anticipation of a divorce. I tore up the letter and threw it in the first trash can I saw after leaving the café. With quick steps I went to see Omran. He welcomed me as graciously as ever and asked how I was and how my wife and daughter were. I answered him tersely, doing my best to suppress the feelings of frustration and despair that constantly torment me, whether I'm alone or with other people! I think I failed in that effort. Therefore, he quickly changed the subject and started telling me about an ancient Greek writer named Aesop. I had never heard his name before. He told me jovially that Aesop was even uglier than my friend Aziz. His head resembled a horn, and he had a snub nose. His belly protruded, and he had knock-knees. Aesop was a slave. Although he had difficulty enunciating words, he woke one day to find himself eloquent. Once he obtained his freedom, he began to travel through Babylon, Egypt, and Greece, helping kings and influential people solve riddles and decipher dreams. He would tell them and also ordinary people tales in which most of the heroes were animals—like Ibn al-Muqaffa' in *Kalila and Dimna*, the French poet La Fontaine, and the British author George Orwell. Because of his sharp tongue, Aesop met a painful, tragic death. When he reached Delphi, he mocked its citizens for preferring to live off offerings to the gods instead of plowing the earth and cultivating it. That remark enraged and infuriated them. Then, even though he tried to appease them by telling them more fables, they cast him from the rocky heights into a deep ravine. Hoping to cheer me up, Omran told me some of Aesop's tales, and I liked all of them a lot. There was one that stuck in my memory more than the others. In it some dogs saw a blob, like a body, floating on the water. After some reflection, the dogs agreed to drink enough of the water to open a path for them to reach it but then perished from choking on all the water they had imbibed.

Omran may have been alluding with these fables to the problems people are facing and to current troubling events in Tunisia, relying on my cleverness and wit to perceive their meanings and interpretation. The problem was that my mind was too muddled to grasp them. When I left his place, I walked on the beach, thinking about Aesop's dogs and his hideous death. My reflections led me to conclude that people often chase phantasms and shelter in these illusions, because they are incapable of confronting the bitter realities of their situation. For this reason, you find that people seek out anyone who will market illusions and lies to them and shun those who reveal their impotence, weakness, and maladies or disclose their hypocrisy, conspiracies, nasty machinations, weird whims, and criminal struggles. That's what is happening in our country now! We have a plethora of merchants of fantasies and empty slogans and vendors of cheap talk. They range from terrestrial folk, who think man has a free will, to celestial folk, who believe that God in the heavens so predetermines everything that nothing escapes Him, no matter how tiny or large. Thus, every deed or motion performed by a man issues from God's inspiration or command. People applaud one group or the other everywhere they settle, celebrating and obeying them in everything they say and do, even if these pundits inflict bodily harm on them and lead them to destruction! Even if their schemes and lies are discovered, people flock behind them obediently and faithfully. In all these respects, celestials and terrestrials are the same. Everyone is insanely enamored of wealth and prestige, striving for them even if

this forces them to betray their principles and ideas they have vigor-
ously promoted to others. Celestials urge jihad against the "infidel,
profligate" West, while allowing themselves to enjoy the West's material pleasures and technological advances. Since their appearance on
the scene in Tunisia after the fall of the old regime, the streets have
filled with the celestials' high-powered autos and trucks, which they
name after camels the Prophet rode during his raids in the Arabian
desert or adorn with verses from the Qur'an, sayings of the Prophet—
inscribed in gold paint, or simply: "This is from God's Grace"—leaving people with the impression that they too will obtain comparable
vehicles if they obey and imitate the jihadis and their fatwas. Indeed,
they may even claim that if people merely recite a verse from the
Qur'an a hundred times before going to sleep, they will be rewarded
with a licit fortune on opening their eyes the next morning.

That day, while I sat in a café, one of their candidates appeared
on television. He had a large bald head, bulging arteries, and red
bulbous eyes. He promised those who dream of fleeing to "the promised paradise" of Europe that he would build a bridge from Tunisia
to Sicily. I feel certain that many viewers believed him and will vote
for him in the next elections to be their deputy in parliament, a government minister perhaps, or a high-ranking government official. I
heard another one promise people a life as happy and prosperous as
those enjoyed by the Swedes and Swiss—if they crown him president
in the Carthage Palace. I've known this man quite well since my
university days, when he used to prowl through the university hostel
with a cudgel and a knife, threatening to discipline "Violators of the
Shariah of God and His Prophet." In that period, he was as dirty
and ugly as rats in dark cellars. Today, he looked prosperous with
a big gut and red cheeks. He issues a new fatwa every day on both
religious and secular topics and sings—on his own special channel—
songs of his Bedouin tribe, to reach even more supporters.

At noon I ate grilled sardines in a working-class restaurant on the
quay of the old port and then headed to a small bar near the large
harbor. I found the eyes of patrons there fixed on Channel France
24, which was broadcasting news of the killing of a militant that

morning. When they showed a picture of him with his bushy mustache and cap, I realized that I knew him well, since he had once lived
in the same university neighborhood I did during my next to last year
at the university. I remember that he claimed to head an extremist
left-wing group. He had dressed, presented himself, and even walked
in a way that he hoped resembled black-and-white photos of Bolshevik militants before they toppled the Czarist regime. In those days,
before the fall of the Berlin Wall, his group, which was fond of the
Albanian president Enver Hoxha and his wife, Nexhmije Hoxha,
would fight bloody battles with Fundamentalists who praised Ibn
Taymiyyah and the Egyptian Sayyid Qutb. These conflicts would
disrupt classes for days or even weeks. I hated both gangs but won't
deny I harbored a secret affection for this militant, who enjoyed con-
siderable personal charm and the ability to sound convincing when
he debated his foes. Unlike his group's other members, who were
always tense and agitated, he was endowed with calm patience and
a gift for dark humor. He memorized beautiful poems and read Russian novels, showing a special appreciation for Gorky. In evening
entertainments organized in the university hostel, he would sing
songs composed by Sheikh Imam, with a mellow voice. When he
became happy and tipsy from bottles of wine or chilled beer, he forgot about Marx, Lenin, Mao Zedong, and Enver Hoxha and his wife
and began belting out the songs of Sulayha, El Hadi El Juwayni, Ali
al-Riyahi, Muhammad Abd al-Wahab, Abd al-Halim Hafiz, and the
Iraqi Nazem al-Ghazali, who was always mournful. I remember he
tried to encourage me to join his group in various ways. Once he realized he would not succeed in this effort, he patted me on the shoulder
when we were in line at the university boarding hall, smiled, and
said, "You're an existentialist, aren't you?"

"What's an existentialist?"

"Don't try to deceive me. I know you understand that word's
meaning very well. The books you read are the best proof of what I
say."

When I smiled, he added, "In any case it's better to be an existentialist, even an oblivious, reactionary, individualist existentialist,

than a Fundamentalist. I respect you for this reason and always tell members of my group to leave you alone!"

That was the last I heard from him. A week later, if my memory doesn't deceive me, he was arrested and sent to perform military service in the South. Since that time, I hadn't had any news of him, and his appearance had gradually begun to fade in my memory until it became a cloud shimmering in time's mirage.

After the regime fell, he appeared again as one of the leaders of the "Tunisian Movement for Freedom and Dignity." Almost every day he appeared on television to warn people about the threat posed by Muslim Fundamentalists, saying: "They can't be trusted. To benefit their own interests, they change more quickly than a chameleon changes color, because they believe God loves them more than any of His other creatures. Thus they are always prepared to commit the most atrocious crimes, in His name." Yes, this is what he was saying! In an interview conducted with him, a militant Fundamentalist leader said that my former friend had been reared with the principles of the first prophets and then threatened to tear his entrails from his belly. This morning, as he left the apartment building where he lived, a veiled man shot him thirty times before fleeing on a motorbike.

Glum and silent, patrons watched news of this assassination on France 24. That was repeated every half hour. Then, suddenly, comments started to pour out. A thin man scratched his gray hair and puffed smoke from his cigarette as he said that this assassination foreshadowed a destructive civil war. A second patron, who was as sad and withered as an autumn leaf, thought our country would soon become another Somalia or Afghanistan. The third, who was as rotund as an overstuffed bag, affirmed that we would be afflicted by the same type of civil war that had consumed our neighbor Algeria twenty years earlier. The fourth, whose face had been deeply furrowed by the passing years, which had also damaged his teeth, emptied his glass of beer into his belly and then started swaying toward the exit as he cursed revolutions that bring devastation, destruction, and anarchy. The fifth man, the youngest, raised his glass on high, shouting jubilantly, "Wine today; we pine tomorrow! Isn't that so, gang?" Then he laughed loudly, all by himself.

At first, I followed the news reports nonchalantly, as if this assassination had occurred in some foreign country and the victim were a stranger with no tie to me at all. At some moment, though, alarm pervaded my soul, and I started to tremble as if I saw a veiled man attacking the bar and firing at all of us. Then he disappeared, leaving behind corpses with their bellies split open, heads crushed, and hands and feet cut off—while the walls became spattered with blood. He might have attacked Omran while he was reading, writing, or strolling on the beach and cut off his head to throw into the sea, where it could be carried off by the waves to the land of the infidels. My terror grew more intense. My digestion was inflamed and upset, and before I could reach the restroom, I vomited everything I had drunk and eaten in one volley. Everyone was outraged, and they started pelting me with tart insults suitable only for dishonorable people who deserve disapprobation and humiliation. The bar's owner tossed me out on the street, cursing my ancestors, my whore of a mother, and the ill-omened day I was born!

I wandered aimlessly, damning evil surprises, until I reached the boulders near the lighthouse. I woke early the next morning to find I had fallen asleep there. The sky was black and lowering, the winds blew strong and cold, and the waves were crashing against the shore wildly. I pulled my shoulders up beside my head and, with plodding steps, proceeded toward the city, feeling that a life like mine was not worth living.

Aziz

Living through yesterday for me was like walking barefoot across an endless desert of thorns: an activist was assassinated by the door of the apartment building where he lived, and his killer fled on a motorbike. People took this assassination as an ill omen but merely shrugged their shoulders disapprovingly when others declared that our country has entered a cycle of terror and creative anarchy comparable to that in Somalia and Afghanistan and that they won't be surprised to wake one morning to find gallows trees erected and squares prepared for stoning and cutting off heads and hands. Every day new fatwas rain down on them, and they experience the torment of hell in this world, not in the next. I don't want to go outside, because I can't bear to see—in the streets, stores, coffeehouses, and markets—all the sorrowful, frightened, anxious faces of people who despair of any immediate or long-term solution. I tried to read but found I couldn't. I similarly didn't feel like watching films—something I do almost every afternoon. I just watched commentaries on the assassination on France 24.

By nine at night I felt restless and went out, meaning to have a drink at my late father's favorite small bar near the port. As I approached it, Saleem appeared before me—cloudy and dark, like a ghost in the fog. I threw myself on him to hug him, but he shoved me away violently, as if I were a stranger he had never seen before. He even tried to slap me when I started to embrace him again. But I was able to dodge his blow. He walked off, cursing and swearing.

I drank four beers and returned to my apartment, where I stayed awake all night, as uncomfortable as if lying on a field of ice, brooding about my friend Saleem. I finally concluded that he is near a complete nervous breakdown!

At dawn, I left my apartment to sit in a coffeehouse that opens early for people heading to work and for others, like me, who had been up all night. After that, I went for a walk on the beach before heading to Omran's house. I was determined to persuade him to return to Paris as soon as possible, lest some harm befall him in Tunisia. I found him busy writing. When I started to leave and apologized for disturbing him, he insisted, "Sit down . . . you came at just the right time!"

I thought he would discuss the assassination. Instead, he began outlining the contents of the essay he was writing. He had chosen as its title "The Deceptive Sanctification of the People."

He explained, "My Dear Aziz, you will have noticed that cultured people and political parties of different orientations flatter 'the people' nowadays and go overboard in glorifying them, praising them, and attributing all the virtues to them. They treat the people like a homogeneous bloc that can do no evil, ever. For these thinkers and parties, the people are always the victim and bear no responsibility for whatever happens to them. These cultured folks and political parties attempt to make us believe that their understanding of 'al-sha'b' differs in no way from what the French historian Michelet meant by 'le peuple'—in other words, that both these Arabic and French terms denote those who suffer, vis-à-vis the bourgeoisie, from poverty and a lack of power and influence. Their concept does not differ from that of Western Romantics who believed that 'the people' are those who launch the revolution, who are always ready to revolt if society needs to emerge from what Michelet termed its 'bad history.' The truth is that these cultured people and political parties attempt to apply these two concepts—that of Michelet and that of the Romantics—to a reality that has not matured sufficiently to digest or receive either of them. You know that use of 'al-sha'b' as a technical term is a recent innovation in Arabic. I do not remember ever reading any reference to it in a book by a medieval Arab author. Nor can I remember any medieval Muslim caliph, sultan, or ruler, great or small, uttering it. Derived Arabic words associated with this three-letter root have negative connotations. A 'branching' or 'divergent' (*mutasha''iba*) road is one that is labyrinthine and twisting; it may lead to loss or destruction. An issue is said to be *mutasha''iba* if it seems difficult to resolve. Branches are said to be mutasha''iba when they separate from each other or intertwine. *Shi'ab* is rough, rocky terrain that is difficult to traverse on account of its pitfalls. Moreover, these same cultured folks and political parties forget that dictators of recent eras, from the French Revolution to the present day, have committed the most atrocious crimes in 'defense of the interests of the people.' In the Arab countries, the technical term '*al-sha'b*' has authorized the perpetrators of sham revolutions to rule people with iron and fire, to plunder fortunes, and to rewrite history. From 'the people' have emerged riffraff and rabble—in other words, those who are said by dictionaries to 'follow every growl and sway with every wind.' From the people also emerge the thugs: stupid, oblivious folk, dictators, and tyrants who abuse anyone who opposes or resists their rule. For this reason, they are not entrusted with any secret, honor, or distinction. They march in every parade and eat at every banquet. "The people" may produce petty elites who mislead the people, toy with their interests, and lead them to destruction and anarchy while the people, entranced by the lies and subterfuges of these petty elites, submit to them obediently. The people may also give rise to tyrannical jurisprudents who use slogans like 'the victory of Islam' or 'command good and forbid evil' to spread civil strife among the people, to incite acts of violence, to shed blood, and to terrorize anyone who disagrees with the jurists' opinion. These jurisprudents promise those who submit to them the paradises of Eden, where rivers flow and houris with beautiful eyes loll.

"For this reason, I caution you against all those who claim to be 'sons of the people' and to defend the interests of 'the people,' claiming they are prepared to sacrifice everything they value and hold dear. Montesquieu used to say that, even in a 'people's' government, power should not be devolved to 'the lowest multitude of the people.'

"I was freed from the sterile concept of 'the people' by the German poet Heinrich Heine. In his intellectual autobiography he wrote: "I have shrunk from anything connected to a link to ordinary people. I can't bear to be near them." He said that, even though, throughout his life, he ceaselessly defended the liberty of the people. One day a "rabid democrat" claimed in Heine's presence that he was prepared to place his hand in the fire to purify it, should it ever touch a monarch's hand. Heinrich Heine responded that should his hand ever be clasped by the hand of 'Their Excellencies the Almighty People,' he would 'wash it.' Heine added that the people, whom he described as 'a king clad in rags,' could always find flatterers more servile than the palace servants of Byzantine and Persian emperors. Such people always like to repeat, 'Oh, how beautiful are the people! How fine are the people! How clever are the people!' According to Heinrich Heine, the people do not possess such attributes. They may be ugly, evil, stupid, and violent, responding only to those who sell them fantasies and lies.

"Because they have been tricked into 'sanctifying the people,' folks now live days of deception when the liar is believed, the truth teller is doubted, the traitor is trusted, and the trustworthy person is thought a traitor."[37]

Omran rose and started pacing back and forth, silently and thoughtfully. Then he stopped in front of me and asked, "What do you think?"

"You always open new vistas for me with new insights."

"What are you reading now?"

"The truth is that I can't focus at present and cannot read more than a few pages at a time . . ."

"Why?"

"The latest assassination has frightened me more that all the previous ones!"

After a brief silence, Omran said, "I'm certain that conditions will continue to deteriorate!"

"Do you mean that there will be more assassinations?"

"Definitely!"

"I'm afraid for you! I think you should return to Paris quickly to remove yourself from harm's way."

"Do you think I'll be immune to their evil there? They're everywhere now!"

"I know . . . but the danger here is greater!"

He fell silent once more. Then he changed the subject and asked, "Have you seen Saleem?"

"Yes . . . I ran into him yesterday when he was coming out of a little bar near the harbor."

"How was he?"

"He acted as if he had never seen me before!"

"I'm sorry he's in such sad shape!"

Shortly before noon, I said good-bye to Omran and walked on the beach for a half hour. Then I headed to the Medina, longing to wander down its narrow alleys and inhale the aromas of people's tasty meals as I had done in my miserable childhood. I stopped before the door of the wretched room where I had lived for eight years with my mother and then ten more years alone. I knocked on the door, which had lost its color thanks to dirt. A scrawny old woman emerged— nothing but bones and blue veins!

She scrutinized my face absentmindedly as her gray head nodded. Then she smiled, letting me see she had lost most of her teeth.

"Have you forgotten me?" she asked in a voice that seemed to rise from a grave.

"Who are you?"

"I'm Dalila!"

"Dalila?"

"Yes. I am Dalila . . . Has time disfigured me so badly that you no longer recognize me, Homely Aziz?"

Yes . . . She was Dalila—Dalila, whose wild beauty had scared me so badly when I was an adolescent that I had never dared to reveal my love to her. I had just gazed at her from the distance and then carried with me for many years its flame, which burned in my heart and belly. She was expert at playing with the affections of her admirers, none of whom could succeed in taming her to make his alone. Many battles in which knives, sticks, and metal knuckles were used had broken out. By the end of each battle, faces were smeared with blood, eyes were swollen, teeth were broken, and souls were weighted down by even more grudges and hatreds. She paid no attention to any of this and continued to play her games of inciting her lovers from our neighborhood (and other ones) to more hard-fisted battles. Out of a desire to win her heart, each admirer did his utmost to satisfy her desires and whims, even as she never stopped toying with his affections, tormenting him, and scorching his heart with her fiery love.

Yes . . . she was Dalila, who had possessed the visual allure of Gina Lollobrigida in her black-and-white films and the voice of Shadia singing romantic love songs. Dalila was especially seductive when she wore short dresses that revealed her curvaceous waist and gorgeous legs, bosom, and neck as she walked barefoot through our filthy neighborhood on hot summer days or sauntered along the shore in a multicolored bikini that revealed even more of her charms. When her silvery laughter resounded, fiery desires ignited in her admirers and even old men were smitten—sparking jealousy, envy, and hatred in the hearts of other young women.

Yes, she was Dalila, who thought that our neighborhood and, in fact, our entire city were not an adequate frame for her beauty. She had fled to the capital, where she lived a dissolute life in its fine hotels and fancy cabarets. When she returned to our neighborhood, after an absence of ten years, to attend her father's funeral, her beauty had begun to fade, thanks to her addiction to smoking, drinking, and nightlife. I did not see her when she returned again for her mother's wake, but people who met her then affirmed she was a shadow of her former self. That was the last I had heard of her, and I had forgotten her like others buried under the dust of time. Here she was now before me—a homely crone, trembling from extreme poverty and feebleness.

"You haven't changed much, Aziz," she said with a smile. "You're still as homely as ever!"

To avoid hurting her feelings, I refrained from retorting that retaining one's homeliness was easier than retaining one's beauty.

"Will you drink some coffee?"

I accepted her invitation, and she prepared two cups. Then she lit a cheap cigarette and began smoking with enjoyment, while sipping her coffee slowly and recounting high points of her life during the many years since I last saw her.

She had worked as a dancer for fifteen years in the top echelon of hotels and cabarets in the capital, in Sousse, in Djerba, and in Hammamet. Then she quit that calling to marry a waiter in a hotel in the capital, but he was addicted to alcohol and gambling. She had two children by him. After he died in a traffic accident between Hammamet and Sousse, she had found herself forced to take menial jobs to raise her children. When the older boy grew up, he migrated to France and disowned her; she no longer heard from him. Her second son had wanted to try his luck at clandestine migration but had drowned, along with ten others, in a storm at sea. One day she found herself unable to pay the rent on the house where she lived in the Muruj area of the capital. Then she had decided to return to her birthplace to live out her final days.

"What about you?" she asked me.

"The same as ever!"

"Did you marry?"

"No!"

"You did the right thing!" Then she lit another cigarette and sank into a funk.

Before I said good-bye, I slipped two twenty-dinar bills in her palm. Then I returned to my apartment to sleep until dawn the next day.

Omran

Plato's maxim, "Do what most concerns you: know thyself,"[38] had served as his principle in years of upheaval and great changes. He had never stopped tracking down ideas that would help him cling to reality and act during multiple events that succeeded each other at an insane speed. Each event clung to the coattails of another one, and days passed as swiftly as wind through windmills. His intellect never stopped searching and investigating, leavened by curiosity and the astonishment and enjoyment of research. Each thought gave birth to another that might destroy whatever had preceded it until he finally discovered thought isn't a struggle or debate with other people so much as with ourselves!

He had known that French gendarmes were keeping an eye on him, watching his every action or pause, waiting for a chance to arrest him again. But none of this stopped him from continuing to publish essays that incited people to continue their nationalist struggle and encouraged them to remain alert and determined in the face of fierce French colonialist acts of terrorizing and suppression.

He had not limited his interests to politics. In fact, he had published literary essays that had excited the admiration of Diogenes and others. For the Ibn Khaldun Society he had delivered a talk on the Iraqi poet Badr Shakir al-Sayyab, another on Enlightenment philosophers who had paved the way for the French Revolution, and a third on Taha Hussein's book *On Pre-Islamic Poetry.* Then, suddenly, signs of change began to appear on the horizon. During the summer of 1954, Mendès France, the first Socialist French prime minister, visited Tunis and announced, from the Palace of Bey Muhammad

Lamine in the port district, his nation's intention to grant Tunisia
home rule: "The French government recognizes the autonomy of the
Tunisian State with no ulterior motives. It is keen, also, to affirm this
as a matter of principle and to work to provide all opportunities for
its success." Then he added, "The degree of development that has
been achieved by the Tunisian people and that we rightfully delight
in, especially since we have fully participated in it, as well as the
notable excellence of its elite, justify the autonomy of this people
to manage its own affairs. In addition to this, we are prepared to
transfer its internal administration to Tunisian figures and institutions." From Chantilly, in France, where he was staying after two
years' imprisonment on La Galite Island, Bourguiba, the leader of
the nationalist movement announced, in keeping with his famous
theory known as a policy of stages, his acceptance of internal autonomy, which he considered "an important step toward full independence." He asked opposition forces to hand in their weapons. Salah
Ben Youssef, the other leader of the nationalist movement, who was
living in Geneva, denounced internal autonomy, which he described
as "a foul and vicious conspiracy against the right of the peoples
of the Maghrib to achieve their full independence" and encouraged
combatants to continued fighting "until final victory."

Grief lifted from the entire country, and people took to the streets
and public squares in the capital to celebrate this significant event.
Women's trills reverberated from balconies, pictures of major nationalist leaders were pasted on walls and distributed in the markets, and
the Tunisian flag fluttered everywhere. Delighted by this, Diogenes
wrote brilliant poems in which he celebrated liberty and "beautiful
Tunisia," which had broken her bonds, allowing her people to enter
history through its vast portal, after centuries of subjugation and
tyranny. Omran, for his part, had started collecting essays he had
written during the bitter years of struggle to publish as a book. The
day Bourguiba returned from exile, Omran set off with Diogenes
and his brother to welcome the leader in the port of Halq al-Wadi.
When Bourguiba disembarked, the crowds, undulating like waves in
the sea, lifted him on their shoulders. Then they accompanied him as

he rode a thoroughbred Arabian steed to the heart of the capital. A large Bedouin straw hat protected him from the fiery heat of the first day of June 1955. That evening Omran hastened with Diogenes to the Canigou Café to celebrate this day of massive victory.

Their overwhelming delight, however, soon soured. On September 13, Omran woke with a headache, an embittered sprit, and a muddled mind. He ate lunch with Diogenes at an unpretentious restaurant in Bab Souika, and then they headed together to the airport in al-'Uwayna, where large crowds assembled to welcome Salah Ben Youssef, who descended from the plane looking sad. Bourguiba approached him, smiling, and embraced him. Then the airport rocked with applause and shouts of long life to the two great leaders, who climbed into a limousine that carried them to the capital in a huge popular procession. That evening, the masses assembled in front of the home of Salah Ben Youssef. When both leaders appeared on the balcony of this house, cheers and trills resounded from everywhere. Then everyone fell silent, their calm tinged with cautious anticipation! Frowning, Salah Ben Youssef took the microphone to announce that the agreements with France were faulty and represented a major danger for the independence and liberty of the country. In response, Bourguiba, who had lost the delighted expression of the airport meeting and was obviously angry, declared that these agreements were a positive step, because they freed Tunisia from colonial administration and did not and would not impede progress toward full independence. Then it became clear to everyone that each of the two major leaders would cling to his own position and that conflicts might erupt between them at any moment and draw the whole country immediately into an inferno of battles against colonial rule and dangerous strikes with unpredictable consequences. Thus, delight was extinguished, and the massive crowds faded away, feeling sad and worried about the country's fate and that of the capital, where there was a funereal atmosphere.

"Where shall we go?" Diogenes asked.

"How about the restaurant of our Spanish friend Mario?"

"Great choice!"

During the Spanish Civil War, Mario's father, who had owned a fine restaurant in the city of Malaga, had supported the Republicans but had not been a combatant. When the Phalangists of General Franco advanced toward Malaga to occupy it, Mario's family had fled to Algeria in a fishing boat and spent a year in the city of Oran before moving to Tunis and the Sidi Bou Said community north of the capital. In the heart of the modern city, on a narrow street, a few hundred feet from Bab el Bhar, Mario's father opened a small restaurant he named "Bolero." This restaurant soon became famous for its gracious staff, reasonable prices, delicious dishes, and fine wines. It was a favorite of the Spanish exile community and for cultured, enlightened expatriates and Tunisians alike. After his father's death, Mario had added another dining room to enhance the restaurant. He had increased its renown so successfully that it became difficult to book a table there toward the end of the week. In keeping with his immense love for Tunisia, Mario married a beautiful girl of Andalusian heritage from the port community. Many discussions with Mario, who was a devotee of Spanish poetry and Flamenco music, had prompted Omran to learn about Spain from reading its major poets and authors like Cervantes, Juan Ramón Jiménez, Machado, Rafael Alberti, and Lorca. He had also read excellent novels about the Spanish Civil War like *For Whom the Bell Tolls* by Ernest Hemingway, *L'Espoir* by André Malraux, and *Les grands cimetières sous la lune* by Georges Bernanos.

By ten o'clock that night the restaurant began to empty of its patrons! Mario sat down opposite them and lit a cigarette. He remarked, "I've heard terrible news!"

"What?"

"The two leaders have not agreed!"

"That's true!"

"What do you two think?"

"The dangers seem major!"

"Do you two fear there will be a civil war?"

"Yes!"

"That's why I'm afraid for Tunis."

"We are too!"

He and Diogenes left the Bolero Restaurant before midnight. When they reached Bab el Bhar. Diogenes proclaimed, "I don't feel like sleeping!"

"I don't either!"

"What shall we do?"

"Let's go to Halq al-Wadi; restaurants there stay open until morning!"

Saleem

I obeyed my wife's request, moved out of our apartment, and booked a room in a small working-class hotel west of the city. There I felt happy for three weeks, enjoying calm and spiritual tranquillity. I slept soundly, without any frightening nightmares. At work, I regained my vitality and confidence in my ability to process all the folders piled on my desk in a short amount of time. Perhaps out of appreciation for this, the director smiled at me more than once when I arrived or left work. My colleagues dropped their sarcastic winks and nods, and some even started to treat me more cordially than ever before. I returned to the hotel directly every day, avoiding coffeehouses and bars. Before going to bed, I spent an hour or more reading *Leaves of Grass* by Walt Whitman, who is one of my wife's favorite poets—perhaps her all-time favorite. She had memorized stanzas from his poems and really loved this one:

> When you read these, I, that was visible, am become invisible;
> Now it is you, compact, visible, realizing my poems, seeking me;
> Fancying how happy you were, if I could be with you, and
> become your loving comrade;
> [Be it as if I were with you. Be not too certain but I am now with
> you.][39]

Once I sensed that I had overcome the severe trial that had afflicted me for many months, I started thinking about an ideal way to restore my relationship with my wife and daughter. In the end, I decided that my wife's birthday, which was coming up soon, might be a golden opportunity to surprise her with an expensive present that would dissolve the thick hostility separating us and release once more cordiality, brilliance, and happiness in our life. But before that, I needed to write a beautiful letter, apologizing to her for all the errors I had committed and promising I would once more be the jovial, loyal spouse I had been during the many years we lived together under one roof. I would conclude the letter with a love poem by one of her favorite authors.

But something suddenly happened to cast me back to the pits of serious and painful disturbances. Nightmares started to torment me again, wrecking my life whether I was asleep or awake. I would be enjoying a sound sleep when a suspicious movement snatched me from it. When I turned on the light, a giant rodent would leap before me and then disappear into the dark night as quick as a flash of lightning. I would search for him under the bed, beneath the pillow, in the folds of the cover, in the clothes closet, in every corner of the little room, without finding any trace of him. The amazing thing was that I could find no trace, in the walls or ceiling, of any hole or opening that would allow a rat his size to enter the room or leave it. Could he have slipped beneath the door? That was also impossible, because the door swept the floor, and only flecks of dirt could slip beneath it. How did he enter then? But had I really seen a rodent? Perhaps I had imagined it. Yes . . . yes . . . perhaps I imagined that! But I had seen a giant rodent! Yes. I saw him leap over the bed, across the floor of the room. Yes. I saw him . . . I saw him . . . I was sure of that. An ugly rodent—large, gray, with crimson nose and paws!

I sat on the bed, brooding dejectedly, while my heart raced violently. Then I fell asleep again. But, almost immediately, a frightening motion woke me. I was so upset and alarmed that I banged my head against the wall, felt dizzy, and fell to the floor. When I was able to rise, I turned on the lights and saw—a few meters from me— the rat, which was black this time and larger than before. Its small, malevolent eyes glared at me. Then it simply dissolved like a grain of salt in water.

The next morning, while I was walking down a long street on my way to work, I saw many gray and black rodents of different sizes—skipping along the sidewalk and slipping under cars and between pedestrians' legs. I succumbed to fear and began trembling. My teeth chattered as if I were walking naked over ice. The old man walking beside me must have noticed, because he patted me on the shoulder in a friendly, congenial way and asked, "Are you cold on such a warm morning?"

"No!"

"But you're shivering."

"I see rodents!"

"Rodents?"

"Yes . . . rats!"

"Where are they?"

"Look carefully around you!"

The old man cast a comprehensive glance around him. Then he said, as if he were concerned about me, "I don't see anything!"

He did not see anything because he was an old man and almost blind. I saw dozens of rodents hopping and leaping beneath the pedestrians' feet, under the automobiles, and along the sidewalk!

The old man looked around carefully. Then he said touchily, "Please don't ruin my day," and walked briskly away.

I continued along while the rodents jumped, danced, and leapt hither and yon, without anyone else noticing them.

All these gray and black rodents slipped into the insurance agency where I work, filling its offices, galleries, hallways, and restrooms, without any of my colleagues noticing. I was the only person who saw them hop, skip, and dance, while they cast me angry, spiteful glances. I tied myself up in knots, I was so disgusted by how ugly they were. I fled repeatedly to the restroom to throw up my meals from the previous day and the day before that. Eventually, all I could vomit was liquid the color of pus.

That evening I returned to the hotel to pass a night during which the rodents played a frightful game of hide-and-seek. The next day, I moved to a tourist hotel on the Corniche. It had reduced rates because it wasn't summer yet, but the rodents pursued me there, night and day, until I no longer remembered what sleep felt like and could not swallow a bite of food. If I did eat something, my stomach immediately cast it back up. I saw them wherever I went . . . in the market, on the streets, in the squares, on the beach: everywhere. I collided with them. Indeed, occasionally, I imagined I saw them emerge from the mouths of pedestrians—from their eyes, nostrils, and ears!

I was in my office one morning when I sensed that all those ugly rodents had slipped into my belly and begun to gnaw on my intestines. With their sharp little teeth, they were shredding my heart and liver. In no time at all they had worked their way up to my head where they greedily began to devour my brain. Then I shrieked with alarm and raced out of the office, screaming: "Rats! Rats! Rats!"

Aziz

Yesterday, along with huge crowds of other residents of the city, I attended the funeral of Madame Zaynab, the wife of my longtime friend Munir. She died of a heart attack on hearing that her only son Nizar, who was twenty-two, had been slain in a battle between armed groups on the outskirts of Benghazi, Libya. With a frozen expression and stare, my friend Munir received condolences. I think his condition will deteriorate, because this calamity is so great that even a person endowed with extraordinary strength and endurance could scarcely withstand it. I say: "My longtime friend Munir" because he is the only son of our impoverished neighborhood in the heart of the Medina who succeeded in his studies; he became a math teacher in the Sciences Faculty in the capital. After he retired, he returned to our city to settle with his wife, who had also retired, in a small villa in the Maryam's Spring neighborhood near the Corniche. Even though time had separated us, each of us had remained fond of the other. That was obvious during our rare meetings, when we would mull over the past, revive memories of a rough period, and drink a toast to it.

I remember Munir told me when Nizar was still a baby: "My wife and I have agreed that Nizar will be our only child and that we will take the best possible care of him and provide him with everything I lacked during my childhood and youth!" Nizar had not disappointed his parents' hopes for him. In school he excelled in all his subjects and even became the model student whom fathers and mothers ask their offspring to emulate. This was not only true of his scholastic achievements but of his upbringing and character as well.

After he completed the baccalaureate, Nizar enrolled in the College of Medicine in the capital. Before finishing his first year of medical school, though, he began to show signs of fatigue and seemed drained. He changed in an alarming and disturbing way and quickly lost his spontaneity and smile. He became a scowling youth who dutifully performed his five prayers a day at the set times. When he returned to the family's home on short or long holidays, he would make a point of staying in his room with the door closed and spoke to his parents only rarely. When he did, he limited himself to mumbling and muttering and avoided looking at them. During his second year of medical school, Nizar stopped visiting his parents. When they telephoned to ask how he was, he would reply rudely: "Leave me and my affairs alone! I'm really busy." Finally, he stopped answering his phone. At that time, Munir rushed to the capital to see what was wrong. The Faculty Office told him Nizar had not attended classes for more than a month. At the university hostel, Nizar's roommate told Munir that his son had put all his belongings in a bag and left, without telling anyone where he was heading.

For the next four months, Munir kept visiting the capital in hopes of finding some trace of his son or hearing news of him. Munir's wife had wept constantly. The day before yesterday, in the morning, when they received the shocking news, she immediately fainted. Before she reached the hospital in an ambulance, she breathed her last.

After the funeral, I went with Murad to The Corsairs. At the door, one of Saleem's colleagues from the firm stopped us and asked, "Have you heard what happened to Saleem?"

"What's happened to him?"

"I think he's gone mad!"

"Where is he now?"

"I don't know . . . perhaps in an asylum in the capital!"

Omran

In the letter that reached him this morning, Sophie had written:

> The bad news from Tunisia frightens me a lot. This latest assassination made me even more fearful for you, my dear teacher. I entreat you to return to Paris as quickly as possible. I know that no place on earth is beyond the harm they cause and the crimes they commit, but I hope you will come back here. I miss you and your riveting discourses very much, as well as our strolls along the Seine and sessions in the Luxembourg Gardens on warm days.
>
> The weather in Paris is very cold nowadays, and that's why I prefer not to go out, except for brief periods to run my daily errands. You ask me: What am I reading now? My reply is that recently I have read three books about Spinoza and his philosophy. My satisfaction with them was increased by the point you made in your last letter that some major works of literature, philosophy, and poetry have been the products of dark and difficult periods. Spinoza's works are examples. From beginning to end, his life was filled with painful events—like the deaths of his mother, brother, stepmother, and sister Miriam. When he was an adolescent, his cousin, the philosopher Uriel da Costa, was lashed before Spinoza's eyes, charged with "doctrinal deviance." He eventually committed suicide. Once Spinoza began to criticize Jewish belief, he was the victim of an attempted assassination in front of one of Amsterdam's theaters. Disturbed by this, he retained the coat his assailant's dagger had slashed

to remind him that religious extremism always leads to insane violence and crime. He would later refer to religious extremists as "the new barbarians." He was banned and excommunicated by the Jewish community in Amsterdam when he was twenty-three. The *cherem* document expressed the desire that God would smite him in His anger and kill him with His curses. That had forced him to move out of his family's home and live shunned by his family, his relatives, and their religious community to the end of his life. To bind his wounds and confront all the dangers that threatened his life and liberty, Spinoza decided to avoid society and plunge into philosophic reflection to find happiness and spiritual tranquility.

Allow me, my dear teacher, to tell you that I have found in the ideas of Spinoza about religion things that reminded me of your lectures on "The Mournful Muslim." Like him, you think that tyrannical, despotic governments and political regimes always need religion to deceive people, delude them, and prevent them from thinking freely and to subjugate them to what we can call "voluntary servitude." Like him, you also affirm that false beliefs are the best way to enslave people and demonize anyone who doubts them or deviates from them. Etched in my memory is the section of your lecture when you said:

The Islamic scholar is shackled with interdictions from head to toe. His perplexity and weakness are increased by his inability to keep pace with modern culture. This has transformed Islamism in the consciousness of its adherents—and especially its fundamentalists—into dead and lethal raving.

I think you sided with Spinoza in his rebellion against petrified Orthodox Judaism when you said in your lecture that fundamentalist thinking is what made submission to a doctrine of predetermined destiny take root in the Muslim's consciousness to the point that this consciousness becomes totally submissive to it. You also believe like him that concern with celestial causes distracts and distances us from our terrestrial reality, leading us eventually to rants and sterile debate!

I found myself in this section of your lecture:

We are influenced in multiple ways by external factors, just as the sea's waves are influenced by the wind's crosscurrents, when we contemplate our destiny and fate.

I lived for a time lost and without a compass, thanks to external factors I could not control. After I met you, your valuable advice made it possible for me to return to myself and perceive that salvation lies hidden in my internal world. It is my job to plunge deeper and deeper inside it to attain happiness, tranquility, reassurance, vitality, and everything I lost during the years I searched for the true meaning of my existence.

My dear teacher, once again, I beg you to return to Paris. I am waiting for you.

He too yearned for Sophie, for her soft laughter and warm, mournful voice. She was always present in his memory. But he would not return to Paris before he finished the final chapter of his new book. He believed that this chapter would be the hardest and most difficult to write. That was why he did not want to hurry it. Besides, he enjoyed, in this isolation, recalling memories of the distant past amid the sound of the sea's surging waves, night and day.

The differences between Tunisia's two nationalist leaders grew more intense, and each toured the country searching for supporters while calling the other the worst and most defamatory names. Each man renounced the humanist culture he had imbibed at the Sorbonne and became a monstrous politician who desired nothing more than to assault his opponent's flesh and slash him to pieces with the daggers and swords of sovereignty. In the final months of 1955, bloody battles broke out between the two leaders' followers, and dozens of victims fell dead on both sides, as the country tottered on the brink of a destructive civil war.

From the start, Omran and Diogenes had shown a cautious aversion to Salah Ben Youssef, who addressed primal, populist instincts and affirmed the reactionary, religious identity of society. For this reason, they did not hesitate to support Bourguiba, especially after he unveiled a Tunisian coed at a celebration of learning attended by enlightened Muslim clerics and with the blessing of Taha Hussein, who was the first Egyptian minister of education to triumph over the shaykhs of al-Azhar and open the doors of schools in Egypt to girls. In his essays and in talks in cultural clubs, he persistently defended free thought, relying on calls to break the chains that shackled women, to separate religion from the state, and to resist all manifestations of backwardness and intolerance. Thanks to his daring positions and thinking, Bourguiba was subjected to attacks and fierce criticism from reactionaries and supporters of Salah Ben Youssef. Some attacked him with sticks more than once, calling him a "freethinker," "infidel," "libertine," and "drunkard." They also did this to Diogenes, who wrote poems mocking "men with heavy turbans" and "black-smudged foreheads," who ruin life with jaundiced fatwas and who authorize swindles and hypocrisy while prolonging the melancholy melodies of the jurisprudence of punishment in the grave.

Early in 1956, Salah Ben Youssef fled to Egypt by way of Libya. Before he crossed the border, he told the Frenchman Charles Saumagne, "Tell Bourguiba that I will teach him a new lesson every day and that the final one will be the end of him."

A few weeks after he fled, the country received its independence, the disturbances died down, and the threat of civil war disappeared. Proud of his victory over his rival, whom he called "the viper," Bourguiba began to build the new state, abolishing the system of beys and establishing a republic. Then pictures of other leaders vanished, and traces of them were quickly erased. In their place, images of "The Great Warrior" adorned offices, cafés, restaurants, and public and private spaces. Bourguiba now seemed to have been the sole architect of Tunisian history. From that day forward, his detractors and foes needed to run their tongues around their mouths seven times, or more, before uttering a word that would detract from his status or attack his leadership!

During those days, which were tainted by fear, upheavals, and sudden dramatic changes, Omran was busy attending to his own affairs. Once he obtained his law degree, he became the youngest attorney in the country since its independence and opened an office. He brought his mother from harsh circumstances in the country-side to live with him and his brother in an elegant apartment in the posh Montfleury district. For several months he was preoccupied by his personal affairs, experiencing an insane infatuation with a Sicilian Italian girl, who disappeared suddenly without a trace. Once he started to frequent the Canigou Café and literary clubs again, he heard the extremely bad news that Salah Ben Youssef's supporters were being abused in confinement. In the cellars of an old house on a narrow street in the Medina they had been subjected to vicious torture. Indeed, at times, they had been forced to eat their own feces and drink their own urine. Ben Youssef's supporters who refused to turn in their weapons were pursued in the southern mountains by French troops, who perpetrated atrocious massacres. His friend Diogenes informed him that the Bey and his family had been treated in a demeaning and humiliating way. When some people condemned their inhumane treatment, Bourguiba, who was a fan of Victor Hugo and Enlightenment philosophers, replied, "They ought to thank God that I didn't erect gallows trees the way the Bolsheviks did for the Czar and his family!"

Omran did not pay much attention to what he heard, believing that history's progress always crushed some victims, especially those who had suffered a bitter defeat and were unable to fight back.

Then came the event that led to Omran's decisive break with Bourguiba and his regime.

On February 16, 1958, one of Salah Ben Youssef's assistants was arrested—someone who was also born on the island of Djerba. The man was armed and carried letters, in the handwriting of Salah Ben Yousef, inciting his supporters to continue fighting. After he was interrogated, he was charged with the serious crime of preparing to assassinate Bourguiba. From the start, it was clear that the regime had devised a plan that guaranteed this courier would not escape the death penalty. But, contrary to what was expected by the regime, which was confident of Omran's loyalty to it, he clung to the spirit of the law and demonstrated in his plea that the death penalty for the accused was not applicable, because the code did not recognize the existence of this crime until it had been committed. That was not the accused man's situation, because he had been arrested far from the location of the planned crime, which was the capital—in fact, more than four hundred kilometers away.

Omran's defense of the accused man won the admiration and respect of some political and judicial circles for its daring and extraordinary ability to reason and convince. The regime, however, was enraged and pressed the court to sentence the accused to immediate execution. In a private session, Bourguiba, after he was briefed on the defense, trembled with extreme emotion and shouted, "This bastard's defense brief is clear proof that he is challenging us and announcing his rebellion against us!"

His misfortunes began then.

Wherever he went, eyes watched everything he did or did not do. Ears heard every word he said. Newspapers and magazines no longer printed his essays, not even ones that were totally unrelated to politics. When he asked for some explanation, editors refused to see him. Fellow attorneys who were loyal to the government, and keen to earn a living, began to avoid speaking with him or being seen with him. Every week—no, every day—his circle of friends grew more constricted. In the end, he met only with Diogenes, who was also convinced that he had been blacklisted after he published, in Lebanon, a poem in which he alluded to a dictatorship that had begun to cast its shadow over the country and its subjects. One day Diogenes disappeared. At first, Omran thought his friend had returned to his village in the South to visit his ailing mother. But, trembling from fear, his brother confided to him that the police had arrested Diogenes in response to a new poem that mocked the regime's current slogan: "Speak the truth and work dutifully!" During the next weeks he toured the city trying to uncover information about Diogenes. But all their old friends and even waiters in cafés and restaurants greeted him with frightening silence and rigid faces. He was having a drink in the Canigou Café, one gloomy, cloudy evening, when a journalist he knew only in passing approached and whispered to him, "Please stop asking about Diogenes. Otherwise, you will meet a fate like his!" After saying this, he departed hastily.

Omran returned home, dragging his feet as if they were shackled by chains. He felt he was Josef K, the hero of Franz Kafka's novel *The Trial*, who died at the end, stabbed by a knife like a stray dog. Without exchanging a single word with his mother or brother, he retreated to his room, where he stayed sleeplessly until dawn. He did not go to his office that day. Instead, he went to a travel agency to purchase a ticket to Paris. At the end of the day, he put his documents and some books in a bag and summoned his brother. After closing the door of his room so his mother would not hear, he told his brother: "Listen: my life has been threatened. If I stay here, my destiny will resemble that of Diogenes or be even more dreadful. For this reason, I have decided to leave tomorrow morning for Paris. It may be many years before I return to this country!"

His brother's eyes filled with tears.

"I ask one thing of you: look after my mother!"

"Trust me with that!" his brother assured him, sobbing.

At noon the next day, which was January 10, 1961, he was walking the streets of the Latin Quarter, feeling that he was soaring like a bird that had just been released from a cage in which it had been imprisoned for a long time. He recited to himself a stanza from a poem by Pablo Neruda:

> We must free ourselves from all our bonds.
> I love the way sailors throw a kiss to the sky
> And set sail.
> I leave even though I feel sad,
> But I always feel sad.[40]

Saleem

He was swimming in an infinite whiteness. Everything was white: walls, doors, windows, beds, sheets, pillows, nurses, and doctors: white on white on white to infinity. Even the words he heard were white. The questions people asked him were white. Their smiles and laughter were also white. All of existence was as white and frozen as Siberia in the film *Doctor Zhivago*. He was a white creature swimming in infinite whiteness, like the patients in *One Flew over the Cuckoo's Nest*.

Aziz

Our trustworthy ancient ancestors related that before Spanyul (meaning Spain) conquered our country in the sixteenth century, black and gray rodents raided our coastal city during a stormy, desolate winter, filling its markets and streets and the dwellings of the wealthy and the impoverished, of pious and depraved citizens. People were alarmed because rodents are harbingers of misfortune, lethal diseases, and the destruction of households and civilizations. They destroy food-stuffs and contaminate every place they frequent. When a stranger appeared at the start of that winter and announced that those rodents were creating the conditions for the arrival of the plague, the city's ruler ordered him imprisoned and beaten on the charge of inciting chaos and fear among the people and poisoning their peace of mind. Only two days after this stranger from parts unknown was incarcerated, the plague spread through the city, sweeping through rich and poor neighborhoods. The first person who died was the ruler's eldest son. When the infection rate skyrocketed and the daily death toll was in the dozens, people's alarm became intense, and they were too terrified to work. No sailors set sail, no farmers tilled the fields, and no craftsman pursued his trade. Every day saw more funerals and more biers going this way or that as corpses were dispatched with wails and laments. In the city, the air was polluted, and its streets, roads, and squares stank. The sea was putrid, and most people preferred dying over living. Once the plague retreated, the ships of the Spanyul appeared. When they occupied the city, their effect on its inhabitants was worse than the plague's. Over the course of many years, they plundered, destroyed, and killed. They raped the most beautiful women and trashed mosques and mausoleums. They even rode their horses over copies of the Qur'an. During this invasion, the country was overwhelmed by a terrible famine caused by a drought, and their livestock perished. Famished people ate carrion, dry sticks, locusts, frogs, and snakes and drank polluted water. Then they contracted scabies, typhoid fever, tuberculosis, and other fatal diseases. Lice nested in their hair, and no one greeted anyone else, on account of all the calamities that afflicted them daily. By the time the Spanyul departed, the city had lost half its inhabitants.

Omran

From inside a café on place de la Sorbonne on the morning of his tenth day in Paris, he gazed at the snow covering the statue of Auguste Comte. Bourguiba had always boasted that, when he was a student, he made a point of placing a bouquet of flowers in front of this statue to show his appreciation for Comte and admiration for his rationalism and positivist philosophy. In the presence of famous Frenchmen, Bourguiba liked to recite Alfred de Vigny's poem "La Mort du loup" and verse by Victor Hugo to establish his commitment to the culture and great symbols of the Enlightenment! But no sooner had he established himself in power than he forgot all about that and began to rule and act like any of those Middle Eastern despots who cannot tolerate anyone differing from their opinion or ideas and consequently punish such persons severely.

Ibn Khaldun was right to point out that power corrupts those entranced by it and transforms them into tyrants who rule by the blade of the sword, attacking even those closest to them. In the history of the Middle East, many examples show that sovereign power drives those who possess it, or aspire to it, to kill even their parents, brothers, friends, and relatives. Patrice Lumumba was killed yesterday in the Congo. Tomorrow, others will be killed in countries that recently obtained their independence. Those who were comrades in arms yesterday, during bitter struggles for freedom, will become enemies who fight each other with the ferocity of wild predators in the forests or deserts to grasp the shiny substance termed sovereignty. The cultured Egyptian gentleman he had met two days earlier in place Saint Sulpice had told him he had fled from his country because

Abdel Nasr, who claimed that he had wrested sovereignty from King Farouq to rescue Egypt and the Egyptians from the corruption of the King and his regime, had quickly become an ugly and frightening dictator who wielded his violence against those who opposed him and employed an army of intelligence agents, opportunists, and people skilled at lying, deceit, and hypocrisy.

He wasn't a coward or traitor, as he had imagined immediately following his departure from his homeland. He had arguably made the better choice, since a dreamy idealist like him could not have done anything against a regime that would not hesitate to trample him underfoot and pulverize him if he attempted to raise his head and speak the truth as he had in his defense plea.

In any case, Omran had learned, from books he had read, a hatred for any form of sovereignty, whether pursued by or imposed on individuals and societies. He had also learned that the battle waged by people brandishing a pen against sovereigns and influential people usually fails. In the end, the price paid is very high. Most Arab poets, writers, and thinkers found themselves forced to offer fealty and obedience to kings and rulers to preserve their lives and safeguard their income. Those who went public with criticism or hinted at any opposition were killed, their books were burned, or they were imprisoned and left to die of neglect or from hunger. When Caesar Augustus wrote verses attacking him, Gaius Asinius Pollio preferred not to reply, saying, "It's not wise to dispute with a man capable of pulverizing me." During a debate he had with Emperor Hadrian, the philosopher Favorinus of Arelate preferred to withdraw, telling his friends, "Mock me if you wish, but do you want me to claim to know more than the commander of thirty legions?"

So, congratulations to Bourguiba for his tight grip on power and complete freedom of action! If he were denied this, his life would have no meaning. Now, in the City of Light, which embraced everyone who fled, like Omran, from tyranny, dictatorship, and violence, he was breathing liberty, feeling it, imbibing it, swallowing it like some tasty dish, seeing it shine forth in the countenances of people in the streets, in cafés, in restaurants, and in the Metro tunnels. The only glum, mournful faces were those of Arab émigrés, who, even though they were far from their homelands, were fettered by bonds that had been passed down through generations and thus proved difficult or impossible to escape.

In the first letter he sent to his brother, Omran informed him that he liked Paris a lot and intended to stay there a long time. He also told him he had found employment in Arabic-language broadcasting in Paris. This consisted of presenting programs about folk art in Tunisia. He asked his brother to contact scholars in that field to send him relevant documents. Because this job would provide him only a meager income, he had written to magazines and publishing houses, proposing to translate intellectual and literary articles and books. At any rate, he didn't aspire to live a life of opulent luxury. Instead, he would be happy with a modest, simple life. His top priority was liberty. Anything beyond that would be grasping at straws. Then he added:

> I know my long absence will torment my mother. That's why I count on you to help her understand my situation. Once she grasps the dangers threatening me back home, I'm sure she will calm down and perhaps even bless what I have done. I know you are under surveillance currently because of me. Even so, I ask you to do everything you can to track down news about my dear friend Diogenes. I think about him all the time. I feel guilty for leaving the country while he is imprisoned at some unknown location.

His brother continued to write him every week and, in each letter, informed him that no one knew what had happened to Diogenes. On October 2, 1961, Omran received this letter:

> Dear Brother,
> I miss you very much, and Mother does too. I think she has begun to understand your situation. For this reason, she has stopped weeping every day—that was really upsetting me. I

suspect it has also upset you, even though you are far away. She asked me yesterday how you are, and I told her you are fine. She replied, "Greet him many, many times for me and tell him: 'When you are fine, I am too.'"

Diogenes has been released, and I met him two days ago at the Canigou Café. I found him in very rough shape. I think that the many months he spent in prison have destroyed him and robbed him of his vitality and youth. He is only a pale shadow of his former self. Throughout the hour I spent with him, he gazed at me and our surroundings with a defeated, hurt expression and avoided answering any of my questions. To keep from upsetting him more, I ceased my inquiries, but then he lapsed into a silence that left me at a loss. So I said good-bye and departed with my eyes welling with hot tears. He did inform me that he has been sentenced to remain in the capital and is required to report daily to a police station to document his presence here. When his mother died a few days after his release from prison, he attended her funeral with an escort of policemen, who brought him back to the capital just as soon as she was in her grave. I won't conceal from you that I had been secretly regretting your departure. Now I am certain you did the right thing. Had you remained here, they would have done to you what they did to Diogenes and many others.

During the summer of his second year in Paris, Omran experienced the independence of Algeria, achieved July 5, 1962, after a vicious war that lasted eight years. He felt that this was one of the most important events of his life. He was extremely happy as he followed, day and night, the Algerians' celebrations of their independence after 132 years of colonial occupation! Men, women, and children had taken to the streets sporting the nation's flag and chanting: "Long live free and independent Algeria!" He thought Algeria might provide hope for the rest of the Arab World, East and West, which was almost devoid of hopes and dreams. For this reason, he decided to leave Paris and to go to "where history was being made."

He became all the more eager once he realized that Algeria had become a destination for the symbols of liberty and the revolutions from all the continents. Activists headed there, determined to change the face of the world and end the hegemony of the empires of exploitative imperialism. Why shouldn't he go there too? Paris provided him the liberty he needed, but if he stayed there too long, he might become isolated from the motion of history in the region that meant more to him than any other in the world and end up depressed and negative, cut off from his original roots!

Before the end of his seventh month in Algeria he was stunned by the kind of shock a person feels after an exhausting struggle to find treasure only to discover that the cavern contains nothing but dozens of hissing vipers. In his case, these vipers were soldiers and civilians struggling and fighting each other and conspirators plotting against each other while attempting to consolidate power in their own hands. Moreover, that fundamentalism, which Albert Camus had warned would shackle the Arabs with more chains and plunge them into darker distress than ever before, rose to the surface in ugly and violent forms. Armed with it, pious shaykhs began to act as if the "Revolution with a million martyrs" had **not** been waged to liberate the country from colonial rule but instead to expel Christians and spread "the magnanimous principles of Islam," by which they meant nothing more nor less than their own fatwas advocating violence, a culture of hatred and loathing, and a rejection of difference. When a major Algerian scholar wrote an essay deploring the suicide of a seventeen-year-old girl forced to marry a man in his sixties, he received threats that he would be lashed and killed. The top authorities in the newly independent state made no attempt to support or defend him. To the contrary, they ordered him to keep silent and to avoid treating subjects that "disturb traditions and cultural norms." The last time Omran met this cultural icon, he told Omran, "I was trying to serve my country, but it seems that the new authorities don't want me to. That's why I'm flying to Paris tomorrow, never to return." In the Aurès Mountains, Berber tribes were threatening to rebel and revolt. In short, Algeria seemed a volcano that might erupt at any moment.

Early on the morning of June 19, 1965, Omran was awakened by pounding on the door of the apartment where he was living on Didouche Mourad Street. He opened the door to find his friend Rachid, who had embraced him when he first arrived in Algiers. Rachid was very tense and agitated.

"What's happened?"

"Minister of Defense Houari Boumédiène has overthrown President Ahmad Ben Bella, who was taken to an undisclosed location, and the Army has occupied the streets."

"What's to be done?"

"Listen, my friend: you know I support Ben Bella. Therefore I am in danger, and you are too, because you're my friend. But I'm going to do everything I can to rescue you before it's too late!"

"How?"

"My older brother is an officer in the Ministry of the Interior and is going to arrange a passport for you. You need to leave Algeria as quickly as possible. But don't return to Paris!"

"Why not?"

"I advise you to go to East Berlin. I have friends there. They will take care of you."

Omran thought: Why not? Becoming acquainted with conditions in a Communist country might allow him to plunge into a new adventure.

Two days later, he was drinking beer in Alexanderplatz in the heart of East Berlin on a scorching hot summer afternoon.

Summer passed, and autumn arrived. Then spring, and the Wall still looked as hideous and frightening as ever: a legendary reinforced-concrete serpent that twisted around spaces and stifled breathing like a hangman's noose. The East German policeman Konrad Schumann, who leapt over its barbed wire on August 15, 1961, preferring to live in West Germany, may have preferred to die from bullets rather than be strangled slowly by the Wall, which was then under construction. After his escape, dozens of people died by guards' bullets or after falling from the Wall. All the same, the Communist authorities insisted on retaining it, as if they were latter-day versions of the Chinese emperor

Qin Shi Huang, whom his country's historians dubbed "the Cosmic Emperor." This emperor, who was a contemporary of Hannibal, erected the Great Wall to protect his vast empire from enemies—as if it were his private garden. He may have thought the Great Wall would preserve him from death and grant him eternal life. He also ordered all books that discussed the past to be burned. Anyone who hid some of them was, if discovered, branded and forced to help construct the Great Wall. But this wall did not prevent enemies from occupying China in later times! Burning books also did not destroy or annihilate thought. Instead, thinking was been born again in every year and place, enlivening the minds of the Chinese. The Cosmic Emperor, for his part, has become a data point from the past he wanted to reduce to rubble and forget forever. The Communist authorities in East Germany clearly did not learn from the example of the Chinese emperor whom history immortalized. Instead, they erected a wall like his, believing that it could protect "The virtues of Socialism from the evils of Capitalism." Although the flight of many people from their jurisdiction proved them mistaken, the Communist authorities rigidly and stubbornly ignored all counterevidence. When Omran passed by their statues near Alexanderplatz, Marx and his comrade Engels seemed to guard a depressing gray fortress surrounded by barbed wire, inside which inhabitants were treated like bestial herds, forced to submit and obey. They did not walk upright but instead crawled on their bellies over cold, barren land. Each inhabitant was obliged to swallow the ideological cudgel with which he was beaten every day.

One Saturday night, he attended a brilliant soirée with workers in a people's tavern. When he asked people there, at the end of the evening, what they thought of Marxism, everyone fell silent and anxiously cast wary glances at each other. Then the oldest man present rose, guided Omran to the wide window, and pointed with his index finger toward the Wall, saying, "There's Marxism!"

Early Sunday morning, he walked along the bank of the Spree River. It was bitterly cold, the sky was cloudy, and the area was as silent as a cemetery. The corpse of Rosa Luxemburg, that short woman who walked with a limp, was thrown into this river. Lenin, who later mocked her, described her as an "eagle" as a tribute to her firmness, forceful personality, and tenacity to her principles.

Time and events would establish, though, that she was as fragile as a sparrow and as delicate as a poet—filled with love, tenderness, and a rare, human nobility. Like all idealistic revolutionaries, she lived simply. She wrote to her lover Leo Jogiches:

> The greatest joy you gave me was when you wrote that we are still young and will be able to organize our personal life. Oh, my golden Dziodzio, if you could only fulfill that promise! [Imagine] our own little apartment, our own little bits of furniture, our own library, quiet and regular work, working together, and from time to time, the opera, and a very small circle of acquaintances whom one can invite for dinner, and going for a trip to the country for one month every year, but absolutely without any work.[41]

From inside prison, Rosa Luxemburg wrote to a female friend:

> Only one thing torments me: that I shouldn't be enjoying so much beauty all by myself. I want to shout out loud over the walls: Oh please, pay attention to this marvelous day! Don't forget, as busy as you may be, as you're hurrying across the courtyard in pursuit of the day's pressing tasks, do not forget to quickly raise your head and cast a glance at those great silver clouds and that silent blue ocean in which they are swimming. Do take notice as well of the air which is heavy with the passionate breath of the last linden blossoms, and take notice of the resplendence and glory that overlie this day, because this day will never, ever come again! This day is a gift to you like a rose in full bloom, lying at your feet, waiting for you to pick it up and press it to your lips.[42]

On the night of January 14, 1919, an essay by Rosa Luxemburg appeared in the newspaper the *Red Flag*. She concluded it with this

sentence: "I was, I am, I shall be."[43] She was arrested the next day
with her comrade in the German Communist Party Karl Liebknecht
and Wilhelm Pieck, her outstanding student in the Party's Gymna-
sium. The three were transported in a cart to Berlin's Eden Hotel.
When they arrived there, they found a large group of agitated and
angry soldiers and officers waiting for them. Their captors spattered
them with nasty curses, screaming, "Here's the old whore!"—referring to Rosa Luxemburg—"She's finally arrived!" After torturing
her in that elegant hotel, within sight and hearing of its residents,
who were decked out in fancy smoking jackets, they dragged her to
the ground, half-dead, and shot her in the head. Then they dumped
her body in a canal.

Omran spent one Sunday afternoon with Lisa in her apartment
on Friedrichstrasse, near the gate separating the two parts of Berlin. He had met her at a party hosted by a cultured Palestinian for
his German wife's birthday. They had discussed, in French, which
she excelled at, Heinrich Heine, Bertolt Brecht, and Thomas Mann's
novel *The Magic Mountain*. Four days later they met again at a small
restaurant on the street where she lived. She confessed, "I must tell
you frankly that I enjoyed speaking with you at that party. That
was the first time I met an Arab who didn't give me a headache by
discussing politics. I love poetry and art. That's it! Talking about
politics really exhausts me. Based on my experience, I would say that
Arabs suffer more from the malady called 'politics' than other people. Perhaps even more than our Communists, who lunch and dine
on empty, boring speeches about the dictatorship of the proletariat
and the class struggle. What wretches they are!"

Their evening discussion lasted a long time. When they were the
last patrons left in the restaurant, she invited him to have a drink
in her apartment. Pictures of her father, mother, and grandmother
adorned her apartment's foyer. Her father was killed in 1943 on the
Russian front, and her mother was raped by Russian troops (while
Lisa hid in the armoire) when they first took Berlin. She was seven at
the time. After that gang rape, her mother's condition degenerated,
and her health quickly declined. On March 2, 1947, she died, a few

weeks before she would have turned forty. Her grandmother, who raised Lisa, had been extremely beautiful and cultured. In her youth she had been fond of artists and poets and had served as a model for well-known artists. She had died at the age of ninety. What his friend had learned from her grandmother still helped her confront difficulties and overcome obstacles. Even though her grandmother hated the Communist regime, she had never revealed that to anyone besides her granddaughter. She would say, "Listen, my little granddaughter: the world is evil and rotten everywhere. I hope to die near the small area where I was born and raised. I'm like a plant that will wither and die if it is uprooted!" Perhaps this had prejudiced her against thinking of escaping to the other half of Berlin, because that would make it impossible for her to continue her simple routines. These included placing bouquets of flowers every Sunday on her mother's and grandmother's graves; watching plays by Brecht, Gogol, and Heiner Müller on the stage of the Gorky Theater; and reading forbidden books that gave her the feeling she could challenge the regime and its surveillance apparatus. Merely laying hands on a forbidden book made her feel she was soaring over the Wall and able to fly anywhere in the world. Had she obtained one of these books in a country where it was widely available, she would not have felt the kind of happiness that possessed her when some man or woman slipped a copy to her, only meters away from a censor or informant! She enjoyed listening with silent sarcasm to empty speeches delivered for large official celebrations on the Alexanderplatz. She would frequently return to her apartment and burst into laughter at the triviality and stupidity of what she had heard and seen. She was presumably a person who understood the true, profound meaning of liberty better (while denied it) than those who enjoyed it!

When Omran decided to visit Prague, Lisa gave him the address of a friend named Dora and told him, "She is my very dear friend and resembles me a great deal. I have told her to take good care of you."

He met Dora Saturday evening in the famous Slavia Café when snow was falling heavily on Prague. Smiling and elegant, she welcomed him. She was approximately forty, and her beauty and delicacy were starting to fade. Hers was the charm of sunshine on an autumn morning. Her gray eyes glittered with a challenging look and a continuing lust for life, even when life was at its cruelest. She gestured toward a man who looked about thirty-eight, was seated alone, and stared silently at the white street. She whispered to Omran, "This is one of our best writers. He's Milan Kundera. Have you heard of him?"

"No."

"I'm sure he will become famous internationally. Now, he's in opposition to the regime. He is under surveillance, because his most recent novel was subjected to withering, stinging criticism by government censors. We also have a great philosopher named Jan Patočka, who was a student of Husserl and of Heidegger. He has also been under surveillance since he was fired from the university, and his works are proscribed. Anyone who visits him is immediately placed on the blacklist. There is another writer named Václav Havel, who is released from prison one day only to return there the next. In short, everyone who disagrees with the regime experiences the same fate as those I have mentioned."

The following day she drove him around rural, snow-covered Bohemia in her vintage car. She said she liked to flee to the countryside because she feels safe there. In Prague, the government's eyes and ears prevent her from thinking freely and dreaming of soaring faraway in her imagination. She asked if he had read George Orwell's novel *1984*, which she had obtained from her friend Lisa. Kafka might have been predicting the nightmares people of her country were experiencing! All the same, she had read no better accounts of the conditions experienced by those living under Communist regimes than in Orwell's novel. She was certain that her country would witness an upheaval like Budapest's in 1956. Yes, this explosion would come, because people could not stand the pressure exerted on them and were fed up with the surveillance to which they were subjected daily, even in their homes and private spheres.

The Arab defeat in the 1967 War caught Omran by surprise when he was in Vienna. For three days he remained in his hotel, because he didn't want to have people look at him with scorn or gloating when he walked along the street. It was natural for them to do that after watching Egyptian troops retreat barefoot over the burning sands of the Sinai Desert and seeing the Israeli flag flutter over the Golan Heights and in Jerusalem after the war, which had lasted only six days. Never in human history had the armies of three nations been vanquished and humiliated by that of a small state with such speed! This political and military defeat had exposed the emptiness of the demagogic rhetoric, which was mixed with lies and fantasies, that corrupt and brutal regimes had propagated over vast areas to mobilize the most chauvinist and primal impulses of peoples who were always sad and scared because of the oppression and despotism they endured. This disaster had also exposed the intellectuals and members of the media who had used hollow language, clichés, and meaningless slogans to drug the masses and blind them to their painful and hurtful reality and to make them easier to lead, like an obedient herd, to a massive slaughter. Indeed, these intellectuals may even have influenced the launch of this self-destructive war.

Omran left Vienna on the night train to Paris. Running through his mind was a poem that the great satirist Karl Kraus had written to eulogize his friend Adolf Loos, who had died in 1933—the same year that saw the rise to power in Germany of the Nazis:

To avoid explaining what I was doing all that time,
I will remain mute and not reveal my reason.
Silence makes the earth tremble.
No single word is satisfactory.
We speak only in our sleep while dreaming of a laughing sun.
Once the word slips away,
It will be clear it wasn't useful.
The word will be extinguished when this era dawns.[44]

He did not stay long in Paris. He fell prey once more to a feverish desire to embark on a new adventure. This time he decided to head to the Near East, which was aflame with revolutions and wars—as if he wished to poke an open wound!

He started in Jordan, where he toured Palestinian refugee camps in Jabal el-Hussein, Irbid, Madaba, Ajloun, and Jerash. He drank tea and Turkish coffee in tents with old women who recounted sad stories about the 1947 Nakba, about the uprooting of their families from their natal villages, which were demolished to destroy any trace of their existence, ever, and to demonstrate that they would never exist again. In their training camps, he spent memorable evenings with young fedayeen, who spoke proudly and arrogantly about their heroic deeds in the battle of al-Karama when they repulsed an Israeli attack. That occurred March 21, 1968. They all believed that this battle, in which "they inflicted heavy losses on the enemy," as they put it, had erased some of the effects of the 1967 defeat and restored their hope of recovering their stolen land. As his relationships with the Palestinian commands of different factions and tendencies solidified, he noticed that they were competing for supremacy. Each group tried to make its message more radical, extreme, and hyperbolic than any other. This propaganda, which day by day grew more inflated and explosive, began to dominate all the factions. Under its influence and with the slogan "Revolution to victory," fedayeen hijacked three civilian airplanes and blew them up while international journalists watched. Considering this incident to be a serious challenge to him and his regime, King Hussein in September 1970 gave his army free rein to commit hideous massacres in the Palestinian camps. Omran himself saw hundreds of corpses rotting in the autumn sunshine and caravans of children, women, and elderly folk wandering in deserts and rocky woods, sapped by hunger and thirst.

During the spring of 1971, Omran found himself in Beirut with the Palestinian factions that had settled in Lebanon. Contrary to what he had hoped, he found the extreme, populist message had grown even more shrill and radical and had become the preferred means of debate. Thought—especially critical thought—was AWOL or almost. Anyone who advocated reflection, calm, and moderation was vilified as standing for cowardice, treachery, and collaboration with the enemy. Indeed, such people might be killed in broad daylight, without their murder causing anyone to feel sorry or repulsed by this crime. A culture of shedding blood and rancor dominated minds and souls and became entrenched in personal and collective conduct. Again, enmity rose to the surface, like rancor among ancient tribes and factions. The past once more dominated the present, and imitation replaced innovation. A destructive culture of jihad and crusade flourished once more, and the delirious message of taking vengeance for "Ravished Palestine" dominated all other messages. The modernity to which some leaders paid lip service was deemed fraudulent and bogus—a mask that disguised a grievous unruliness of thought, a disgusting narcissism, and painful false starts. Now the true heroes were hijackers of airplanes, hostage takers, and people like Che Guevara, that model revolutionary, whose reckless adventures were ended by a tip from an elderly Bolivian farmer. The heroes were also perpetrators of rash operations like that during the Olympic Games in Munich in the fall of 1972. In response to those operations, Israel assassinated some of the brightest minds among the Palestinians: people like Ghassan Kanafani, Wael Zwaiter, Muhammad Mahmoud Hamshari, Kamal Adwan, Kamal Nasser, and Muhammad Youssef al-Najjar. Because of the proliferating differences and splits inside the Palestinian factions, numerous revolutionary "shops" began selling fantasies, empty slogans, and false promises, which they sold and purchased in bulk. Weapons were no longer aimed at the enemy but directed at the comrade who had been a friend only a few days before. Meanwhile, people living on "petrodollars," which flowed from so-called reactionary and agent states, had bellies that bulged large, necks that grew thick, and faces that became swollen, and they began—like raging Spanish bulls—to butt heads with their foes.

His stinging denunciations of extremism and armed violence became known in Beirut, and all the Palestinian factions united to attack him fiercely. He was called "a coward," "as feckless as Bourguiba who threw him out of Tunisia like a stray dog," and "an agent of Western embassies." He was even labeled a spy for Mossad—like

Eli Cohen who had held a high post in the Syrian state before he was discovered and executed in 1965.

As these accusations escalated, his life was threatened. A few months before the Lebanese Civil War broke out, he made his way surreptitiously to the Beirut Airport at dawn and boarded a plane to Paris with a disappointed, defeated spirit.

For the next five years he kept a very low profile. Every day he went on long walks, before returning to his small apartment to immerse himself in reading and writing. Silence and isolation were his only responses to those who continued to combat him with prejudicial rumors and accusations.

Toward the end of 1980, he heard that his friend Ibrahim, who had fled three years from the Bourguiba regime before he did, had been hospitalized after a heart attack. When he went to visit him, Ibrahim embraced him warmly and said, "I've been thinking about you a lot this morning. I guessed you would come. Now the day has been illuminated by your visit!"

When Omran told Ibrahim about his failed adventure in the Levant, Ibrahim asked, "Do you remember what I told you before you went there? I told you the Middle East had become a shipwreck, ruins, and rubble and that the Arabs have stepped out of the flow of history, because of their superstitious mentality, from which they will never recover!"

He looked down at the floor thoughtfully and added, "We too have lost everything. All our dreams and hopes have been shattered. We have grown old, and only death, loneliness, and forgetfulness lie before us. Isn't that so?"

As Omran prepared to leave, Ibrahim asked, "Can you visit me tomorrow?"

"Certainly!"

"I have a request . . ."

"What?"

"Bring me a book—just not one that's big and complicated. I want it to be entertaining and as easy to read as children's books."

The next afternoon he went to the hospital with a copy of *Alice in Wonderland*. When he arrived, the nurse informed him his friend Ibrahim had died at four that morning. This painful calamity shocked him, and he suffered from insomnia for months thereafter. Finally, acting on advice from a physician, he returned to his own country, after an absence of twenty years.

Aziz

I walked along the beach, leaving the city behind me and the house where Omran lived. Yesterday Murad told me that Saleem had escaped from the asylum and attacked his wife with a knife when she was returning with her daughter to her apartment in the evening after work. If passersby had not overpowered him and then delivered him, with his hands bound, to the police, he would have killed her. The little girl fainted from the terror of the shock. Murad told me that he arrived on the scene when things were winding down and that Saleem had looked like Anthony Perkins in Hitchcock's famous film *Psycho*. Moments ago, I passed by the house where Omran stays to tell him about Saleem's attack on his wife, but he wasn't there. Instead, I found tire tracks in front of the house and these words, painted in thick black letters, on the door: "Death to freethinkers and libertines!"

I continued walking along the beach. When I finally looked back, the city had disappeared behind the thick forest. I sat down on the sand and took out the piece of paper I had found in front of the house where Omran stayed. Putting on my glasses, I read:

Life is ruined. The whole world is a mess. Perhaps man will soon lose the ability to enjoy the beauty of nature, which will be methodically destroyed by rich and poor people alike. Because of all this, forests will be erased from existence, and orchards and gardens will disappear, as the earth becomes a barren desert, like the Empty Quarter. Pure air will vanish, and men will die on their feet. Rivers and lakes will dry up, and the seas and oceans will become stagnant, foul-smelling swamps devoid of fish! Yes, all this may happen. Even so, politicians and theorists in large, rich states will glorify what they term "scientific and technological progress," oblivious to the devastation occurring everywhere in the world. Inquisitions will return. Books will be burned again. Poets will be slain. Philosophers will be banished. Women will be stoned. Swords will be raised to behead those who love life. The Assassins we thought extinct will reappear, armed with blind rage and unrivaled ferocity and hostility, spreading death and terror around the world until scarcely anyone is secure from their evil.

I folded the paper and put it back in my pocket.

All I heard then was the wind rustling through the trees of forest and the calm sea's murmuring waves.

I closed my eyes and reflected: We live once and cannot retrace our steps or bring back our happy times—not even the painful ones. As the ancient Greek philosopher, whom my late friend Ahmad admired, said: "We never swim in the same river twice!"

"*Salam* to the dead, and peace to the living!"

Finished:
Hammamet, Tunisia,
Sunday at dawn,
November 11, 2018

Notes

Bibliography

Notes

1. Carson McCullers, *The Square Root of Wonderful: A Play*, 67.

2. Earl Shorris, *Literary Life among the Dinka*, 104–5.

3. Carson McCullers, *Illumination and Night Glare: The Unfinished Autobiography of Carson McCullers*, 14.

4. Carson McCullers, *The Heart Is a Lonely Hunter*, 358–59.

5. McCullers, *Illumination and Night Glare*, 15, 16.

6. McCullers, *Illumination and Night Glare*, 32.

7. McCullers, *Illumination and Night Glare*, 21.

8. McCullers, *Illumination and Night Glare*, 35.

9. McCullers, *Illumination and Night Glare*, 36.

10. McCullers, *Illumination and Night Glare*, 59.

11. McCullers, *Illumination and Night Glare*, 64.

12. McCullers, *Heart Is a Lonely Hunter*, 359.

13. This fictional Tunisian night spot is called "The Corsairs," just as the real restaurant in Stanley, North Carolina, is called "The Woodshed." See woodshed steakhouse.com.

14. See Ovid's *Tristia*.

15. Michel de Montaigne, "That to Think as a Philosopher Is to Learn to Die," chap. 20 of *The Essays of Michel de Montaigne*, 1:103–23.

16. Al-Mutannabi (d. 965 CE) was a renowned early Muslim Arab poet. He and his companions were attacked and slain by "brigands." For more information, see Julie Scott Meisami and Paul Starkey, eds., *Encyclopedia of Arabic Literature*, 2:558–60; and Margaret Larkin, "The Gap of Bavvan."

17. Henry Miller, *Black Spring*, 23. One of the anonymous readers for this book pointed out that Mosbahi's translation of this English text into Arabic makes it sound like an imitation of the style of the Qur'an: "the obscene, the boisterous, the thoughtful," and so forth.

18. This song, which was sung for Prophet Muhammad when he entered Medina, was sung when the Islamist political leader Rached Ghannouchi, cofounder of

Ennahda Party, returned to Tunisia on January 30, 2011. See https://en.wikipedia.org/wiki/Rached_Ghannouchi.

19. El Ghorbah is also a cemetery for foreigners, not to be confused with El Grhiba, the synagogue on the island of Jerba.

20. Kharbaqa is a Tunisian game that is played with squares (drawn in the dirt) that players take turns filling with their "men," which may be pebbles or date stones and the like.

21. Qur'an, Al-Dukhan (The Smoke), 44:43–50.

22. Abu al-Qasim al-Shabbi.

23. Antoine de Saint-Exupéry, *The Little Prince*, 49.

24. Saint-Exupéry, *The Little Prince*, dedication page.

25. Saint-Exupéry, *The Little Prince*, 64.

26. See Antoine de Saint-Exupéry, *Le Petit Prince*.

27. Saint-Exupéry, *The Little Prince*, 54.

28. C. G. Jung, *Memories, Dreams, Reflections*, 189.

29. See Stefan Zweig, *The Right to Heresy: Castellio against Calvin*.

30. "Report on an Investigation of the Peasant Movement in Hunan" (Mar. 1927), in *Selected Works*, 1:28, https://www.marxists.org/reference/archive/mao/works/red-book/quotes.htm.

31. Michel de Montaigne, *The Essays of Michel de Montaigne*, 1:252.

32. See https://www.frenchtoday.com/french-poetry-reading/french-poem-liberte-paul-eluard-audio/.

33. Plato, *Apology*, 30e.

34. Cited in Plato, *Cratylus*, 402a. See also https://plato.stanford.edu/entries/heraclitus/.

35. Ovid, *Tristia*, I:XI, line 36ff, https://www.poetryintranslation.com/PITBR/Latin/OvidTristiaBkOne.php#anchor_Toc34214747; https://archive.org/details/ovidtristiaexpon011949mbp/page/n99/mode/2u.

36. See Costica Bradatan, "The Philosopher of Failure: Emil Cioran's Heights of Despair."

37. See Heinrich Heine, "The Liberation," https://www.gutenberg.org/files/37478/37478-h/37478-h.htm.

38. Plato, *Charmides*, 164d and elsewhere.

39. Walt Whitman, "Full of Life, Now," in *Leaves of Grass*, https://whitmanarchive.org/published/LG/1867/poems/62.

40. Pablo Neruda, "Farewell y los Sollozos" (Farewell and Sighs), http://www-personal.umich.edu/~jlawler/curveoflove-rev.pdf. Haj Ross: "I am going away. I am sad: but I am always sad."

41. Rosa Luxemburg, *The Letters of Rosa Luxemburg*, 113–14.

42. Luxemburg, *Letters of Rosa Luxemburg*, 429.

43. https://prruk.org/rosa-luxemburg-murdered-15th-january-1919-i-was-i-am
-i-shall-be/; https://en.wikipedia.org/wiki/Rosa_Luxemburg#Last_words:_belief_in
_revolution.

44. See Massimo Cacciari, *Architecture and Nihilism*, 163.

Bibliography

Bradatan, Costica. "The Philosopher of Failure: Emil Cioran's Heights of Despair." *Los Angeles Review of Books*, Nov. 28, 2016.

Cacciari, Massimo. *Architecture and Nihilism*. New Haven, CT: Yale Univ. Press, 1993.

Jung, C. G. *Memories, Dreams, Reflections*. Edited by Aniela Jaffé. Translated by Richard and Clara Winston. Rev. ed. New York: Vintage Books, 1989.

Larkin, Margaret. "The Gap of Bavvan." In *Al-Mutanabbi*, by Margaret Larkin. London: Oneworld Academic, 2008. E-book.

Luxemburg, Rosa. *The Letters of Rosa Luxemburg*. Edited by Georg Adler, Peter Hudis, and Annelies Laschitza. Translated by George Shriver. London: Verso, 2013.

McCullers, Carson. *The Heart Is a Lonely Hunter*. 1940. Reprint, Boston: Houghton Mifflin Harcourt, Mariner Books, 2000.

———. *Illumination and Night Glare: The Unfinished Autobiography of Carson McCullers*. Edited by Carlos L. Dews. Madison: Univ. of Wisconsin Press, 1999.

———. *The Square Root of Wonderful: A Play*. Boston: Houghton Mifflin; Cambridge, MA: Riverside Press, 1958.

Meisami, Julie Scott, and Paul Starkey, eds. *Encyclopedia of Arabic Literature*. London: Routledge, 1998.

Miller, Henry. *Black Spring*. New York: Grove Press, 1963.

Montaigne, Michel de. *The Essays of Michel de Montaigne*. Translated by George B. Ives. New York: Heritage Press, 1946.

Mosbahi, Hassouna. *Solitaire*. Translated by William Maynard Hutchins. Syracuse, NY: Syracuse Univ. Press, 2022.

Nasr, Hassan. *Return to Dar al-Pasha*. Translated by William Hutchins. Syracuse, NY: Syracuse Univ. Press, 2006.

Saint-Exupéry, Antoine de. *The Little Prince.* Translated by Richard Howard. 1943. Reprint, San Diego: Harcourt, 2000.

———. *Le Petit Prince.* 1946. Reprint, Paris: Gallimard, 1999.

Shorris, Earl. *Literary Life among the Dinka. Harper's* (Aug. 1972).

Zweig, Stefan. *The Right to Heresy: Castellio against Calvin.* Boston: Beacon Press, 1951.

Hassouna Mosbahi, who was born in 1950 near Kairouan, Tunisia, is a writer, literary critic, and poet, as well as a freelance journalist for Arab and German newspapers and magazines. Following his university studies, he taught French in Tunisia but lost his position for political reasons in the 1970s. He settled in Munich in 1985 and lived there, working for *Fikr wa-Fann* until 2004. In 2005 Mosbahi returned to Tunisia. In Arabic he has published several collections of short stories, novels, and works of nonfiction. He has additionally made a name for himself as a travel writer, biographer, and translator into Arabic—translating Henri Michaux, René Char, Samuel Beckett, and Jean Genet. His biography of Saint Augustine was published in Arabic in Tunisia in 2010. In 2012, he wrote and lectured in the United States. Mosbahi won the Tunisian Broadcasting Prize in 1968 for some short stories and the National Prize for the Novel from Tunisia in 1986. He was awarded the Tukan Prize in Munich in 2000. His short story "The Tortoise" was short-listed for the Caine Prize for African Writing in 2001. *A Tunisian Tale* was his first novel to be published in English (in 2011). A translation of his novel *Solitaire* was published by Syracuse University Press in 2022. His short story "Paranoia" appeared in the *Brooklyn Rail*, February 5, 2015, and his short stories "Delirium in the Desert" and "Truman Capote" appeared on that journal's website, InTranslation, in September 2015.

Mosbahi has written, "Two things have always fascinated me: the rhythm of the Koran, which I learned by heart without understanding the meaning of its verses, and the storyteller's freedom. He was the only person who could talk about taboo subjects like women and love. Villagers hung on his every word when they gathered around a fireplace and a teapot."

Mosbahi's Arabic novel translated here as *We Never Swim in the Same River Twice* won the 2020 Comar Prize for a Tunisian Arabic novel.

William Maynard Hutchins is a serial translator of Arabic literature and a professor emeritus in the Philosophy and Religion Department of Appalachian State University. He has translated *Solitaire* by Hassouna Mosbahi and *Return to Dar al-Basha* by Hassan Nasr, another contemporary Tunisian author, for Syracuse University Press, as well as *The Fetishists* by Ibrahim al-Koni and *Ibn Arabi's Small Death* by Mohammed Hasan Alwan, among other works of Arabic fiction.

Printed in the USA
CPSIA information can be obtained
at www.ICGtesting.com
CBHW020519170924
14319CB00004B/5